REQUIEM FOR A MEZZO

A show-stopping performance...

With dashing Scotland Yard detective Alec Fletcher at her side, Daisy Dalrymple is enjoying a splendid performance of Verdi's *Requiem* featuring her neighbour Muriel Westlea's celebrated sister, Bettina, when what emerges from the star's gifted vocal chords is literally a dying gasp. The doomed diva was notoriously difficult and had more than her share of enemies, including a philandering tenor, a burly Russian bass and even her own vocal coach husband, with whom she had a turbulent relationship. Did one of them poison the singer? Or was it someone determined to see that Daisy's investigation ends on as bitter a note as Bettina's last performance...?

REQUIEM FOR A MEZZO

REQUIEM FOR A MEZZO

by

Carola Dunn

Magna Large Print Books
Long Preston, North Yorkshire,
BD23 4ND, England.

British Library Cataloguing in Publication Data.

Dunn, Carola
    Requiem for a mezzo.

    A catalogue record of this book is
    available from the British Library

    ISBN   978-0-7505-3149-8

First published in Great Britain in 2009 by Robinson,
an imprint of Constable & Robinson Ltd.

Copyright © Carola Dunn 1996, 2009

Cover illustration by arrangement with
Constable & Robinson Ltd.

Published in Large Print 2011 by arrangement with
Constable & Robinson Ltd.

Magna Large Print is an imprint of Library Magna Books Ltd.

Printed and bound in Great Britain by
T.J. (International) Ltd., Cornwall, PL28 8RW

To Keith,
for smoothing the rough edges,
as an editor should.

CHAPTER 1

As Daisy reached a second time for the gleaming brass knocker, the dark green front door opened.

'Oh, it's you, Daisy. Do come in,' invited Muriel Westlea, an apologetic smile on her thin, perpetually worried face. A faded woman in her early thirties, she was drably dressed in a brown spotted challis well past its prime. 'I'm sorry you had to wait, but it's our parlour maid's day off. You haven't even got a coat.'

'It's all right, I only live next door after all, and it's a simply spiffing day. The daffodils are about to burst into bloom. I adore spring.'

Daisy stepped into the house. The sun, shining through the Victorian stained-glass fanlight and panels on either side of the door, cast green and purple blotches on white walls and polished parquet. On the hall table stood a vase of crimson hothouse roses.

'From one of Betsy's – Bettina's – admirers,' said Muriel, following Daisy's gaze.

'They never have the fragrance of the real thing.'

'No, but they're jolly pretty. Your sister's real name is Elizabeth, is it?

'Yes. She was always Betsy as a child and I can't get out of the habit.'

'I know, it took me ages to stop calling Lucy by her school nickname, which she hates so much I shan't even repeat it to you.' Daisy held out her empty jam jar. 'I'm afraid I've come begging. I started to make a birth-day cake for Lucy and discovered too late that I'm short of flour. Do you think your cook can spare a quarter of a pound or so?'

'Of course. Let's go down to the kitchen.' She led the way towards the service stairs at the back of the hall. From somewhere in the depths of the house came the sounds of a piano and a female voice. 'When is Lucy's birthday?'

'Tomorrow. I'm making a sponge because it's light and she's always watching her figure. I wish I had her strength of mind,' Daisy added mournfully. 'I shall never attain the no-bosom, no-bottom look.'

'It wouldn't suit you,' Muriel comforted her, 'and anyway the fashion will change one of these days.'

She opened the green baize door and suddenly the music was louder: Carmen warning her lover, *'Si je t'aime, prends garde à toi!'*

'Your sister's voice is lovely.'

'That isn't Betsy, it's Olivia Blaise, one of Roger's pupils.'

'Blaise? Sounds familiar. I think she came to Lucy to have her portrait taken,' said Daisy as they started down the stairs. 'Mr. Abernathy has referred quite a few of his pupils to her. Jolly decent of him. It must be wonderful to live surrounded by music,' she added as the piano started on the introduction to another of Carmen's arias.

Muriel sighed. 'If only one might have the music without the artistic temperament! I'm afraid "If I love you, watch out," or better still, "If you love me, watch out," nicely sums up most of them. That's the soloists, of course. Humble chorus members like me keep our heads down.'

Daisy was dying to ask whether, as she suspected, Bettina was one of the artistically temperamental majority. She was saved from the temptation to dispense with tact by their arrival in the kitchen.

The cook filled Daisy's jam jar with flour and, when Daisy admitted to never having made a sponge before, gave her a few hints. 'The kettle's on the boil, Miss Westlea,' she said then. 'You'll be wanting tea?'

'Will you stay for a cup, Daisy?' Muriel asked hopefully.

'I'd love to but I've already turned on the oven and broken all the eggs into a bowl. I think I'd better get back.'

'I suppose so.' Disappointed, Muriel ushered her back up to the hall.

This time the singing was on the other side of the baize door, coming from a room off the hall at the front of the house.

> *'Judex ergo cum sedebit,*
> *Quidquid latet apparebit:*
> *Nil inultum remanebit!'*

Though Daisy didn't understand the words, she thought the rich voice sounded positively spiteful.

'That's Betsy. Verdi's *Requiem*, the part about the Day of Judgement when "nothing will remain unavenged." She's going to sing in it at the Albert Hall. Most of her appearances are with provincial opera companies so it's a great opportunity for her to be heard by the people who count.'

'I hope it goes well,' Daisy said with more politeness than truth. She had only met Bettina Westlea – alias Mrs. Roger Abernathy

12

– a couple of times but she wasn't frightfully keen on her. In fact, she had put the singer down as a bit of a blister.

'She has a beautiful voice,' Muriel said loyally, 'and she's beautiful, too, perfect for an opera heroine. It's just a matter of the right people hearing her. Oh, do you think Lucy would like a pair of tickets to the concert as a birthday present? Betsy has a few complimentary tickets to spare. It's next Sunday, a matinée. To be precise, 3:00 P.M., 18th March 1923, is to be Bettina's moment of triumph.'

'I don't know about Lucy. *I'd* love to go.'

'Then you shall have them.' Muriel's smile made her look years younger and almost pretty. 'They're down in the music room. I'll bring them round later.'

'Topping! Will you be singing?'

'Yes, it's the ProMusica Choir. Roger's our choirmaster, you know.'

As Muriel reached for the door handle to let Daisy out, the knocker rat-tatted. The gentleman on the doorstep was tall and lithe, youngish, and rather good-looking. His pale grey lounge suit was the last word in natty men's tailoring. However, a shock of brown hair much too long for fashion brushed his collar, where a white silk cravat supplanted a tie, and his shirt and the handkerchief in his breast pocket were lilac. Clearly he laid claim to belonging here in Bohemian Chelsea.

Daisy did not recognize him, though the motorcar visible behind him out in Mulberry Place was familiar, a maroon Leyland Eight with the distinctive long, square bonnet.

He raised his grey Homburg. 'Good afternoon. I've come to fetch Miss Blaise.'

'You had better come in and wait.' Muriel's voice was colourless, her face set as she moved aside. 'Miss Blaise should be up any minute. Daisy, do you know Mr. Cochran? He's to conduct the Verdi. Our nextdoor neighbour, Miss Dalrymple,' she introduced Daisy as the conductor bowed slightly, giving the jam jar of flour a puzzled look.

'You live next door?' he said. 'You must be the photographer Abernathy recommended for my publicity photos.'

'That's my friend, Miss Fotheringay. She's very good.'

'I'd have given her a shot, but my wife decided on a West End chap she had patronized before.'

As Daisy nodded, the drawing-room door was flung open. 'Muriel, for heaven's sake, how do you expect me to practise with all this noise?' Bettina demanded petulantly.

14

'Who...? Oh, it's you, Eric.' Her smile was the smile of a cat with a live mouse beneath its paw. 'Have you come to meet dear Olivia? I do hope she'll be glad to see you.'

Mr. Cochran's answering smile was decidedly weak, not to say unhappy. He appeared unimpressed by golden curls surrounding a perfect oval face and wide eyes of celestial blue with long lashes judiciously darkened. Bettina's blue silk dress, belted at the hips, its embroidered hem skimming the ankles in the latest fashionable length, matched her eyes and flattered her svelte figure. Beside her poor Muriel looked shabby, gaunt, and middle-aged.

'Hello, Bettina,' said the conductor lamely. 'Working hard on the *Requiem*, I trust?'

The singer gave him a scornful look.

Daisy was torn between dashing back to her oven and lingering in the hope of finding out what was going on between Eric Cochran, Bettina Westlea Abernathy, and Olivia Blaise. As a writer she had a duty to satisfy her insatiable curiosity about human relationships. At least, it was a good excuse.

But the gas bill would be horrendous if she left the oven burning. She was turning to Muriel to take her leave when footsteps at the back of the hall drew everyone's attention.

Olivia Blaise was the essence of chic. As she came closer, Daisy realized that her pale yellow coatdress was too short for the new style and made of a cheapish jersey, yet she looked inarguably elegant. Perhaps it was the way she walked, with a supple grace eloquent of vitality restrained, Daisy thought enviously. Probably she'd look equally marvellous in rags. Her smooth, dark, bobbed hair and rather sharp features gave her an elvish air. Daisy remembered that Lucy had raved over her bone structure and predicted a brilliant career as a model should she come a cropper as a singer.

Olivia grimaced as she saw the four standing in the hall.

Stepping forward, Cochran blurted out, 'Olivia, let me give you a lift.'

'Oh, all right,' she said ungraciously. 'I suppose it's better than taking the bus.'

Behind her, emerging from the shadows at the back of the hall, trudged Roger Abernathy, a stocky middle-aged man, balding, with thick-lensed hornrimmed spectacles. His face was drawn with pain and his lips had a bluish tinge.

'Roger!' cried Muriel, darting to his side. 'You came up the stairs too quickly again. Sit down.' Her arm around his shoulders,

16

she urged him to a chair by the hall table.

Olivia swung round. 'Gosh, it's my fault. I was in a hurry, hoping to avoid ... this.' She gestured at Cochran and Bettina. 'What can I do, Miss Westlea?'

'He hasn't got his medicine.' Muriel was feeling in Abernathy's inside coat pockets. 'If you wouldn't mind, Miss Blaise, there's a spare bottle of pills in the cloakroom, and a glass of water...'

'My own fault,' Abernathy muttered as Olivia hurried past him with a compassionate glance. 'Better in a moment.'

'When you're *quite* recovered, Roger,' Bettina snapped pettishly, 'I need your help with the *Liber scriptus*.'

'Of course, my love.' His gaze followed his beautiful wife, his wistful, doggish devotion obvious despite the heavy spectacles.

She disappeared into the drawing room, shutting the door with an irritable thump. A moment later, a piano chord sounded, followed by the richly glorious mezzo-soprano voice: *'Liber scriptus proferetur,'* taking the awkward fifth leap in its stride.

Olivia Blaise returned with Abernathy's medicine. Cochran hovered awkwardly on the threshold, uncertain whether to remove his obviously unwanted presence. Daisy

17

decided it was past time to remove hers.

'I'm off, Muriel,' she said. 'Thanks!'

Busy with the pill bottle, Muriel gave her a distracted smile. 'I'll see you later, Daisy.'

Daisy dashed back to the 'bijou' residence next door and down to the cramped semi-basement kitchen. Weighing out flour and sugar in advance, as advised by Muriel's cook, she set about vigorously beating up the eggs.

An hour later, she was at the kitchen table, just finishing a cup of tea with Mrs. Potter, the daily who 'obliged' her and Lucy, when the doorbell rang.

'So I up and I tells 'im, "not on your life you don't," I says,' the charwoman finished her story. Draining the last heavily sugared drop from her cup, she heaved herself to her feet. 'I'll get the door, miss. Time I was scrubbing out the bathtub. Now don't you go peeking in that there oven, mind, or Miss Lucy's birthday sponge'll end up flat as a pancake, mark my words.'

Her weighty tread mounted the semi-basement stairs. Daisy stared longingly at the gas range. Surely if she just opened the oven door a crack, no harm would come to the cake? But the Abernathys' cook had said the same, and how Lucy would rag her if she made a hash of it after her airy claim that nothing was easier!

'It's miss from next door, miss,' Mrs. Potter yelled down the stairs.

'Don't come up, Daisy, I'll come down,' Muriel called. Light footsteps pattered down. 'I've brought you the tickets.'

'Thanks, Muriel, you're a brick. Sorry I hopped it like that but I felt a bit *de trop*. I'd have stayed if I'd thought you needed help.'

'That's all right. Poor Roger has a weak heart but all he needs is his pills. He ought to carry them, only he forgets. Betsy knows his turns are not serious,' she added in defense of her sister.

Daisy, her opinion of Bettina reinforced by the scene she had witnessed, said tactfully, 'I'm glad Mr. Abernathy isn't gravely ill.'

'So am I. He's always been very kind to me.' Muriel's thin cheeks pinkened. 'I'm sorry you ... that is, I'm afraid it was all rather awkward.'

'You mean with your sister and Mr. Cochran and Miss Blaise?'

'Yes. You see, Miss Blaise expected to get the mezzo part in the Verdi, and then it was given to Betsy. I'm afraid there are hard feelings.'

That was the least of it, Daisy thought.

19

Hoping to hear the rest of the story, she said, 'Would you like a cup of tea? This pot is stewed, but I can easily make some more.'

'I'd love to,' Muriel said regretfully, 'but I must get back. With Beryl out, there's no one else to answer the door. I'll see myself out. I don't want to tear you away from your baking. Mmm, your cake smells delicious.'

'Oh Lord, I'd forgotten the time!' Frantic, Daisy checked the clock. 'Whew, still five minutes before I dare peek. If it turns out halfway decent, you must come over to-morrow and have a slice.'

'I'd love to. Four o'clock? Betsy will be out all afternoon.'

'We'll see you at four,' Daisy agreed, sup-pressing with difficulty the temptation to say she'd meant eleven. It would only upset Muriel. If she chose to allow her sister to ride roughshod over her, it was none of Daisy's business.

CHAPTER 2

The sponge cake came out looking quite edible, success enough to satisfy Daisy considering it was her first attempt. The black bit round the edge of the bottom could easily be scraped off and she would fill the dip in the top with jam. Leaving it to cool on a rack, she took the *Requiem* tickets and went out to Lucy's photographic studio in the back garden.

Practically overnight, the forsythia had burst into bloom, a fountain of gold against the mellow red brick of the converted mews. Daisy wished some clever inventor would hurry up and invent a simple and satisfactory colour photography process.

The small studio was as usual cluttered with cameras, tripods, backdrops, and props. The desk in the corner was piled high with photos and bills, paid and unpaid, beneath which the appointment book undoubtedly lurked. Lucy was talking about having a telephone put in; she'd probably use it to hang up the black cloth she draped over her head when she shot portraits. How anyone who invariably emerged from beneath the black cloth without a hair out of place could stand the mess had puzzled Daisy for years.

'Lucy?'

'I'm in the darkroom, darling. I'll be out in a jiffy.'

'Right-oh.' Daisy sat down at the desk and began in a desultory way to sort out the jumble. She helped out in Lucy's business when things were particularly busy so she knew pretty much what was what.

Among the heaps, she came across a photo of Bettina and her husband. Roger Abernathy, standing behind his seated wife, gazed down upon her with a smile so fatuously adoring it made Daisy snort with disgust. Too sickening! Some men simply couldn't see past a head of golden curls, or perhaps, in this case, a golden voice. She buried the photo at the bottom of a pile.

The papers were all neatly stacked by the time Lucy emerged. She had already taken off her white darkroom coat and combed her dark bob. No chemical stains had been permitted to yellow her fingers to match her amber eyes. Tall and sleek, she wouldn't have been caught dead in last year's calf length hems, though her budget was as limited as

Daisy's; she made her own clothes and spent on materials and trimmings the equivalent of what Daisy put into books and gramophone records. Daisy's best hat, from Selfridge's Bargain Basement, always made her shudder.

'Angel!' she said as she caught sight of her tidy desk. 'You shouldn't have.'

'I jolly well couldn't bear looking at it while I waited.'

'Then you know how I feel looking at your hair. The best birthday present you can give me is to have it bobbed.'

'I'll think about it.'

'Come on, Daisy, you've been havering for months.'

Daisy sighed. 'All right, I'll do it. Tomorrow morning. I've invited Muriel for tea – I hope you don't mind.'

'Muriel? Oh, that poor prune next door. Why on earth...?'

'I had to borrow some flour for your cake, and then she offered two concert tickets for your birthday.'

'A concert!' Lucy groaned. 'You didn't go and tell her I'd be thrilled?

'No, darling, I said I didn't know about you but *I'd* be thrilled, so she gave them to me. You needn't think I'll try to make you go with me.'

'You'd better invite Philip.'

'Philip! He'd accept because he thought I needed an escort, and like you he'd be bored to tears. There's nothing worse than going to a concert with someone who's bored. It's impossible to enjoy it. No, I'm going to ask Alec Fletcher.'

'Oh Daisy, not your tame policeman! He'll be as bored as Philip and not gentleman enough to hide it.'

'A fat lot you know. You haven't even met him yet. Alec is a perfect gentleman, and what's more, he likes good music. He invited me to a concert at the Queen's Hall, but it was last week while I was in Suffolk doing the research for the third *Town and Country* article.'

'But really, darling, a bobby! Too, too *déclassé*, even if he is a Detective Chief Inspector. A policeman simply cannot be quite ... well, quite. And when Philip's dying to marry you!'

'He's not dying to marry me, he simply feels duty-bound to take care of me because of Gervaise,' Daisy said crossly. Her brother, Philip Petrie's closest chum, had been killed in the Great War and she didn't appreciate the reminder every time she had this argument with Lucy. 'Just because you think Binkie's bloodlines are reason enough to encourage him although he's a complete fathead...'

'Philip's not the brightest star in the firmament,' Lucy retorted.

'So why are you pushing me at him?'

Lucy sighed. 'It's not so much pushing you at Philip as trying to wean you from your detective. Lady Dalrymple would have forty fits if she knew you were seeing a common copper.'

'Mother has forty fits whatever I do. She needs something to carp at. It's what keeps her going.'

'True,' Lucy said ruefully. 'Well, I won't carp at you any longer just now. I've got someone coming for a sitting – if you've unearthed my appointments book, you might look it up and tell me if they're due at quarter past or half past.'

'Quarter past. I'll get out of your way. Don't despair, darling. Remember Alec's a widower who lives with his mother and daughter, both of whom may hate me on sight.'

'No one ever hates you on sight, darling. They're more likely to pour their troubles into your ears as you step over the threshold.'

Laughing, Daisy returned to the house. It

was true people tended to confide in her, though she wasn't sure why. Alec, who had twice revealed to her more details of a current case than his superiors or he himself thought quite proper, muttered accusing reproaches about guileless blue eyes. She protested that her eyes were no more guileless – less guileful? – than anyone else's, and besides it made her sound like a halfwit.

Be that as it might, people told her things, and whatever Alec said, she had helped him solve both cases.

She was dying to ring him up about the concert, but she didn't want to disturb him at Scotland Yard. Didn't quite dare, actually. Detective Chief Inspector Fletcher could be quite formidable when annoyed.

It was a pity she and Lucy really couldn't afford to have a phone installed in the house. That evening, after an early supper of toasted cheese, Daisy nipped out to the telephone kiosk on the corner and asked the operator to put her through to Alec's home number.

A young girl's voice answered with a conscientious repetition of the number.

'This is Daisy Dalrymple. May I speak to Mr. Fletcher, please, if he's at home?'

'Gran, it's Miss Dalrymple!' The voice was muffled, as if the speaker had turned away from the mouthpiece. 'You know, Daddy's friend. I can't remember, should I call her "Honourable" or what?'

So Alec had talked about her at home. At least Belinda hadn't slammed the receiver into its hook on hearing her name.

'Miss Dalrymple.' The girl sounded breathless now. 'This is Belinda Fletcher speaking. Daddy ... my father's just come home and gone upstairs. If you don't mind waiting just a minute, I'll run and fetch him.'

Daisy contemplated the six minutes' worth of pennies lined up on the little shelf by the apparatus. 'Could you ask him to ring me back right away, please? I'm in a public booth. If you have a pencil, here's the number.'

'We always have a pencil and pad by the telephone in case there's an urgent message from Scotland Yard,' Belinda said proudly. 'Daddy says I'm very good at taking messages.'

'I'm glad to hear it.' Daisy read off the number. 'Thank you, Miss Fletcher. I'm delighted to make your acquaintance, even if at a distance.'

'Me too. I mean, I want awfully to meet you properly. I'll go and tell Daddy right away.'

She rang off, leaving Daisy to wonder

whether such enthusiasm wasn't worse than outright hostility. How on earth was she to live up to whatever exaggerated idea of her charms Belinda had got into her head?

Fortunately no one came to use the telephone booth before the bell shrilled. In fact, Alec rang back very quickly.

'Daisy! Don't tell me you've fallen over another dead body?'

'Certainly not. When I do, I'll phone up the Yard.'

'I trust that won't be necessary. What's up?'

Daisy had sudden qualms. Among close friends in her set, it was perfectly acceptable for a girl to ask a man to escort her to an event if she was given free tickets, but perhaps middle-class mores were different. Could Lucy be right that it was a mistake for her to have made friends with Alec?

No, though he might laugh at her, he wouldn't think her forward or pert or any of those ghastly Victorian notions. At least, not more forward or pert than he already considered her, and he seemed to like her anyway.

'I've got free tickets to the Albert Hall,' she said tentatively. 'On Sunday afternoon, three o'clock. Would you like to go with me?'

'What's on? A boxing match?' His grin

came down the wire as clearly as if she could see it.

'Don't be a chump, it's a concert. Verdi's *Requiem*. My neighbour's singing the mezzo solo.'

'I'd love to go, Daisy, and I'll do my utmost to keep the afternoon free, but though things are quietish at present you know I can't give you an absolute promise.'

'I know, you might be called out to a murder in Northumberland. I'll keep the ticket for you. If you can't make it, I can always rope in Phillip at the last minute.'

'I'll make it,' Alec said grimly. He still wasn't convinced Phillip was no more to her than a childhood friend. 'By hook or by crook.'

'What an unsuitable phrase for a police-man!' Daisy teased. 'Phillip'll be very relieved if you do. He'd hate it.'

'I wouldn't want to be responsible for his agonies. May I take you out to dinner after-wards?'

'I'd like that, if you swear you won't leave for Northumberland between the soup and the fish.'

'I swear. Even if it's John o' Groats I'm called to, I shan't desert you till after dessert. I'll pick you up at two.'

'Spiffing.' Daisy would have liked to go on chatting but if he had just come in from work he must be tired and hungry. Complimenting him on his daughter's telephone manners, she said cheerio.

On Sunday, Alec's small yellow Austin Seven, its hood raised against a wintry downpour, pulled up outside the house promptly at two. Daisy saw it from the window of the front parlour, where she was pretending to read *The Observer*. She dashed into the hall and jammed her emerald green cloche hat onto her head, tugging it down as far over her ears as she could, practically down to her nose. Then, in more leisurely fashion, she put on her green tweed coat.

The doorbell rang. She opened the door and Alec smiled at her from beneath a huge black, dripping umbrella.

'You're all ready to go?' he said, raising dark, impressive eyebrows. 'No hurry, we've plenty of time.'

'Yes. No.' Flustered, she hoped he didn't think she wanted to avoid introducing him to Lucy, who was out anyway. 'Come in a minute while I find my gloves. Shall I take an umbrella?'

'Mine is plenty big enough for two. And

there's no wind; you don't need to pull your hat so low. I can scarcely see your face. Or is that the latest style?'

'No.' In fact, now that he was close she couldn't see his face at all, nothing above the Royal Flying Corps tie in the open neck of his overcoat. She pushed the cloche up a bit. 'Oh Alec, I had almost all my hair cut off – I promised Lucy – and it feels so peculiar and draughty. My ears feel positively *naked*. I don't know what you'll think...'

'Nor do I, since I can't see a single lock. The hairdresser did leave you *some* hair, I trust?'

Bravely Daisy took off her hat and presented her shingled head for his examination.

'Hmm.' Chin in hand he studied her, a twinkle in his eyes. 'Just like Lady Caroline Lamb in the portrait by Phillips.' Alec had studied history at university, specialising in the Georgian era.

'The one who chased Lord Byron? Didn't she go mad?' Daisy asked suspiciously.

'Yes, but she wrote a very successful book on the way, a scandalous *roman-à-clef*. On second thought, the chief similarity is the hair. Caro Lamb had short, honey brown curls like yours, but she had brown eyes, not blue, if I'm not mistaken. As for her expression of haughty wilfulness, only the wilful part applies to you.'

'Mother would agree, but I'm not wilful, I'm independent.'

'Same thing. No one could describe you as haughty, at least.' He grinned. 'And I don't suppose Caro Lamb ever had a single freckle on her nose, either.'

'Blast, are they showing?' Whipping out her powder-puff, Daisy sped to the hall mirror and anxiously examined her roundish face. 'No. You beast!' She dabbed a little extra powder on her nose anyway. 'You haven't said if you like it, Alec.'

He came up behind her and set his hands on her shoulders, gazing at her in the looking glass. 'It's utterly enchanting,' he said softly.

Daisy blushed, to her own extreme annoyance – too fearfully Victorian! 'Here are my gloves, in my pocket,' she said. 'Let's go.'

A few minutes later the massive rotunda of the Royal Albert Hall loomed before them through the rain. The huge auditorium had been planned by Prince Albert as the centrepiece of a corner of Kensington to be dedicated to the arts and sciences. Not completed until a decade after his death, it had for half a century been a major venue for everything from political and religious meetings to concerts and sports events. Colleges and museums clustered around it, and usually the streets were busy. However, it was a wet Sunday afternoon and they were early so Alec had no difficulty finding a place to leave the Austin quite close to the entrance.

In the lobby he bought a programme, and the usher directed them around the circular passage to the inner entrance nearest their seats.

The seats were perfect, neither too far from the stage nor too close, and a little above its level. Daisy could never understand why anyone would pay the premium prices to be in the front rows. All one could see was the conductor, the soloists, and the first ranks of violins and cellos, and just about all one could hear, too. That was where people sat who cared more for showing off their furs and hats than for the music. Not the place for her green tweed and the Selfridge's Bargain Basement cloche!

Behind her and Alec and to either side, and even behind the stage, the tiers of seats rose towards the distant glass dome, now a dingy grey. A full house was about eight thousand, someone had told her. At the moment the vast hall was thinly populated, but people were gradually filing in through the many doors around the circle.

'Good,' said Alec, 'there's a translation in the programme. My Latin isn't up to it, hasn't been for years.'

Together they studied the words of the *Requiem*.

'Gosh, look at that,' Daisy exclaimed, and read aloud, '"*Confutatis maledictis:* When the cursèd all are banished, doomed to burn in bitter flames, summon me among the blessèd." Talk about holier-than-thou!'

Alec laughed. 'It is rather, isn't it? You have to consider it as opera. The story may be questionable but the music is divine. Listen to this. 'Day of wrath, day of terror, day of disaster and anguish, that great, hopeless, exceeding bitter day." Just like one of those operas which ends with bodies strewn all over the stage.'

'Ghastly! I'm not all that keen on opera.'

'Nor am I.'

They finished reading the programme as the orchestra players started to wander in. Odd notes, chords, and twiddles of melody arose in a tantalizing cacophony. A momentary silence fell as the leader came in and bowed to the audience, to a wave of applause. The first oboe sounded an A and the serious tuning of instruments began.

Daisy regarded the leader, Yakov Levich, with interest. A Russian Jew in exile, he was beginning to make a name for himself as a solo violinist – she had read a glowing review of his recent recital at the Wigmore Hall. Tall and almost painfully thin, he had curly black hair greying at the temples and a long, serious face with prominent cheekbones and a high-bridged nose.

An expectant hush fell as the choir filed in. Daisy turned her attention to picking out Muriel and pointing her out to Alec. She had more colour in her face than usual and the severe black of the choir uniform unexpectedly suited her. She opened her music score with a look of joyful anticipation. Obviously singing was one of the few pleasures in her life.

Eric Cochran appeared, baton in hand, his longish hair the only sign of Bohemian proclivity now that he was clad in formal tails. He led in the soloists. First came the soprano, Consuela de la Costa, a voluptuous figure in crimson velvet cut dashingly low on the bosom.

'More appropriate to the opera than a requiem mass,' Alec whispered.

'Perhaps she represents one of the temp-

tations which lead the damned to Hell?'
Daisy whispered back.

'Or the fiery furnace itself.'

Behind Miss de la Costa, Bettina Westlea
was a cool, slender beauty in blue satin with
a more respectable neckline. Gilbert Gower,
the tenor, came next. A handsome Welsh-
man, he had been a staple of the English
opera stage for years, never quite achieving
the summit of the profession, but well res-
pected. Next and last, the bass was another
refugee from the Bolshevik Revolution. A
Russian bear of a man with a full black beard,
Dimitri Marchenko had as yet found only
small rôles in England, chiefly in oratorio.

'I've heard him in the *Messiah*,'Daisy muttered to Alec. 'His low notes have to be heard
to be believed. "Why do the nations..."' she
hummed.

'"...so furiously rage together?" Most
appropriate.'

They settled back, clapping, as conductor
and soloists bowed. Cochran raised his
baton, brought it down with infinite deli-
cacy. The pianissimo first notes of the
Requiem murmured through the hall.

The music swept Daisy away. She forgot
the grim words except to wonder at the
brilliant way Verdi illustrated them. After the

momentary annoyance of latecomers entering at the end of the *Kyrie*, the *Dies Irae* was gloriously terrifying. Marchenko's *Mors stupebit*, reaching down into the depths of the bass range, sent a shiver down Daisy's spine. Consuela de la Costa's voice was as vivid as her appearance. Mr. Abernathy had given Bettina whatever help she had needed and she sang the *Liber scriptus* with a thrilling intensity. Gower's clear tenor was a touch off-key in the *Quid sum miser*, but his *Ingemisco* was so beautiful it brought tears to Daisy's eyes.

The first half of the concert ended with a hushed 'Amen' dying away into slow chords and silence. For a long moment Daisy, along with the rest of the audience, sat in a near trance before a roar of applause burst forth.

Soloists and conductor bowed and departed. The chorus began to file out.

'My hands hurt from clapping,' Daisy said to Alec as they made their way out to the circular passage to stroll about during the interval.

'It was worthy of sore palms,' Alec said, smiling. 'Thank you once more for inviting me. I must write a note to your friend Miss Westlea, too.'

'I'm glad you could come: She linked her

arm through his, surely justifiable as the eddying crowd threatened to part them. 'You do still mean to take me out to dinner, don't you?'

'Yes, I'm incommunicado as far as the Yard is concerned.'

'Spiffing!' said Daisy.

'Hungry? There's the bar over there. Would you like a drink?' Alec asked. 'I expect they have salted almonds or something else to nibble on.'

'No thanks, I'm not thirsty and I'll save my appetite.'

'Did you notice Bettina Westlea had a glass under her chair she kept sipping at when she wasn't singing?'

'Her throat must get fearfully dry.'

'The others managed without, not to mention the chorus. I wonder if that might annoy conductors enough to explain her lack of success. She has a lovely voice.'

'I suspect she's just generally difficult to work with.' Daisy decided not to describe Bettina's peevish self-importance in case it spoilt his pleasure in her singing.

They completed the circuit of the hall just as the bell sounded for the end of the interval. The second half began with a lengthy section for all four soloists. They sat down; the choir rose. Daisy glanced down at the programme: the *Sanctus* was next.

As she looked up again, she saw Bettina reach beneath her chair for her glass. Thirsty work, singing.

Bettina took a big gulp and choked. Her face turned bright red. With a strangled cry she sprang to her feet, the glass flying from her hand as she clutched her throat. Gasping, she doubled over, spun around in a grotesque parody of a ballerina's pirouette, and collapsed.

Her sprawling body writhed, jerked convulsively twice. For a moment her heels drummed a desperate tattoo on the stage. Then the blue figure lay still.

CHAPTER 3

Alec leapt up. 'Police!' he said sharply, pushing past knees to the aisle.

The trumpets' staccato introduction, the basses' resolute opening 'Sanctus,' died away. Half the choir sat, the rest remained uneasily standing, except for Daisy's friend Muriel Westlea, who scurried down from the ranks, threading her way between woodwinds and violas.

'Betsy!' she cried, and fell to her knees at her sister's side.

From somewhere in the audience came a belated scream. People started to stand up. Though the hall was still quiet, any minute there would be a hubbub followed by a stampede for the doors, and Alec had no way to stop it.

The conductor still stood on the podium, gaping down at his supine soloist. 'Police!' Alec rapped out again as he reached the rapidly emptying front row of seats. 'Mr. Cochran, make an announcement, please. No one is to leave.'

Cochran shook his head dazedly, visibly pulled himself together, and swung round to face the audience. 'Your attention, please, ladies and gentlemen,' he began in a carrying voice. 'There has been an accident...'

Alec turned towards Bettina Westlea, just in time to stop a short, stout man stepping on the damp patch of floor littered with broken glass.

'I'm a doctor,' the man declared, reaching for Bettina's wrist, which dangled limply over the edge of the stage. Blank eyes bulging, her lips were blue though her face was suffused

40

with blood. 'No pulse. I'm afraid she's dead.'

'Cause of death?' Alec demanded.

'I shan't commit myself, but it looks to me very like cyanide poisoning.'

Alec bent down and sniffed. A strong smell of bitter almonds met his nostrils. He nodded.

Above his head, a shriek rang out: '*¡Asesino!*'

He looked up. Miss de la Costa, her face a mask of horror, was pointing a quivering, accusatory finger at Gilbert Gower. Did she know something, or was she merely being irritatingly foreign and operatic?

From audience, orchestra, and choir arose a swelling clamour. Two more men hurried up to announce themselves as doctors.

'Damnation!' Alec muttered. Here he was, a Scotland Yard officer miraculously witness to a murder — an apparent murder, he corrected himself — and he had far too much to do to be able to observe the reactions of the horde of presumed suspects on the stage.

As the three doctors conferred, Alec glanced at the victim's sister. Muriel Westlea sobbed, her face buried in her hands. Beside her knelt Daisy, a comforting arm about her shoulders.

'*Damnation!*' Alec repeated, softly but

41

vehemently. He ought to be resigned by now to the inevitability of Daisy involving herself in whatever was going on around her. At least she was looking about her, and she was a keen observer and meticulous reporter – when she didn't decide for reasons of her own to keep information from him.

Shrugging, he turned back to the doctors.

'Cyanide,' confirmed the tall, scrawny, elderly one. 'Flushing, collapse, cyanosis, all typical symptoms.'

'It could have been a natural seizure,' the third suggested tentatively. A youngish man in gold-rimmed spectacles, he was very pale, his forehead gleaming with sweat. Amazing how many doctors couldn't cope with sudden, unprescribed death.

'The odour, Doctor!' said the first, disdainful. 'The odour of bitter almonds is unmistakable.'

'I can't smell it.'

'Some can't discern cyanide,' the elderly man agreed.

The stout doctor nodded. 'Cyanide it is,' he said.

Two out of three and the evidence of his own nose were enough for Alec. 'If there's nothing you can do for her, gentlemen,' he said, 'I'll ask you to return to your seats. I shall need official statements later. By the way, I'm Detective Chief Inspector Fletcher, Scotland Yard.'

'Scotland Yard!' came a groan from behind him. Alec was just in time to stop the groaner stepping on the shattered glass. A tubby man with a bristling moustache, his forehead was bedewed like the young doctor's but his complexion was florid. 'Jove, you fellows are fast! Peter Browne, Major, Albert Hall manager.'

'Tell your ushers to close and guard all exits, at once, please, Major. I need a telephone.'

'My office.' Browne started off.

'Just a minute. You there!' Alec beckoned to the nearest cellist. 'I need a couple of music stands.'

Mystified, the man passed down two stands. Alec arranged them crosswise over the damp patch and the glass shards. That would have to do for the moment.

Catching Daisy's eye, he mouthed, 'Telephone.' She nodded. He hurried after the manager.

When Bettina fell, Daisy had been watching Muriel. She saw her expectant delight in the music turn to dismay, to horror. As Muriel hurried to her sister's side, Daisy followed

43

Alec past the knees of their stunned neighbours and down the aisle.

The leader, Yakov Levich, had risen to his feet and stood there indecisively, holding his violin. While Alec spoke to Cochran, Daisy called softly, 'Mr. Levich, help me up, please. I'm a friend of her sister's.'

Levich set down the violin and bow on his chair and leaned down to offer a lean, long-fingered hand. He was stronger than he looked. With his aid Daisy scrambled onto the stage, blessing short skirts and the demise of corsets. She crossed behind the podium, where Cochran was asking the audience for calm, and joined Muriel just as the short, stout doctor declared Bettina dead.

Muriel broke down in tears. Daisy, her arm about Muriel's shoulders, looked up as Consuela de la Costa gave a theatrical shriek, '¡Asesino!'

The curvaceous Spanish soprano's quivering finger accused Gilbert Gower of the dire deed.

'Here, I say!' stammered the startled tenor weakly. Up close, he was much older than he had appeared from the auditorium, in his fifties, with thinning hair discreetly Marcelled and deep lines in his face, though still passably good-looking. 'You don't want to go

about saying things like that, my sweet.'
Moving closer, he said something Daisy
couldn't hear above the growing noise of the
agitated throngs.

Miss de la Costa promptly flung herself
into his arms, sobbing hysterically. 'Oh, *mi
querido, mi amor*, I mistake. I not mean.'

Holding her rather closer than was strictly
necessary to comfort her, he murmured
soothingly in her ear.

Daisy glanced at the bass soloist. Dimitri
Marchenko was still seated, hands on knees
in apparent stolid calm. However, his eyes
glittered with what looked like satisfaction,
and in a soft, malicious voice he sang a reprise of his *Confutatis maledictis:* the damned
condemned to the flames. There was one
person who was not sorry Bettina lay dead.

Eric Cochran, on the other hand, was
aghast, practically tearing his hair. Daisy
remembered the curious scene in the Abernathys' front hall, when Bettina had taunted
Cochran, and Olivia Blaise was so obviously
less than thrilled to see him. And later Muriel
had told Daisy the conductor gave the mezzo
part to Bettina although Miss Blaise expected it. Yet Cochran had gone to the house
to meet Miss Blaise, and he hadn't seemed
attracted to Bettina. Nor did he seem grieved

now by her death – more appalled. Curiouser and curiouser, thought Daisy.

While she contemplated the reactions of those around her, consoled Muriel, and tried to avoid looking at Bettina's congested face, Daisy was aware of Alec talking to several men. One of them muttered something about a seizure, but the others insisted on cyanide. That explained the almondy smell. She was familiar with it from Lucy's darkroom, where a solution of cyanide of something-or-other was used as a fixing agent.

So Bettina's glass had contained deadly poison. It lay smashed on the floor below the stage now, shards scattered across a damp patch of carpet already drying in the warm air of the hall.

Daisy wondered how much of a substance Scotland Yard's forensic lab needed for chemical analysis. Luckily the odour made identification obvious. Nonetheless, Alec had barricaded the spot with music stands; he probably hoped one of the larger pieces of glass would provide what his sergeant, Tom Tring, referred to as 'dabs.'

He'd caught her eye, mouthed, 'Telephone,' and gone off with a plump, red-faced man – leaving Daisy to cope with a stageful of questionable characters, she thought indignantly.

One of the characters now approached, though actually she was predisposed in favour of the helpful Yakov Levich. His bony face was sensitive, his dark eyes kind, troubled now as he regarded Muriel's bent head.

It was a bit soon for condolences. 'I think Mr. Levich wants to speak to you,' Daisy murmured in Muriel's ear. 'Shall I tell him to go away?'

'No!' Looking up, her face blotched with tears, Muriel gave the violinist a tremulous smile. Daisy helped her stand up and she held out her hand.

Levich took it in both his. 'My dear Miss Westlea,' he said, his diffidence evident despite a strong accent, 'I regret so much.'

'Thank you, Mr. Levich.' Muriel spoke shyly but she gazed up at him with a glow which transformed her face.

Oh dear, another complication!

'Betsy!' The despairing cry momentarily hushed the milling orchestra members. A way opened between them and Roger Abernathy stumbled through. He stopped beside his dead wife, staring down. 'Betsy, no!' His anguished voice broke. 'Oh, my dearest girl!'

His thick spectacles misted over. His lips were bluish in his suddenly white face, and he clutched at his chest in a gesture horribly reminiscent of Bettina's clutching at her throat.

'Come and sit down, Roger.' Calm, gentle, yet decisive, Muriel took his arm and made him sit on the nearest chair. To the hovering Levich she said, 'Please, a glass of water.'

'I fetch.' He strode off.

'Shouldn't he lie down?' Daisy asked as Muriel felt in Abernathy's inside pocket and produced the pill bottle.

'No, he can't breathe if he lies down when this happens. Oh, drat! Only one left. Here, Roger dear, put this under your tongue.'

Obedient as a child, he opened his mouth while tears trickled down his cheeks.

'He has his pills?' Olivia Blaise materialized beside them.

'Only one,' Daisy told her, unsure how many were needed.

'I know a couple of people in the choir who use the same stuff. Just a minute.'

Both choir and orchestra were beginning to leave the stage, but Miss Blaise found whomever she was looking for and came back with half a dozen tiny tablets.

'Bless you!' said Muriel, scooping them into her brother-in-law's little bottle. She and Miss Blaise sat down on either side of him, leaning protectively towards him.

Levich returned with a glass of water. Miss Blaise glanced round, her gaze going past him and taking on such a depth of contempt that Daisy turned to see what she was looking at.

Eric Cochran was talking to a woman whose silver fox fur coat hung open over a heavily embroidered silk dress. The river of diamonds sparkling at her throat was not quite the thing for a matinée performance. Despite expertly applied cosmetics, she was clearly several years older than the young conductor.

'My career's over, Ursula,' he said to her in despair. 'No important orchestra will hire me after this.'

'Stuff and nonsense,' she responded bracingly. 'Just because the little ... an unfortunate young woman has met her end when you happened to be conducting, there's no reason to give up.' She cast a look of venomous dislike at Bettina's body, lying there for the moment ignored, unmourned.

Daisy felt it was rather indecent to leave the dead singer sprawled in undignified death. To her relief, because her eyes *would* keep sliding back to the horrid sight, one of the uniformed Albert Hall ushers appeared with a cloth to cover the body.

However, Alec would not appreciate any effort to straighten the contorted limbs before the police had done whatever they had to do. Daisy stepped forward to warn him.

'Chief Inspector's orders, miss,' said the usher. 'I shan't touch, just cover her up, like. You'll be Miss Dalrymple? He said to tell you to hold the fort; he'll be back soon as he can.'

Pleased at the hint of Alec's appreciating her assistance, Daisy helped the usher spread the wide, oddly shaped green baize.

'Piano cover, miss,' the man explained.

Enveloped in the trappings of music in death as in life, Bettina disappeared beneath the strange shroud.

When Daisy turned back to see how the new widower was doing, the youngest of the three doctors was bending over him, consulting with Muriel. 'Quite right, Mr. Abernathy should not lie down,' he said, 'but we must get him to a more comfortable chair, where he can relax. The name's Woodward, by the way.'

'He's not fit to walk, Dr. Woodward,' Muriel protested.

Yakov Levich laid his hand on her arm. 'I help to carry,' he offered.

50

The doctor nodded. 'Thank you, sir, we'll manage between us. But where to?'

'The conductor's private room,' Miss Blaise suggested, not without a glint of malice. 'I know the way. Follow me.'

Muriel came over to Daisy. 'Will you come with me?' she begged, her eyes anxious. 'Poor Roger's in a bad way and...'

'I would,' Daisy said apologetically, giving her a hug while watching another new arrival on the stage, 'but Al ... Chief Inspector Fletcher sort of depends on me to keep an eye on things here. I came with him, you see. He'll be back shortly, and I'll come and find you.'

'Oh *please* do.' Muriel followed the others.

The woman who had just arrived was middle-aged, plain and plump, her clothes of good quality but dull and dowdy. Her lips tightened as she regarded Gilbert Gower, still locked in a barely decorous embrace with the gorgeous Consuela de la Costa.

Gower caught sight of her and let go of the soprano like a live wire. A nervous hand smoothed his waved hair.

'Jennifer, my dear.' He came over to the woman, took both her hands in his, and kissed her cheek. She must be Mrs. Gower. 'Miss de la Costa was fearfully shocked, practically hysterical. I've been trying to calm her down. These foreigners, you know.'

'They do tend to be emotional, don't they?' Mrs. Gower said dryly.

'I ... er ... I didn't know you were coming.'

'The children were invited out to tea and tennis so I decided to make use of the ticket you gave me.'

'I'm glad.' Suddenly the aging tenor clung to his wife. 'It's the deuce of a mess, old dear. The police are here already. I gather they suspect Bet ... Miss Westlea was deliberately poisoned.'

Mrs. Gower started to speak, but Daisy was distracted by Alec's return. She sat down on the edge of the stage, legs dangling, to talk to him.

'Any trouble?' he asked in a low voice.

'Not exactly, except Bettina's husband's weak heart playing up. I've got lots to tell you, though.'

'I was sure you would,' he said, resigned. 'Don't think I'm not grateful, but I hope you aren't expecting...'

'...To involve myself in the case?' Daisy said guiltily. 'I wasn't exactly *expecting* to, but I'm afraid Muriel wants me to be with her.'

Alec groaned. 'I might have guessed. I suppose if I send you home, I'll be accused of bullying a female witness. I have to speak to her, of course, and the husband. He's the choirmaster, right?'

'Yes. They're both fearfully upset, though I must say Muriel calmed down right away when Mr. Abernathy was taken ill. She's used to coping with his attacks, but one of those doctors is with him, too. A Dr. Woodward.'

'I suppose I'll have to take medical advice on whether he's fit to be questioned.' He ran his fingers through his hair, which, dark and crisp, showed no sign of disarray. 'I've got bobbies from the local division on their way to man the doors, and most people will only need to leave their names and addresses. The trouble is going to be deciding whom else I ought to see.'

'The other soloists, for a start.' Daisy looked around, but by now the stage was empty except for the baize-covered body. The nearby area of the auditorium had cleared, too, though many people had remained in the upper reaches rather than move out to the doubtless crowded passage and lobby.

'Yes, I gather the soloists all shared a suite,' Alec said. 'The organist used it, too. The manager, Major Browne, thinks Mrs. Abernathy's glass may have been there during the interval. An usher was posted at the door during that period to keep out the unauthorized, but I've not had a chance to speak to him yet, nor to see the room. Browne has locked it and given me the key.'

'It wasn't kept locked during the performance?'

'No. One doesn't exactly expect late-arriving concert-goers to pinch the soloists' handbags, let alone to poison them.'

'Rather not!'

'I'm praying I shan't have to trace late-comers. This place is a nightmare in terms of universal access to everything. With the circular construction, there's no proper backstage. The dressing rooms – if that's the proper term – are around the outside of the building, with performers and audience mingling in the passage. Chaos! Still, I have to concentrate on the most likely suspects.'

'You'd better have a shot at the conductor,' Daisy suggested. 'He's been behaving a bit oddly. He...'

'Save the details for later, please. Any more?'

'His wife, I should think, and Olivia Blaise, who's – who *was* a rival of Bettina's. And Gilbert Gower's wife, perhaps, though I don't know that she had anything to do with Bettina. That's her with him now. I can't think of anyone else.'

54

'With the organist, the three doctors, and Browne, that's plenty. They're not the sort of people I can leave Tom Tring to handle on his own, either.'

'Is Sergeant Tring coming?' Daisy was pleased. She and the elephantine sergeant had a mutual soft spot for each other.

'I telephoned him and Ernie Piper at their homes, and they'll both be here as soon as they can. I'm assuming the case will be assigned to me, as I'm on the spot, though the local divisional Super could insist on jurisdiction.'

'He's a chump if he does.' She recalled Cochran's abject despair, Marchenko's glittering eyes, Consuela de la Costa's hysterical accusation. 'I've a feeling you're going to find yourself up to your ears in artistic temperament!'

CHAPTER 4

Daisy took herself off to join Muriel Westlea as Major Browne hurried up to Alec with the glass jar he had requested.

'It had olives in it,' the pudgy manager

apologized, 'at the bar. I had them wash it out.'

'Thank you, it will have to do.' Alec crouched and, his hand protected by his handkerchief, picked up the larger fragments of glass and put them in the olive jar, screwing the lid on tight. 'Did you find a good, sharp knife?'

'Yes, but I really must protest, Chief Inspector. I can't believe it's necessary to cut a hole in the carpet!'

'Sorry, sir, but our laboratory chaps will need all I can give them of the residue of Mrs. Abernathy's drink.'

'Mrs...? Oh, Miss Westlea. The late Miss Westlea,' he corrected himself with a nervous glance at the baize-shrouded mound on the stage. 'Well, if you must, you must.'

Wringing his hands, he watched Alec slice out a good-sized patch of damp carpet and roll it up with the smallest slivers of glass embedded in it. The almond smell was still strong. The unfortunate Bettina must have been given a massive dose, Alec thought, taking the shallowest breaths possible.

Where the deuce were the local coppers?

Heavy footsteps behind him provided the answer. 'Chief Inspector Fletcher?' The uniformed sergeant saluted, the constable at his heels following suit, as Alec nodded. 'Sir, all the exits are guarded, like you asked on the telephone.'

'Thank you, Sergeant. They know no one is to leave without giving a seat number, or at least row number, name, and address?'

'There won't be any trouble about that,' said Browne dolefully. 'They'll be only too happy to leave word where to find 'em. Seven thousand odd ticket refunds, that's what I'm looking at. It'll make mincemeat of my budget.'

With his somewhat callous concern for his carpet and his budget, Browne seemed an unlikely poisoner. However, Alec might need his knowledge of the internal working of the Albert Hall.

'I won't keep you just now, Major,' he said, 'but I must ask you to stay in the building for the present. Be so good as to send to the soloists' suite the usher who was on duty at that door during the interval.'

'Right you are, Chief Inspector.' The manager trailed away, disconsolate but not visibly alarmed.

Alec turned back to the sergeant and gave him the names of the others who were to be asked to stay.

'I want them gathered in the choir's room,'

he said as the man laboriously wrote in his notebook. 'It's next to Browne's office, which will be a good place for interviews. As soon as you've notified all those, circulate word that the rest can go. I'm going to the soloists' suite now. When Detective Sergeant Tring arrives, send him to me.'

'Sir.'

'And you' – Alec turned to the constable – 'you're to stay here to make sure no one interferes with the body or these items of evidence. A police surgeon and photographer will be along soon.'

Several times, as he made his way through the crowded passage outside the auditorium, anxious or irate concert-goers stopped him, recognizing him as the man who had taken charge. Alec soothed them with promises of being able to depart very shortly. At last he reached the soloists' suite, where a weedy youth in uniform nervously awaited him.

'You were here during the interval?'

'Y-yes, sir,' the usher bleated. 'I d-didn't see anything, honest.'

'I'm not going to bite. I just want to ask you a few questions.' Alec unlocked and opened the door. 'Come in here a minute.'

He threw a swift glance around the small room. An array of easy-chairs covered in 'tartan' tweed in singularly hideous shades of burnt orange and olive green met his eyes. Worse than the worst of Tring's abominable suits, he decided. To his left, in the corner, a table held small coffee and tea urns; a silver samovar; a carafe half full of water; a round silver tray with a cut-glass decanter; cups, saucers and glasses, some used, some clean – one full of tea, scummed on top, appeared untouched; a plate of digestive biscuits; and an empty ashtray.

Anyone standing at the table would effectively hide with his back whatever he was doing with his hands.

'Don't touch anything,' Alec said sharply as the usher followed him in. Closing the door, he pointed at two others, one on each side of the room. 'Where do those lead?'

'The one on the right's to the ladies' dressing room and lav, sir, and t'other's the gents'. There's mirrors and that, and the ladies' has a couple of chaze longs so's they can lie down.'

'Who came in here while you were on duty this evening?'

'Well, all the soloists, sir. That's Miss Costa, Miss Westlea that's dead – as was reelly Mrs. Abernathy and her sister's Miss Westlea, but that's arteests for you – and Mr. Gower and

Mr. Marchenko.'

'And the organist?'

'Mr. Finch? That's right, though you don't hardly notice whether he's there or not. A nice, quiet-spoken gent.'

'Those are all the authorized people. Did you let anyone else in?'

'Mr. Abernathy, though he only popped in for a minute or two. In the choir room next door he was mostly. Then there was Miss Muriel Westlea, she was here the whole time, doing this and that for her sister. Sings in the choir, she does. Major Browne dropped by like he always does, to see they've got all they need, and so did the conductor, Cookham, is it.'

'Cochran.'

'Him. Then a lady came by said she was his wife.'

'Did you let her in?'

'Yes, sir. I'd got no reason to think she wasn't what she said, had I? Fancy dresser that, di'monds and all. And there was another one, proper dowdy-looking, claimed to be Mr. Gower's missus.'

'She went in too?'

'Summun came up and asked me summat, and she must've slipped past me, 'cos she came out a couple of minutes later. Said Mr.

Gower was back there in the dressing room and she wouldn't wait. I asked did she want to leave a message but she said no.'

'Mrs. Cochran. Mrs. Gower.' Alec had to admit that once more Daisy had proved right when she advised him to see those two ladies.

'Then there was Miss Blaise. She's another singer. She'd left summat at Mr. Abernathy's house when she went for her lesson, and Miss Muriel'd promised to bring it in for her today. And the only other one I can think of's Mr. Levich.'

'Yakov Levich? The violinist? The orchestra's leader?' Not on Daisy's list.

'Right, and he's another nice, quiet chap even if he is a furriner. Always a friendly word though you can't hardly tell what he's saying. Not like some I could name.'

'What did he want in this room?'

'I didn't ask. The leader mucks in with the rest of the orchestra in their room so he doesn't properly belong in here, but I wasn't going to stop him when he came along, was I? I seen him around. I know who he is.'

'Reasonable,' Alec conceded. 'I hope he hasn't left, but I suppose I can always find him later. All right, my lad, you...' He stopped as someone knocked on the door.

'Chief?' Around the opening door appeared

61

a large, bald head, the face beneath adorned by way of emphasis with a splendid grey walrus moustache. 'Ah, there you are.' Sergeant Tring came in, a massive figure in his favourite suit of tan and yellow checks.

'That was fast, Tom,' said Alec.

'Mate of mine had dropped by for a cuppa, him and his wife. He's got a motorbicycle so he ran me in.'

Alec's mind boggled at a vision of Tom's bulk squeezed into a sidecar, or worse, balanced on the back of a motorcycle. 'A brave man, your mate. Give him my thanks when next you see him. Tom, first thing, find the local man and tell him to add Yakov Levich, the orchestra's leader, to the list of people I want to stay. Then come back here.'

'Right, Chief.' The sergeant withdrew with his curiously soft, light tread.

Turning back to the usher, Alec dismissed him. 'I may have more questions for you later, but I assume Major Browne has your address, so you can go. You've been helpful. Thank you.'

'My pleasure, sir,' said the young man with a slight bow, regaining the suave manner of one accustomed to dealing with the public.

The door clicked shut behind him. Alec turned to the table. The array of refreshments reminded him that it was teatime, that he was not likely to be offered any, and that his dinner with Daisy was not going to reach the soup, let alone dessert. Still, since she had somehow managed to involve herself in the investigation, she could hardly take umbrage. Thank the Lord for small mercies.

Absently nibbling on a rather limp digestive biscuit, he studied the various items before him.

The door opened again. 'Living dangerously, Chief!' said Tom Tring.

'She was poisoned with a drink, not a biscuit. Look, this is labelled with her name.'

The cut-glass decanter sported a silver tag engraved 'Bettina Westlea.' Only a few dregs remained in the bottom. Wrapping his fingers in his handkerchief, Alec delicately removed the stopper, sniffed, and beckoned to Tom.

'Cyanide right enough, Chief. But that almond smell's strong enough with only a drop or two left, you'd think she'd've noticed before she took a swig.'

'Not everyone can smell it, as I was reminded by one of my self-appointed medical consultants.'

'Ah.' The sergeant helped himself to a biscuit and chewed it ruminatively. 'Dabs?'

'Yes, you have your kit? Good. Fingerprint this room and the two adjoining, and look out for anything which might have contained the cyanide before it was put in the decanter. A photographer and a police surgeon should arrive soon. I don't know who's on call today.'

''Cepting it weren't you and me.'

'That's life – I hope you conveyed my apologies to Mrs. Tring. Anyway, I'm putting you in charge while I start interviewing. I'll use one of the local lads for note taking until Piper gets here.'

'You going to search 'em all for whatever they brought the stuff in?'

'I thought about that, but the easiest form of cyanide to obtain is the potassium or sodium salt, as a pesticide or photographic fixing agent. The crystals could be carried in an envelope to be flushed down the lavatory. Our murderer has had every opportunity to dispose of the evidence.'

'Ah.'

'Keep an eye out for any unexplained container, all the same. It's always possible he used prussic acid, which would require a glass vial. I'm off.' He paused. 'Oh, by the way, Tom, I ... er ... I don't believe I mentioned on the phone that I came to the concert with Miss Dalrymple?'

Tom grinned. 'Ah.'

'I'm afraid she ... well, she's managed to get mixed up in things again. One of our suspects is a friend of hers.'

'Dunno how she does it,' said the sergeant admiringly.

'So don't for pity's sake let her interfere!'

With those heartfelt words, Alec stepped out into the passage. The crowd had thinned considerably. At the two nearest exits, constables scribbled down particulars of the audience, orchestra, and choir members in the slowly shortening queues.

As Alec turned towards the manager's office, Ernie Piper hurried towards him. The wiry young detective constable was out of breath, the shoulders of his brown serge suit damp and his tie awry.

'I came quick as I could, Chief,' he panted. 'Ran all the way from the Tube.'

'Perfect timing. I'm just about to start interviewing.'

'Ready, Chief.' Piper's notebook and three sharp pencils instantly appeared. Alec sometimes wondered if he slept with them in his pyjama pocket.

Browne was in his office, gloomily contemplating figures in a large ledger. 'You want my room, Chief Inspector?' he said. 'You can have it, and the bloody job, too. What a balls-up! My only hope is to persuade people they had half the concert so they can't expect more than half a refund.'

'Can't you reschedule the concert and offer replacement tickets?'

'Possibly, but there's all sorts of extra costs involved, and whether people'll want to come after the stupid bitch – ahem – the unfortunate woman got herself murdered in front of an audience...' He brightened. 'Still, knowing the great British public, it might even bring 'em in. Who can guess?'

'You didn't care for Mrs. Abernathy?' Alec asked.

Browne looked at him in alarm. 'Now don't you go making something of a slip of the tongue!' he begged. 'Except for meeting her a couple of times when they rehearsed here, I only knew her by reputation. I'd heard she was difficult, and by George, she was. Too hot, too cold – as though I could change the Hall's heating system just to please her! I tell you, if it wasn't one thing, it was another, but I'd no cause to bump her off.'

'Who picked her to sing in the Verdi? Who chooses the soloists?'

'Well, I'm consulted, though the conductor

has the final say. Something like the *Requiem*, the choirmaster's generally asked for suggestions. Roger Abernathy – his ProMusica sings here quite often – he's tried before to talk a conductor into giving his wife a chance. Dotes ... doted on her, he did. He's a good chap, mind you, but I've generally managed to put a spoke in his wheel in the interests of peace and harmony.'

'This time you failed.'

'Could have knocked me down with a feather. I'd had a quiet word with Cochran and he agreed absolutely that Bettina Westlea was more trouble than her voice was worth. Next thing I know, he's done an about-face and won't consider any other mezzo.'

Confirmation of Daisy's remark that Cochran had been behaving oddly, Alec thought. 'Did he give you any reason?'

'No, just he'd decided her voice was perfect for the part whatever her drawbacks.' The Major sounded resigned. 'These artistic types, you simply can't count on 'em, you know. Give me a boxing-wallah any day. Crooked as corkscrews, every one of 'em, but you know where you are. Speaking of which, care for a whisky, Chief Inspector?' He opened a drawer of his desk.

'Thank you, not on duty.' Alec had to

assume he was on duty. He hadn't yet heard from either his own or the local division's superintendent, though the local duty officer had responded with admirable speed to his request for manpower. If the case was later taken out of his hands, at least he could lay a solid foundation for whoever took over.

He asked the manager a few more questions about the organization of the Albert Hall in general and the Verdi concert in particular, then let him go.

'Privilege working with you chaps,' said Major Browne, sketching a military salute. He gestured at Alec's tie. 'Royal Flying Corps, were you? They stuck me in the Army Service Corps, worse luck, but I saw a bit of action, all the same.' He hefted his ledger and reached for an appointment book. 'I shan't buzz off yet. I'll just take these through to my secretary's room, have another go at the blasted figures and check a few dates, so halloo if there's anything more I can do for you.'

'Not next door, if you don't mind, sir.'

'Oh? Right! Least heard, soonest mended, eh? The ticket office'll be just the ticket then, haw haw.' Pleased with himself, he went off.

'The three doctors next, I think,' Alec said

to Piper. 'It never does to keep professional men waiting.'

'All together, Chief?'

'Yes. They're not suspects, I just need a written report of their diagnosis. They should be with the rest in the choir room, next door.' He gestured at the wall opposite the door to Browne's secretary's room. 'Oh, but one of them is taking care of Abernathy, I believe.' According to Daisy. 'Er ... I ought to warn you, Ernie, that Miss Dalrymple has got herself mixed up in this business.'

'Our Miss Dalrymple's a right 'un!' said Piper with enthusiasm.

Alec sighed and sent him to fetch the medical men.

The subsequent talk of hyperpnea, dyspnea, hypopnea, vertigo, convulsions, cyanosis, nausea, hypotension, asphyxia, and syncope strained Piper's shorthand to the utmost. All three doctors admitted to never having seen a death from cyanide poisoning before, but the symptoms were consistent with what they had read. Together with the bitter almond odour, the conclusion was obvious.

'I'll have statements drawn up for you to sign, gentlemen,' Alec said at last, 'but I needn't detain you any longer at present –

except you, Dr. Woodward, just a moment, if you please. I'd like your advice about Mr. Abernathy.'

There was something slightly odd about Woodward's reaction to his request. However, thanking the other two, Alec failed to analyse it and it had passed by the time he turned to their younger colleague.

'Mr. Abernathy is not officially my patient, Chief Inspector,' Dr. Woodward said at once, 'but I can tell you that he is a sick man. The shock of his wife's sudden death has brought on an acute attack of angina, possibly even a mild heart seizure. It would be most remiss of me to allow you to question him without protest.'

'Shall I send for an ambulance?'

'No, he is resting in moderate comfort at present and he is best left thus as long as possible.'

'Would you be kind enough to go and see whether I could have just a word with him in a few minutes? If not, I shall leave him till last, or even postpone talking to him until another day if you think it absolutely necessary.'

'Probably, but another hour may see him much improved. I'll stay with him.'

'Thank you, Doctor.'

The man's gold-rimmed spectacles glinted as he nodded. Piper showed him out.

'Who's next, Chief?'

'The victim's sister, Miss Westlea. She's the one Miss Dalrymple has taken under her wing this time. I don't suppose you'll be able to separate them, but you might try suggesting to Miss Dalrymple that her presence is unneeded.'

Piper grinned. 'I'll try, Chief.'

Alec was not at all surprised when Daisy followed Miss Westlea into the office. As he had guessed, her protective instincts had been aroused. Ignoring her for the moment, he concentrated on Muriel Westlea. A slight, brown-haired woman, meek-looking, her eyes red and puffy from crying, she none-theless seemed quite composed. She had taken charge at once when her brother-in-law had his attack, according to Daisy.

According to Daisy. Sometimes he wondered wryly how the deuce he had managed over the years to solve so many cases without her help! Of course, he hadn't had to contend with her interference, either.

'You don't mind if Miss Dalrymple stays with me, Chief Inspector?' Miss Westlea asked anxiously.

'Not at all,' he said stoically, beetling his

71

eyebrows at Daisy's smile. 'Please be seated, ladies.'

They took two chairs facing the manager's desk, and Alec sat down behind it. Piper, notebook at the ready, stationed himself near the door, slightly to Miss Westlea's rear. Daisy turned her head to smile at him – she had more than once acted as Alec's stenographer when he interviewed a suspect.

'Allow me to express my condolences, Miss Westlea,' Alec said.

'Thank you. It was a great sh-shock.' Her voice wavered but she pulled herself together.

'You must have been close to your sister. I understand you made your home with the Abernathys.'

'Yes, I've lived with Betsy and Roger ever since they were married.'

Jealous? Alec wondered. It wouldn't be the first time a plain spinster had fallen in love with her beautiful sister's husband. Add envy of a voice and career Muriel Westlea could not aspire to, and the victim's reputedly demanding nature, and the result was an explosive mixture.

Nothing could have looked less explosive than the quiet woman sitting opposite him, her earnest eyes fixed on his face.

As often happened, his contemplative silence brought explanations from the other's mouth. 'It was convenient for everyone,' Miss Westlea assured him. 'Our parents would never have let Betsy marry Roger and leave home if I hadn't promised to look after her. I wanted to come to London as much as she did but I couldn't afford to live alone, and Betsy had no interest in running a household, which I'm quite good at. And then, she likes ... liked to have me with her at concerts, rather than her maid, whenever I wasn't at a rehearsal or performance myself.'

'I understand you were helping Mrs. Abernathy in the soloists' room today, although you were also performing.'

'Yes, well, I didn't have anything else to do in the interval.'

'What did you do for her?'

'Nothing much. She just likes me to be there. I brushed her hair, sewed on a loose button, brought her– Oh!' She clapped her hands to her mouth and gazed at him in horror.

'Brought her a drink?' Alec asked. 'From the decanter?'

She nodded dumbly.

'It seems probable that anything she drank during the interval was all right – she did drink during the interval?'

'Yes, at least half a glass.'

'Which had no apparent effect on her? No. Most likely the poison in the drink she took on stage was enough to kill her virtually instantly.'

'I poured that, too,' Muriel blurted out. Daisy reached out to take her hand. Alec waited. 'Betsy always insisted on having a drink beside her on stage during a performance, to soothe her throat and revive her energy. She had her own glass, matching the decanter. No one else would have used it. No one would have helped themselves from the decanter, either. Everyone knew she liked ratafia, and it's too sweet for most people's taste.'

Ratafia? To Alec the word suggested elegant Regency ladies delicately sipping while the gentlemen downed port and claret by the bucketful. 'A liqueur?'

'Yes.'

'Rather old-fashioned,' said Daisy, having held her tongue as long as she could. 'I remember my grandmother always having ratafia biscuits for tea. They tasted of almonds, like macaroons.'

'I believe they actually use peach or apricot stones to make the liqueur,' said Miss

Westlea, 'but yes, the aroma is like almonds.'

'Great Scott, no wonder Mrs. Abernathy didn't notice the smell of cyanide!' Alec exclaimed. 'That just about puts paid to any theory the poison might have been meant for someone else. Whoever put it in the decanter knew exactly what they were doing. Miss Westlea, you say "everyone" knew. Whom do you mean, exactly?'

'Oh, conductors, other soloists, people who had worked with her. I'm afraid there was sometimes a bit of a fuss about her drinking on stage.'

'Can you give me names, especially any of those present today who had reason to feel enmity towards your sister?'

'Enmity!' Muriel Westlea burst into tears. 'Betsy never had any enemies!'

Daisy jumped up, put her arm around her friend's shoulders, and glared at Alec. He shrugged his shoulders. Interrogating a weeping woman made him feel a brute and was usually unproductive besides, especially when she had a resolute protector to hand.

And Daisy was as resolute a protector as anyone could ask for.

CHAPTER 5

On his way to find out if Mr. Abernathy was fit to see Alec, D.C. Piper ushered Daisy and Muriel towards the choir room. Alec had said Muriel was free to leave the Albert Hall, as long as she notified the police if she went anywhere other than home.

'But I shan't leave until Roger is well enough to go, too,' she told Daisy, drying her eyes. 'Oh Daisy, it's an awful lot to ask, but do you think you could possibly come and spend the night? I ... I don't think I can bear to be alone with Roger when he's so utterly devastated, and besides, people will talk.'

'Of course I'll come. It won't take a minute to fetch my things from next door.'

'You're an angel. I feel as if you've been transformed practically instantaneously from a pleasant neighbour into a dear friend.'

Daisy had no answer to that. Fortunately she wasn't required to find one. Piper opened the choir-room door for them and stopped for a word with the uniformed constable on duty there, while Daisy and

Muriel went on in.

Intended for several score performers to gather in before proceeding on stage, the long, slightly curved choir room now held fewer than a dozen people. The Gowers were at one end, the Cochrans at the other, perched uneasily on folding chairs. In between, Olivia Blaise was talking to Yakov Levich, with an impassive Dimitri Marchenko on his own at a distance. Consuela de la Costa stalked up and down, declaiming to herself in passionate Spanish with agitated gestures. Very operatic, Daisy thought.

The organist, John Finch, was there too, a puny man who somehow coaxed magnificent sound from his instrument. Though his long, thin fingers twitched, his faraway look did not suggest disquiet, only that he was lost in a musical daydream.

As Daisy and Muriel entered the room, Mr. Levich came to meet them, his face anxious. He held out both hands to Muriel. 'Miss Westlea, you are not harmed?'

'No fear!' said Daisy indignantly. 'Mr. Fletcher would never hurt anyone.'

'Excuse, please,' he apologized, clasping Muriel's hands as he turned to Daisy. 'In Russia, police are very bad men, cruel, savages. Bolsheviks, Okhrana – Tsar's police –

all same. Especially for Jews.'

'Well, you're in England now. Our police are fair whether you're an Englishman, a Chinaman, or a Hindu. Most of them, anyway,' she added in a rush of honesty, recalling a certain inspector whose unfairness had made her call in Scotland Yard, in the person of Alec.

Mr. Levich didn't appear altogether convinced. 'You are friend of this Chief Inspector, Miss Dalrymple,' he said forgivingly.

'That doesn't mean I'd stand by and let him harm Muriel.'

'Daisy is my friend, too,' Muriel assured him. 'She'll come home with me to stay the night when Roger's well enough.'

'*Khorosho.*' He nodded approval. 'You always taking care of others, must sometimes let others to take care.'

Muriel blushed, and extracted her hands from his clasp as Piper returned.

'Dr. Woodward says Mr. Abernathy needs to rest a bit longer, miss,' the young detective told Muriel. 'He'd like to see you.'

'Poor Roger. I'll go to him.'

'You're Mr. Levich, sir? If you wouldn't mind, sir, Chief Inspector Fletcher will see you now. This way, if you please.'

Such an abundance of courtesy surely

ought to reassure the apprehensive Russian Jew, Daisy considered, smiling at Ernie Piper. Not that she blamed Mr. Levich for having the wind up. Though she didn't follow foreign news closely, she had heard of the Bolsheviks' Cheka and OGPU – and that they were worthy successors to the Tsars' brutal and anti-Semitic secret police.

Piper led the reluctant violinist away.

'Shall I go with you?' Daisy asked Muriel.

'No, thanks, but you won't leave, will you?'

'Gosh, no.' With a roomful of suspects quite possibly dying to reveal all to her? Not likely!

She went across to Olivia Blaise.

'Got a fag?' the rival mezzo-soprano asked as Daisy approached. Sitting down beside her, Daisy shook her head. 'Oh well. I don't really smoke, it's frightfully bad for the voice, but there are times... You're Daisy Dalrymple, aren't you? We haven't been properly introduced but I expect you've gathered I'm Olivia Blaise.'

'Yes. I heard you singing a bit of *Carmen* the other day, at the Abernathys'. It sounded simply marvellous.'

'Thank you. I owe an awful lot to Roger – Mr. Abernathy. It's no earthly use having a good voice if you don't train it and I couldn't afford lessons, but he reduced his fees for me. He's a first-rate teacher, you know, as well as the kindest of men.'

'How did you meet him?'

'I was in the ProMusica. I simply had to sing, though I was always pretty tired in the evenings after earning my living as a steno.'

'I hated stenography,' Daisy said with deep sympathy.

'I still do some part-time, but I pick up enough in singing fees to make up the difference. The trouble is, to have a chance with the major opera houses one needs someone with influence fighting on one's side, and dear as he is, Roger can't be described as forceful. Anyway, that bitch Bettina would have put paid to any attempt of his to fight on my behalf.'

Bursting with questions, Daisy said cautiously, 'She does seem to have been an awkward sort.'

'Awkward! I spent enough time in that house to see that she treated Roger and Muriel like doormats. Maybe Muriel had no way to escape, but Roger was too infatuated with Bettina even to try to break free. Poor old Roger, he looked awfully queer, didn't he? I hope the stupid bitch's getting herself murdered isn't going to do for him.'

'Dr. Woodward said he'll be well enough to see Mr. Fletcher later, or at least to-morrow.'

'Mr. Fletcher? The copper? He's a friend of yours, isn't he? You know, I've never been interrogated by the police before.' Olivia shifted restlessly, her animated, pixyish face irresolute. 'Damn, I wish I had a cigarette.'

'Mr. Cochran's smoking. I expect he'd give you one.'

'I wouldn't take a fag from Eric Cochran if I was going to be shot at dawn!'

'I thought he seemed rather keen on you.'

'So did I, until Bettina threatened to tell his wife about us if he didn't give her the Verdi mezzo part. Ursula Cochran holds the purse strings, you see, and dear Eric's career would be nowhere without her moneybags. But I never cared so much for the money, only his influence. All that time I've wasted on him!'

'You mean you... Oh dear!'

'A girl with no money and no family does what she must to get by.' Olivia grimaced. 'But I'm sorry I've shocked you.'

'Not really,' Daisy lied valiantly. Who was she to cast stones? She claimed to earn her own living, but it was eked out by the small income left her by an aunt. Besides, if things got too ghastly she could always run to her mother at the Dower House, or her married sister, or even the cousin who had inherited Fairacres and her father's title. 'I ... I'm sorry it didn't work out.'

'I won't pretend it was all work and no play. I was quite keen on Eric. But he *promised* me the part and what use is a man you can't count on? He gave in without a chirrup to Bettina's blackmail. It's not as if Bettina was pure as the driven snow!'

'No?'

'Oh no, I'm not washing other people's dirty linen in public. I do have my standards.' She hesitated. 'I suppose you'll tell your chief inspector all this.'

'Yes, I can't keep it from him in a murder investigation.'

Olivia shivered. 'Never mind. Someone's bound to spill the beans, and I'd rather it was you than Eric, or myself, come to that. Here's that rather sweet little detective back again. Who's for the rack next?'

'Miss Blaise?' said Piper. 'May I trouble you?'

With a wry backward glance at Daisy, Olivia departed. Daisy decided she quite liked her in spite of her shocking behaviour. She looked over at Mr. Cochran. He was gazing after Olivia with hopeless longing mingled with dread. That he wanted her was plain, and that he feared what she might tell the police.

The expression vanished in a moment as he turned back to his overdressed wife. Beneath the mask of makeup, her face was unreadable. Whether she had noticed anything amiss, Daisy could not tell.

'*¡Señorita!*' Miss de la Costa subsided with dramatic grace onto the folding chair beside Daisy, momentarily lending it the glamour of a royal throne. Her crimson velvet dress seemed an extension of her vivid personality. Glancing at the Gowers – Gilbert Gower studiously avoided looking at her – she spoke in a low voice, throbbing with passion. 'To you I will esplain all!'

'All?' said Daisy cautiously. She wasn't quite ready for a confession of murder.

'All! *¡Todo!* I was madly, wildly jealous! *Mi querido Gilberto*, he meet often this Bettina with the golden hair, you understand. How I hate her! With pleasure I scratch out her eyes! When she drop dead I am glad, glad!'

'But if you were glad because you'd have him to yourself...'

'*¿Perdóneme?*'

'With Bettina dead ... Mr. Gower ... is ...

all yours' – except for his wife - 'so why did you accuse him of murder?'

'But this is what I come to esplain! When I cry to him, "*¡Asesino!*" you are near, I know you hear.'

So did anyone else within range of the soprano's powerful voice. 'Yes, I heard,' Daisy admitted.

'First I think Gilberto kill her because he not wants to be her lover still, he wants to be all mine, like you say. *Bien entendido*, for this I am happy, I protect him with my life, never I cry to him, "*¡Asesino!*" I look at him to admire and he sees I know. He has fear; he esplain. Is long time he is not Bettina's lover. He sees her often because he made a promise is impossible to keep. Always she asks him, when you do this, when, when?'

'Do what?'

'Is nothing to me.' Miss de la Costa shrugged her superbly eloquent shoulders. 'But now I know, is because she is a nuisance he kill her, not for me. So I cry to him, "*¡Asesino!*"'

Baffled by such convoluted' reasoning, Daisy stuck doggedly to the point. 'For whatever reason, you think Mr. Gower killed Bettina?'

'I?' Had she been on stage, the soprano's

astonishment would have been clear to the furthest reaches of the gods. 'Gilberto did not kill Bettina. This he tell me. So, I have esplain, now you will tell your friend, *el jefe de policía.*'

'Miss de la Costa.' Piper had reappeared. 'The chief inspector would like a word with you, if you please, ma'am.'

And Miss de la Costa swept out like a heroine going to the scaffold, leaving Daisy thoroughly confused. Perhaps the pride of a Spanish hidalgo – if that was the right word – would not let him disavow a killing, and the Spanish soprano imputed the same sense of honour to the Welsh tenor. Gower denied murdering Bettina, so in Señorita de la Costa's view he had not done it.

Of course, Alec wouldn't swallow it, and Gilbert Gower didn't expect him to, to judge from the nervous look the tenor sent after his current mistress.

The Gowers exchanged a word, and stood up. Mr. Gower headed down the length of the room towards the Cochrans, while his plump, drab wife came over to Daisy.

'I hope you don't mind,' she said apologetically. 'We haven't ... that is, you must wonder ... you don't know me from Adam, but...'

'Yes, I do. You're Mrs. Gower, aren't you? Mr. Gower's solo nearly made me cry.'

'The *Ingemisco?* He did sing well, didn't he?' Her eagerness to snatch at the compliment to her philandering husband made Daisy nearly cry again.

'Won't you sit down?' she said hastily. 'I'm Daisy Dalrymple. The Abernathys and Muriel Westlea are my next-door neighbours.'

'Oh, do you share a house with Miss Fotheringay, the photographer? Mr. Abernathy recommended her to Gilbert for a publicity shot, and it was so good we took the children to her for a family portrait.'

'Lucy is pretty good, and Mr. Abernathy has been kind enough to recommend her to a number of friends.'

'The poor man! My heart goes out to him. How very fortunate he has no children, but Gilbert says he was very fond of his wife.'

The more shame to Gilbert for his affair with Bettina, Daisy thought indignantly – assuming Miss de la Costa had understood correctly. 'So I gather,' she said dryly.

'He was taken ill, wasn't he? Do you know how he is?'

'Improving, the last I heard.'

'It looked like angina. I work as a volunteer in a clinic in the East End – I myself prefer to deal mostly with the children, poor little things, but on the adult side we deal with angina cases quite frequently. A tablet of trinitrin will usually ease the pain at once.'

'Oh yes, I remember. I worked in a hospital office for a while during the War, and I couldn't help learning a bit. Mr. Abernathy took a pill, but he's not well enough yet to speak to the police.'

'What a dreadful business this is! I suppose the police want to see Gilbert because ... because of what Miss de la Costa said.'

'Chief Inspector Fletcher doesn't explain everything he does to me, Mrs. Gower, though we are friends.'

'I saw you talking together.' Flushing, her eyes on her twisting hands, she went on, 'You must ... you must wonder why I didn't make a fuss about Gilbert publicly embracing that ... that Spanish hussy. One must make allowances for the artistic temperament.'

'I suppose so,' Daisy said doubtfully.

'The truth is, his infidelities are no secret and I'm resigned to them. There's something about foreign divas – the young, beautiful ones – he seems unable to resist. But at the end of the opera season they go back to wherever they came from and Gilbert comes home to me and the children. He's a good father. It wouldn't be right to make the children suffer for the sins of the parents. There's no sense in making a great to-do.'

Patient Grizel in person. Daisy had no patience with such weak-kneed forbearance – she distinctly remembered being disgusted with the story at school. Though she rather thought Chaucer's Grizel had been separated from her children.

So Gower was a good father and always returned to his wife and children. It didn't excuse his hurting Roger Abernathy by his affair with Bettina. Mrs. Gower didn't seem to know about that. Did Abernathy know? Did Muriel know? What had Bettina wanted Gower to do, and was her persistence cause enough for him to murder her?

Or had the melodrama-loving Consuela de la Costa made up the story out of whole cloth?

'I make him comfortable and don't enact any tragedies,' said Mrs. Gower wearily, 'and he comes back. I know you modern girls don't regard a husband as head of the household in quite the way I was brought up to. Whether it will make your lives any easier, I can't guess. One does one's best.'

'Yes, of course. I... Oh, here's D.C. Piper again.'

'Mrs. Gower, if you wouldn't mind giving the chief inspector a few minutes of your time?'

'But I wasn't anywhere near her! I never so much as exchanged a word with her!'

'It'll be all right, Jennie,' said Mr. Gower uncertainly, starting towards her.

'It won't take long, ma'am.'

Daisy expected Gower to insist on accompanying his wife. She knew Alec would let him, but the thought apparently didn't cross his mind. As Mrs. Gower trailed out, looking panicky, the tenor joined Daisy.

'I say, it is all right, isn't it?' His slightly bloodshot eyes anxious, he sleeked down his hair with an agitated hand. 'I mean, the bounder won't bully her or anything?'

'Mr. Fletcher is a perfect gentleman,' said Daisy coldly.

'Yes, yes, of course. Saw you chatting with the fellow in there, in the auditorium. Er ... my wife say anything?'

'She said a good deal.'

'Ah. Yes. Mentioned Miss de la Costa, did she?'

'Mrs. Gower appears to be under no illusions about your friendship ... with Miss de la Costa.' Dying of curiosity, Daisy decided to take the bull by the horns. 'She doesn't know about Bettina, though.'

'Good, that's good. I say, you don't think I did Bettina in, do you? It was all over between us. If you ask me, it was that Russkie bass chappie, Marchenko.'

'Marchenko? Why should he kill Bettina?'

'No one told you yet? It's no secret. Marchenko fancied her and she played him up, led him on, you know. He gave her all sorts of jewellery, good stuff he'd smuggled out of Russia. Then one day at a rehearsal, right in front of everyone, he whispered something in her ear and she slapped his face, called him a disgusting Russian pig. There was something about face fungus, too; I don't remember exactly.' He cast a sidelong glance at Marchenko, who glared back, his black beard bristling.

Daisy remembered the bass's sotto-voce reprise of *Confutatis maledictis* with Bettina lying dead at his feet. 'He certainly had cause to dislike her,' she agreed.

'Dislike! He detested her, and these foreigners are very emotional, very excitable, often downright unstable. Believe me, I know.' He preened his hair again, this time with a self-satisfied smirk. The habitual gesture must be good for the cash register of the hairdresser responsible for preserving his

Marcel wave. 'You'll tell the coppers about Marchenko, won't you?'

'Why don't you?'

'Oh. Well. After all, it's only speculation. I haven't got anything they'd consider evidence. Wouldn't want them to think I was just making trouble.'

Or trying to get himself off the hook. 'I'll pass your speculation on to the chief inspector,' Daisy promised. Along with the news of his affair with Bettina and her pestering him to keep his promise.

'Exhausting, that's what they are, foreigners,' said Gower in a burst of candour. 'In the end, give me good old English reticence every time.' He stared longingly at the door whereby his plain, dull wife had left.

As if in answer to his stare, it opened and Jennifer Gower came in. Their reunion was spoiled by Piper.

'Mr. Gower, your turn, sir.'

He gave her a peck on the cheek in passing. She looked much calmer, no doubt reassured by Alec's most soothing manner. She started towards Daisy but veered off to talk to the Cochrans when Dimitri Marchenko beat her to Daisy's side.

The massive Russian looked down at her grimly. 'You police spy,' he growled.

'No I'm jolly well not!'

'*Tak*, not spy – informer, *nyet?*'

'I'm not an informer, either. I happen to have a friend who is a policeman. I make no secret of it, and if people choose to tell me things, that's their lookout.'

'*Shto* lookout?' He sat down heavily, the chair creaking beneath his weight. 'Lookout is spy.'

'I mean,' said Daisy slowly and carefully, 'if people who know the chief inspector is my friend give me information, they should not be surprised when I tell him.'

Marchenko ruminated on this for a moment, then nodded. 'Informer. I tell you, you tell policeman.'

She gave up. 'Yes.'

'I tell you, Yakov Levich kill Bettina.'

'Mr. Levich?' Daisy was dismayed. She rather liked what little she had seen of the violinist. 'How do you know?'

'Is dirty Jew. Jews all murderers. Kill *Khristos,* kill *khristianskiye dyeti* – childs. To Jews, kill *khristianin* is nothing. Also, Levich is *Russkiy.*'

'So are you.'

'*Nyet! Ya ukrainets.* Live in Russia, speak Russian, but *ukrainskiy* blood. Russians spit on Ukraine, I spit on Russians.' He seemed

92

about to act upon his words but fortunately collected himself in time. 'Also,' he said in a low sinister rumble, 'Levich is Bolshevik spy!'

Daisy didn't believe a word of it. He had spies on the brain. Besides, Levich could not, presumably, rejoice in both Jewish and Russian blood. 'He had no motive, no reason to kill Bettina,' she pointed out.

'Is reason! Good reason. Levich like Bettina's sister. Bettina call him money-gubbing Yid, say will tell parents sister like heretic, try to stop meeting.'

'She tried to stop Muriel's seeing Mr. Levich?'

'*Da*. They talk, she come: "Do this, do that. Fetch this, fetch that." Is reason, *nyet?*'

'A pretty feeble reason!' said Daisy uneasily. Better than that Yakov Levich was a Russian Jew and a Bolshevik spy, she acknowledged to herself. Had Bettina really tried to spoil her sister's romance?

'Pretty reason, yes! Pretty damn good. You tell big policeman. He believe you better. To policemans I do not talk.'

'Mr. Marchenko?' Piper was back. 'If you wouldn't mind, sir.'

Marchenko looked at him blankly.

'PLEASE ... COME ... SIR.' Piper obviously subscribed to the opinion that if

93

you speak to a foreigner loudly enough, he's bound to understand. In case his voice wasn't loud enough to penetrate, he beckoned, too.

Pretend as he might that he understood no English, Marchenko had to respond to the gesture. He heaved himself to his feet and went off muttering into his beard.

Alec was going to have a tough time getting anything out of him, or so Daisy hoped as her suspicions crystallized. The first two or three might have been coincidence, but Marchenko was the last straw. Every time Piper came in he summoned – presumably on Alec's orders – whoever was with her.

The rotter was trying to stop them talking to her!

CHAPTER 6

When Marchenko lumbered into the office behind Ernie, Alec was speaking on the phone. At last his superintendent had rung him up to say all was squared with the local division and the case was his.

He wasn't at all sure he wanted it.

For a start, Daisy's involvement was cause enough for qualms, though at least he'd be on the spot to save her from herself.

As for his suspects, so far he might as well have interviewed a flock of sheep for all the information he had got out of them. The artistic temperament prophesied by Daisy had been absent – except in the flamboyant Spaniard – unless it was manifested in a certain Bohemian cast of mind which made them wary of the police.

He couldn't even say they were lying, since none of them told him anything.

No one was aware of any reason why anyone should have poisoned Bettina Abernathy. No one had ever had anything to do with cyanide. No one had seen anyone interfering with the decanter or glass. All but Mrs. Gower had been far too occupied preparing their thoughts and recruiting their energies for the second half of the concert to concern themselves with anyone else's whereabouts.

And those who did not belong in the soloists' room all had acceptable reasons to go there, including Mrs. Gower. She had gone to congratulate her husband on his performance. Miss Blaise confirmed the usher's report that Muriel had promised to bring a sheet of music she'd left at the Abernathys'.

95

Levich, not finding Cochran in the conductor's room, had gone in search of him to ask something technical about the second part of the *Requiem*. Alec was sure Cochran would have an equally musical explanation, and his wife, of course, had been looking for him, while Abernathy had wanted to see *his* wife.

All perfectly reasonable, and utterly unhelpful.

Nor did Marchenko look promising. His face impassive, as far as one could tell through the luxuriant black beard, he stood stolidly in front of the desk, his gaze fixed on the wall behind Alec. Alec almost turned to see what held his attention, but he knew there was only a plain office clock of no conceivable interest.

'Please sit down.' The only response was a blank stare. Alec waved at a chair. The Russian bear sat.

Alec looked at Ernie Piper, who shrugged. He'd been told to fetch whomever Daisy was talking to, so presumably Marchenko had managed to communicate with her.

'I must ask you a few questions, sir.'

'*Nye ponimayu*,' growled the bear.

'*Vous parlez francais?*' He knew a lot of Russian exiles spoke French, as did any decently educated girl of Daisy's class.

'*Govoryu tolko po-russki.*' The deep bass voice made his every word weighty.

'It seems we need an interpreter. Piper, see if Mr. Levich is still here, will you?'

'*Nyet!*' Marchenko surged to his feet and leant with his fists on the desk, looming over Alec. Piper took a step forward but Alec, unimpressed, waved him back. 'Levich *nyet!* Zhid *nyet!*'

Zhid – Yid? If the man had an irrational hatred of Jews, they'd never get anything out of him by using a Jew as an interpreter. Let him stew in his own juice overnight and face him with an official interpreter tomorrow. Who could tell, he might suddenly find he understood English after all.

A calendar hung on the wall to Alec's right. He beckoned Marchenko over to it, pointed at him, at himself, and at the next day's date. 'Tomorrow, Monday, we talk with an interpreter,' he said slowly and clearly. 'Now, you may go.'

He escorted the disconcerted Russian to the door and saw him out.

'I'd swear he was talking to Miss Dalrymple, Chief.'

'Very likely, but there was no sense sitting here all night waiting for him to decide to talk to us. I've others to see. The Cochrans,

Finch, and if possible Abernathy. Off you go, Ernie.'

When Alec robbed Daisy of the interesting, if rather alarming Marchenko, the Gowers came over to her to say goodbye. Gilbert Gower had an air of bravado about him, but he hung onto his wife's arm as though it were a lifeline.

They went on to exchange a few words with the Cochrans, then left. Cochran went to speak to Finch, startling the little organist out of his reverie, while Mrs. Cochran approached Daisy.

'You don't mind if I introduce myself?' Her tone made it plain no objection of Daisy's was going to weigh with her. 'I'm Ursula Cochran. And you're Miss Dalrymple?'

Daisy was frightfully tempted to say, 'Yes, the *Honourable* Miss Dalrymple,' just to see if Mrs. Cochran's high-and-mighty attitude changed. But that might cut off the anticipated flow of confidences.

'Yes,' she said, 'I'm Daisy Dalrymple.'

'How do you do.' Mrs. Cochran sat down.

Her cosmetics really were exquisitely applied, even if they didn't quite conceal her age, and her fox furs were too divine. The diamonds must be worth a fortune. Maybe she wore them to distract attention from her face, Daisy thought charitably. It must be difficult living up to a much younger and good-looking husband, whether or not she knew of his pursuit of Olivia.

'This is a dreadful business,' the conductor's wife continued.

'Dreadful. I'm afraid poor Muriel and Mr. Abernathy are absolutely shattered.'

'Oh. Yes, naturally, one must feel for their bereavement. But it can't have been poison, as the police seem to believe. It's unthinkable! If Miss Westlea merely suffered a seizure, the scandal won't be nearly as bad. At least it shouldn't get into the morning papers, so we'll have time to think what to say.'

'I'd be very surprised if the morning papers don't have the story,' said Daisy. 'I suspect I saw the *Times* music critic racing for a telephone. Even so highbrow a gentleman must have recognized the news value of a soloist dropping dead on stage.'

'Disgraceful! It shouldn't be allowed. The Press have no sense of decency whatever. I dread to think what the effect will be on my husband's career.'

'Will it harm him? What about the other soloists?'

'The foreigners have nothing to worry about. They can always go back where they came from – the sooner the better as far as poor Jennifer Gower is concerned, I feel sure,' Mrs. Cochran added condescendingly. 'What the unfortunate creature has to put up with! As for Gilbert Gower, he's fading fast anyway. His voice just isn't up to the mark any longer. Dissipation, I'm afraid. Whereas Eric is a rising star and it will be too bad if Miss Westlea's demise ruins his chance of a knighthood.'

'A knighthood!'

'Why not? Many conductors are knighted; look at Hallé, Wood, Cowen, Henschel, Costa. Sir Thomas Beecham was knighted, even though a year later he inherited his father's baronetcy. My father, Sir Denzil Vernon, was a baronet, you know.'

'How unfair that you couldn't inherit his title,' Daisy ventured. Though she didn't care much about titles, she sometimes pondered how different her life would be had she been able to inherit Fairacres.

'Exactly.' Mrs. Cochran nodded her appreciation of Daisy's understanding. 'Eric's knighthood will be some compensation.'

'Unless this scandal puts paid to his hopes. I dare say you are right and Bettina had a seizure, but if not, who do you suppose might have killed her?'

'Oh, the sister, I expect. Bettina left everything to her and she hasn't a penny of her own.'

'How on earth do you know that?'

Mrs. Cochran waved a vague hand. 'One hears these things. Besides, it's usually money, isn't it? Ah, here comes that little man again. The Inspector has sent for my husband, I expect, though I can't imagine why he insisted on Eric's staying. He can't have anything useful to tell.'

'Mrs. Cochran, ma'am, Chief Inspector Fletcher would like a word with you, please.'

'With me!' She sounded outraged, but Daisy thought she saw a flicker of dismay in the hard eyes.

'If you please, ma'am.'

'Oh, very well! I must say, the police seem to grow more tyrannical every day.'

Cochran met her half-way to the door and murmured something, then turned back to Daisy, abandoning Mr. Finch to his internal music.

'Miss Dalrymple, I believe?' The handsome conductor bowed slightly. He had obviously forgotten Muriel's introduction in the Abernathy's hall. 'I'm afraid it would be the height of false modesty to introduce myself. May I join you?'

'Do, Mr. Cochran. Of course I know who you are. I was enjoying your concert until...' Daisy let her voice die away.

'A most unfortunate occurrence. Poor Abernathy is very much distressed, of course.' He said all the right things, but too smoothly, somehow, as if he was only saying them because they were the right things. 'Bettina was all the world to him. I expect he'll give up teaching and directing the Pro-Musica after this. A great loss to the profession.'

'I don't see why he should give up. He'll need his work to take his mind off his loss.'

'If it were only the loss of his wife! But he's losing his sight, he can scarcely see beyond the end of his nose, poor chap. He can't read music any more, so he has to stick with pieces he knows by heart. He'd have to give up the choir soon, in any case, since he can't teach them anything new.'

'How absolutely frightful for him!'

'It's very sad. I shall have to offer to conduct a benefit concert for him. No pensions in our business, alas. Since he's on his way down, too, one must hope Gower has enough salted away. I must admit I rather doubt it.

He has an expensive taste in women.'

Unlike Cochran himself, Daisy thought. All Olivia had wanted from him was a hand up the ladder.

'But I ought not to mention such things to a wellbred young lady.'

'I'm not naïve, Mr. Cochran!' Daisy said tartly, sure that he was keen to talk about Gilbert Gower. 'I saw him with Miss de la Costa.'

'So you did. She's the sort he favours, the sultry southern beauty. We were all rather surprised when he took up with Bettina Westlea. Bettina Abernathy, that is. Not at all his type.'

'You know about that?'

'The world of classical music is small enough, and that of opera and vocal music smaller still. Within it, there are few secrets.' No doubt his bitterness was genuine, considering the use Bettina had made of her knowledge of his liaison with Olivia. 'Gilbert ought to have known better. Mrs. Abernathy's reputation was warning enough.'

'I've heard she wasn't the easiest person in the world.'

'A splendid understatement!'

'Why, what did she do to Mr. Gower?'

'Oh, she ... er ... succumbed to his charms

on the understanding that he'd get her the coveted entrée to Covent Garden. She can't have realized he was on the way out – no influence with the management whatsoever. He's been there forever, of course, and in his heyday he might have done something for her, though he never sang the important rôles.'

'So Bettina was angry when she found out he couldn't keep his promise?'

'I gather she never did quite find out. Even after their affair ended, he kept making more promises – the opera season hasn't started yet, of course – but he must have been afraid she'd land him in the soup by going direct to the powers that be. They wouldn't appreciate his having boasted of his influence with them and it would probably have put a speedy end to what's left of his career. It's a pity it should have led him to murder.'

'You think Mr. Gower murdered Bettina?' Daisy had seen it coming for some minutes. She disliked him more and more. 'If so, at least he won't have to worry about the lack of a pension.'

'Always supposing the police find out.' He looked at her meaningfully.

'They will – if it's true.' For the first time that evening, Daisy was pleased to see Piper come in.

'Mr. Cochran?'

She breathed a sigh of relief. The conductor was almost as bad as Marchenko
with his wild accusations, and not nearly as
interesting.

Mrs. Cochran had returned from her
interrogation looking pleased with herself. 'I
have an idea,' she said to Daisy. 'I shall open
my house for refreshments after Miss
Westlea – Mrs. Abernathy's funeral. There's
bound to be a large turnout and I don't
imagine that meek little sister is capable of
doing it properly.'

The offer would have been more impressive
had Daisy believed it to be motivated by
charitable instincts. Mrs. Cochran's smug expression suggested she revelled in an
opportunity to play Lady Bountiful while
displaying her talents at entertaining a crowd
in style.

'It's true the Abernathys' house is not large
enough to accommodate vast numbers,'
Daisy said, 'so Muriel and Mr. Abernathy
may welcome your help, but the parents are
still around, I believe. They may have their
own ideas.'

'I'm sure they'll be glad to have the
trouble taken out of their hands,' said Mrs.

Cochran determinedly.

Daisy decided she wasn't madly keen on either of the Cochrans.

Major Browne came into the choir room. 'Ah, you're still here, ladies,' he said cheerfully. 'I've found an evening I can squeeze a repeat performance into, with a bit of juggling. If you offer people a free ticket they can't demand their money back. I hope your husband is available tomorrow week, Mrs. Cochran?'

'My good man, I haven't the faintest idea. He has a secretary to deal with that sort of business.'

'All right, I'll ring up in the morning,' said the Major, unoffended. 'What about you, Miss Dalrymple? You and the chief inspector will be able to come, I trust, if it works out?'

'I shall, I expect. I can't answer for Mr. Fletcher.' She thought mournfully of the dinner she should have been eating with Alec at this very moment. 'He's always jolly busy and things come up unexpectedly.'

'Dashed good chap. Have everything cleared up in a trice, I shouldn't wonder. Abernathy hasn't surfaced yet, eh? Well, I doubt the ProMusica has another performance so soon and Monday's their rehearsal night so there shouldn't be any problem with the members. I'll just have a word with Finch. Excuse me, ladies.'

Daisy watched him accost the organist, rousing the little man from his phantom practice, which ended with two silent, crashing chords in annoyance at the interruption.

Mrs. Cochran sat in silence for a few moments, toe tapping impatiently. At last she burst out, 'I can't think why that man is keeping Eric so long!'

'It's only been a few minutes.'

'Quite long enough. Eric has no more to say to him than I did. Really, the police are getting quite above themselves these days.'

'Chief Inspector Fletcher has a murder to investigate,' Daisy reminded her.

'Fiddlesticks! The more I consider it, the more certain I am that Mrs. Abernathy suffered a seizure. Ah, here's Eric now.'

Cochran conferred briefly with Browne and Finch, then Mrs. Cochran bore off her husband, Piper bore off Finch, and the Major rejoined Daisy.

'I think it's going to work out,' he said jubilantly. 'I wish I could offer you a drink to celebrate, but the booze is in my office with the chief inspector.'

'Thank you, but even if you could get at it, I don't think it would be a frightfully good idea on an empty stomach.'

'My dear young lady, you must be starving! My secretary keeps a tin of biscuits in her desk. Now just you wait here one minute.'

He bustled off, to return shortly with a tin of assorted Peek Frean's. Munching on Maries and gingersnaps, they chatted – carefully avoiding the subject of murder – until the choir-room door opened yet again and Muriel and Mr. Levich came in.

Muriel hurried across to Daisy. 'Your chief inspector's with Roger now,' she said. 'Dr. Woodward stayed.'

'Alec won't press Mr. Abernathy beyond what he's fit for,' Daisy assured her, pulling her down onto the next chair, 'and you'll feel much better – well, at least a bit – if you'll just eat a biscuit or two. I'm sure you will. I do.'

'Oh, I couldn't.'

'Eat, my dear,' said Levich, taking the tin proffered by the major and presenting it to Muriel. 'Will not help Mr. Abernathy if you ill.'

Muriel gave him a wavering smile and took a wafer, which she nibbled while he returned the biscuits to the major.

'Help yourself, Mr. Levich,' Browne invited. 'I'll have to replace the tin anyway, after the hole Miss Dalrymple and I've made in it.'

Levich hesitated, nodded, and pulled up a chair, and they had a little tealess tea party. Daisy, at least, tried hard not to think of poor Roger Abernathy, inevitably under suspicion for the death of his beloved wife.

In the conductor's room, a few doors down from the choir room, Alec sat down in a ghastly orange and green tweed chair like those in the soloists' room. Roger Abernathy slumped in a similar chair opposite him. He looked twenty-five or thirty years older than his dead wife, but making allowances for illness, Alec thought he was probably the elder by no more than fifteen years.

Though he was not to have appeared on stage that afternoon, like the performers he wore evening dress. It fitted his stocky frame awkwardly, not ill-made but draping a body on which nothing ever hung quite right. A French phrase came to Alec: '*Il n'est pas chez soi dans sa peau*' – something like that. Roger Abernathy wasn't quite comfortable in his own skin, and from all Alec had heard, marriage to Bettina would not have helped him to feel more comfortable.

At least it seemed unlikely that Daisy's friend could be madly in love with her brother-in-law.

'Mr. Abernathy is a sick man, Chief Inspector,' Dr. Woodward reminded him unnecessarily. Though also seated, he gave an impression of hovering over his patient.

Alec nodded. 'Tell me about your wife, sir,' he said gently.

'I loved Bettina,' said Abernathy in a low, hesitant voice. The glass of his spectacles misted with tears. 'I'm aware she was no angel, but it was a constant joy to look at her, to hear her, and to know she was mine. I was privileged to discover her glorious voice. When she agreed to marry me, I could scarcely believe my good fortune. How I shall go on living without her I can't... I can't...'

'Enough!' snapped the doctor. 'I really cannot allow this, Chief Inspector. After Mr. Abernathy has had a good night's rest, you may consult his own practitioner about the wisdom of a further interview.'

Alec gave up. 'Shall I telephone for a taxicab?' he asked. 'I'll send my sergeant home with Mr. Abernathy and Miss Westlea to lend a hand and make sure they have no difficulties en route.' Not to mention to speak to their servants. Tom Tring, though devoted to his equally mountainous wife, had a way with female servants. He could weasel out information they didn't even know they knew.

CHAPTER 7

Daisy easily read Tom Tring's expression as he came into the choir room. 'Did you miss your tea, Sergeant?' she asked, holding out the major's tin of biscuits.

'Just sitting down to a nice pork pie we was, miss, me and the wife and a couple of friends, when the chief telephoned. Ta, don't mind if I do.' A piece of shortbread vanished in a single crunch. He turned to Muriel. 'You'll be Miss Westlea, ma'am? There's a motor cab waiting to take you and Mr. Abernathy home, and I'm to go with you to see all's well.'

'Is my brother-in-law all right?'

'Not to say all right, miss, but the doctor says he'll do. If he's looking queer when we get him home, we'll ring up his own doctor, otherwise the morning'll be time enough for that. Are you ready to leave, miss? Dr. Woodward and Detective Constable Piper are helping Mr. Abernathy to the taxicab.'

'I'm coming too, Sergeant,' said Daisy as they all stood up. 'Miss Westlea asked me to spend the night with her.'

'Very wise, too, miss. She'll want another woman with her, I don't doubt.' The twinkle in Tom's eye told her he reckoned her kindness was mixed with a determination not to be shut out of the case.

Daisy was equally sure Alec hadn't sent him only to help Roger Abernathy. She oughtn't to be so critical of Mrs. Cochran, who just might genuinely wish to be of assistance as well as to show off.

Alec met them in the lobby. 'We're all off, now, Major,' he said. 'You're at liberty to lock up the Hall. I'll have to keep the keys to the soloists' room for a day or two.'

'Right-ho, Chief Inspector.'

After an interested look at Muriel and Levich, their heads together saying goodbye, Alec turned to Daisy. 'I have to go to the Yard. I'll run you back first but it would be much easier if Tom saw you home, if you don't mind.'

'Don't worry, Chief, I'm going to stay with Muriel anyway.'

He frowned. 'That's not...'

Daisy interrupted quickly, before he could attempt to forbid her. 'I've got an awful lot to tell you.' She nearly said, 'in spite of your efforts to part me from the suspects,' but he looked so weary she refrained.

'Will you have lunch with me tomorrow? I'm sorry about dinner, Daisy.'

'Well, all you promised was not to vanish in the middle, presumably leaving me with the bill, so I suppose you've kept your promise. Shall I hop on a bus and meet you at the Yard?'

Alec grinned. 'Somehow I've a feeling my convenience isn't all you have in mind. I'll show you around one day, but tomorrow I'm hoping to clear up my business there in the morning and to see your friends – among others – in the afternoon, so I'll pick you up.'

'Spiffing.'

'Tom, I'll see you at the Yard first thing tomorrow morning.'

'Right, Chief. Ready, Miss Westlea?'

Muriel was looking up at Yakov Levich with shocked dismay. 'I've just realized,' she blurted out, 'I'll have to telephone my parents. To tell them about Betsy.'

'If you like, Miss Westlea,' said Alec gravely, 'I'll call them up and break the news before you have to speak to them. Just give me the name and telephone number. If they're out, I'll keep trying until I get through, and I'll advise them to ring you so you don't by chance catch them before I've told them.'

'Will you really, Mr. Fletcher?' Muriel's face cleared. 'It's Bury St. Edmunds six-five-three. The Reverend Albert Westlea.'

A clergyman! No wonder Bettina's threat to inform her parents about Mr. Levich had worried Muriel. The general prejudice against Jews was bad enough. Heaven alone knew what a parson would make of his daughter's romance.

As Alec assured Muriel he would telephone right away, Daisy tried to remember who had told her of Bettina's interference. Marchenko, she thought. She hadn't believed much of what the Ukrainian told her, but that had rung true.

'I'll pick you up at one,' Alec said to her, and they all went out into the dark, rainy evening.

On the way to Chelsea in the taxicab, Sergeant Tring perched on the small pull-down seat, facing backwards. His bulk overflowing on each side, he kept up a soothing stream of platitudes about the weather and the increasing number of motor vehicles on the streets of London.

When they reached Mulberry Place, Tring handed Daisy and Muriel down and then gave his arm to Roger Abernathy. Daisy saw a light in the window of the little house next door.

'I'll just pop in and tell Lucy what's up,' she said to Muriel, 'and fetch my pyjamas and toothbrush. I'll be with you in half a jiffy.'

Lucy and her frequent escort, Lord Gerald Bincombe, were in the kitchen, which meant Binkie was in one of his impecunious phases. Like the Honourable Philip Petrie, Binkie did something in the City, though he was more successful at whatever it was than poor Phil. At least, his car was a newish Alvis in contrast to Philip's aged Swift, and he usually managed to take Lucy out to dinner and a show instead of helping her wash up after a cheese omelette.

'What-ho, Daisy,' said Binkie, a hefty, taciturn ex-rugger Blue of about thirty with a gloomy outlook on life, who was wearing an apron over his elegant lounge suit.

'Hallo.' Daisy sat down at the kitchen table and reached for a slice of Lyons Swiss roll. Major Browne's biscuits had merely whetted her appetite.

'I thought your copper was taking you out to dinner,' Lucy said, adding hopefully, 'Have you had a tiff?'

'No! As a matter of fact, I'm helping him

with another case.'

'Another murder? Darling, it's not true.' Dropping her tea-towel on the draining board, Lucy sat down. 'What happened?'

'In the middle of the concert, Bettina next door dropped dead of cyanide poisoning. It was rather ghastly, actually.' She'd been too startled at first, and then too busy, to realize just how ghastly: now Bettina's flushed face, clutching hands, convulsing body rose before her. She felt sick. 'As a matter of fact, it was perfectly horrid.'

In silent sympathy, Binkie poured a glass of cheap South African sherry and set it down in front of her.

'If you haven't eaten,' said the more practical Lucy, 'you'd better not drink that yet. There's an egg left, isn't there, old bean?'

'Two. I'll scramble 'em. Toast?'

'No, don't, Binkie, thanks. I promised Muriel I'd spend the night with her, and I think I'd better make sure she and Mr. Abernathy have something to eat, which'll mean eating with them. I'll tell you more tomorrow, Lucy.' Wearily, Daisy started to rise. 'I'd better go and get my things.'

'You sit right there, darling. I'll pack a bag for you.'

A few minutes later, Daisy was admitted

to the house next door by the house parlour maid, a pudding-faced girl more excited than upset.

'Ooh, miss, isn't it awful?' the maid greeted her. Ushering Daisy into the drawing room, she went on, 'Miss Westlea said please to make yourself comf'table for a minute or two and to help yourself to sherry. She's gone with that p'leeceman to help Mr. Abernathy to his room. If you'll excuse me, miss, I've to make up your bed.'

She scurried out, leaving Daisy a bit disappointed not to have a chance to talk to her. Just as well, she decided. All very well for the police to start questioning grieving relatives and their households right after a death, but it wasn't really quite the thing for a friend and guest to follow suit. Unless, of course, those concerned wanted a friendly ear into which to pour their concerns.

On the whole, the drawing room was stiffly formal, fashionably though not expensively furnished. Amid the conventional, the one incongruity was a baby-grand piano, which took up close to a third of the room. Daisy wandered over to it and played a few notes, vaguely wishing she had practised more in the days of obligatory lessons.

She closed the lid over the keys as Muriel

came in, pale and strained.

'He just sits there,' she said without pre-liminaries. 'When I asked him if he wanted something to eat, he didn't even hear me. Sergeant Tring's getting him to bed, and he says if I put a tray in front of Roger he'll probably eat automatically. What a nice man Sergeant Tring is!'

'Yes, he's a jolly good sort. Muriel, I don't want to be in the way. If you want to be with Mr. Abernathy, don't mind me.'

Muriel shrugged helplessly. 'He doesn't notice I'm there. I told Beryl to take up a tray and I'll pop up later to see how he's doing, but... Won't you have some sherry or a cocktail?'

'No, thanks.' Did she look so desperately in need of alcoholic refreshment? Muriel cer-tainly did. 'But why don't you have a spot?'

'Oh, I couldn't,' Muriel said with a shud-der. 'After ... after seeing Betsy, I don't think I'll ever touch another drop of *any* drink.'

'I know what you mean. You must eat, though. As Mr. Levich said, it won't help if you fall ill, too, and a couple of biscuits are *not* enough to sustain your strength.'

'Nor yours, Daisy. However little I feel like eating, I've no intention of starving you, I promise. I had a cold supper laid out in the dining room for after the concert, so let's go in.'

She led the way across the hall. 'I asked Sergeant Tring to join us, but he prefers to eat in the kitchen.'

'I'm sure he does,' said Daisy dryly. She had more than once heard Alec expatiate on Tom Tring's way with female servants. If the cook, the house parlour maid, or Bettina's personal maid knew anything useful, he'd discover it.

In the dining room, Muriel hastily cleared away the third place setting and they helped themselves to the cold ham, salad, bread and butter, and chutney set out on the table. While satisfying her own ravenous hunger, Daisy made sure Muriel ate properly despite her tendency to fall into a brown study. Her musings did not appear to be all unhappy. Perhaps she was thinking as much of Yakov Levich as of her dead sister.

Beryl came in to clear the dishes, then returned with a rice pudding, its pallid surface dotted with pale yellow sultanas like disembodied cats' eyes.

Muriel stared at it with a strange look on her face. The moment the door closed behind the maid, she said in a tight voice, 'We ate a lot of rice pudding at the Vicarage.

Betsy always had to have it after a concert.'

'Perhaps it reminded her of her childhood, when life was less complicated.'

'Perhaps.' She started crying, hiding her face in her hands. 'I'm sorry,' she sobbed.

'It's all right, honestly. I can't imagine how I would feel if it had happened to my sister.'

'No, you can't possibly imagine, because you love your sister, I expect, and I didn't love Betsy. I did when we were children. I thought I still did. It was when I saw her lying dead, and a great burden rolled off my shoulders, I knew that for years all I'd felt was a sense of responsibility for her. That's why I cried, because I found out I didn't love her. I can't grieve, not properly, only for Roger's and my parents' grief. And I loathe rice pudding!'

'So do I,' said Daisy inadequately, and she moved the dish to the far end of the table where the sultanas couldn't look back at her. 'You felt responsible for Bettina? You can't have been much older than her, and she was an adult.'

'She was still a spoiled child. Our parents doted on her, and all I can remember from the moment she was born, when I was four, is having it dinned into me that I must look after my little sister. She had golden curls

120

and I had straight mousy hair. She had round, rosy cheeks, and mine were thin and pale. She bounced and prattled, and I was quiet and ... and mousy. But I *did* love her.' She looked in appeal at Daisy.

'I'm sure you did. A spoiled little girl can be lovable. A spoiled grown-up is another matter.'

'Yes,' Muriel mused, 'I suppose it was when we came to London things began to change. At home it always seemed natural to do things for Betsy, to give up what I wanted for her sake.'

'Because your parents felt that way, I expect. Didn't you say they didn't want her to marry and come to live in town? How on earth did she ever meet Mr. Abernathy?'

'He was on a walking tour. His heart wasn't so bad then, ten years ago, and gentle exercise was supposed to strengthen it. One Sunday he came to the morning service at my father's church, chiefly to hear the music, I'm sure. Betsy and I were both in the choir, but any solo parts were always given to her, although the organist said my voice was just as good. Father thought more of his congregation would attend church to see a singer who looked like an angel.'

'Men!' said Daisy in disgust. 'Bettina –

Betsy – sang a solo when Mr. Abernathy was there, I take it?'

'Part of Mozart's *Exsultate, Jubilate*. Do you know it? Roger fell in love with her on the spot. Not that he said anything about that then. He said she ought to have proper voice lessons and if she came to London he'd be happy to teach her for free.'

'And your parents wouldn't hear of her leaving home and going off to the wicked city.'

'That was when Roger proposed, of course. Betsy agreed to marry him at once if that was the only way she could get to be a star in grand opera. Even then he was making a decent living as a teacher and choir director, besides having a little money of his own, so in the end Father gave in to her, as always. He gave his permission – as long as I went along, too, to make sure Roger didn't mistreat Betsy. As though he would! He worshipped the ground she trod, just like Father and Mother.'

'Even when she trod on him.' The words slipped out. 'Oh, I'm frightfully sorry, Muriel, I shouldn't have said that.'

'It's true, all too true. I'd better go up and see that he's all right. Beryl will bring coffee to the drawing room. There's a gramophone there, if you want to put on a record, and some magazines. I'm afraid it's going to be a dull evening.'

'I've had quite enough excitement for one day,' Daisy assured her. 'A magazine and some nice, soothing music will be just the ticket.'

Unsurprisingly, the record collection strongly favoured vocal music, but Daisy found a set of Beethoven piano sonatas played by Schnabel. She wound up the gramophone and changed the needle in case the old one was worn. Lulled by the beginning of the 'Moonlight', she picked up the latest *Town and Country* and settled into a chair to admire again the spiffing photos she had taken of Occles Hall. That article had led to the commission she was presently working on, a piece about the Victoria and Albert Museum, conveniently just up the road.

Beryl brought in a tray with a vacuum flask of coffee. 'Cook thought it best, miss, seeing everything's at sixes and sevens. Shall I pour?'

'No, thanks, I'll wait for Miss Westlea.'

The maid had just left when Sergeant Tring knocked and entered, padding in with his unnaturally silent tread.

'Just you here, miss?'

'Yes, Miss Westlea went up to see Mr. Abernathy. Are you finished here? Have the servants told you anything useful?'

'Now, miss, having a bite to eat in the kitchen I was, on Miss Westlea's invitation.' Though the sergeant's tone was injured, his little brown eyes twinkled.

'Bosh,' said Daisy. 'Do sit down and tell me everything.'

'The chief'd have me guts for garters.' But he cautiously lowered his bulk into a chair. 'Well now. Cook never set eyes on Mrs. Abernathy, seemingly, nor heard aught but complaints, and she reckons Miss Westlea didn't pass on the half of 'em and softened them she did.'

'That's no surprise.'

'The housemaid – house *parlour* maid, begging her pardon – she says all anyone ever heard from Mrs. Abernathy was complaints, family included. If it weren't Miss Westlea who gave her orders, young Beryl'd've handed in her notice long since.'

'What about Mrs. Abernathy's personal maid?' Daisy asked impatiently.

'Ah.' Tring ruminated. 'Well, it's not what I ought to be saying to a young lady, but Miss Elsie Pitt did let on as Mrs. Abernathy wasn't no better than she should be. The which Beryl confirmed. And that's as far as I'm prepared to go, miss.' He levered himself out of the chair. 'I'll leave the chief to tell you the rest – supposing you don't ferret it all out for yourself! I'm off home now. 'Night, miss.'

'Good night, Sergeant.' Accompanying him to the front door, she directed him to the nearest bus stop.

The rain had stopped at last; the night was mild, with a westerly breeze delivering fresh air to the smoky city. Daisy lingered on the doorstep, reluctant to return to the troubled atmosphere indoors. Binkie and Lucy came out of next door and exchanged a chaste good-night kiss. Lucy went in. Departing, Binkie saw Daisy, gave her a sheepish wave, and zoomed off in his nippy Alvis sports car.

Daisy turned back into the house. As she closed the door behind her, Muriel came down the stairs.

'I was just seeing Sergeant Tring out,' Daisy explained. 'How is Mr. Abernathy?'

'He's eaten a little and thinks he'll be able to sleep. Have you had coffee?'

'No, I waited for you.' She preceded Muriel into the drawing-room.

'Good. I need a cup.' Pouring coffee from the flask into two dainty little demitasses, Muriel asked, 'Daisy, how on earth did you

125

come to know a detective chief inspector?'

'I sort of got mixed up in a couple of his cases. He says I interfered, but he had to admit I helped him, too.' Daisy sipped her coffee, hesitating. 'Dimitri Marchenko accused me of being a police spy. I'm not, but I shan't conceal from Alec anything which might help catch Bettina's murderer. So if you'd rather I left...'

'No, stay, please. After all, neither Roger nor I killed her. Betsy was ... difficult, but she didn't deserve to die like that. She ... she was my sister.' The telephone rang in the hall. Muriel's cup clinked against the saucer as she set it down, slopping coffee over the rim. 'Oh gosh, that must be Father.'

She went out, leaving the door ajar. Daisy heard the maid's voice: 'Shall I get it, miss?'

'No, that's all right, Beryl.' The ringing stopped. 'Chelsea two-two-six-one. Hallo? Yes, this is Miss Westlea. Who? Oh but... No!' Muriel's voice went shrill and indignant. 'Mr. Abernathy is ill but he is *not* on his deathbed. And I have nothing else to say. Good-bye!'

Red-faced, she marched back into the drawing room.

'The Press,' Daisy guessed.

'*The Times*, wanting to verify information!

Wouldn't you expect *them* to have more consideration?'

'It's a scoop. I thought I saw the *Times* music critic – I met him at a dinner party once. None of the other papers will have the news yet, I imagine, but perhaps you'd better take the receiver off the hook for the night.'

'I have to wait for Father to telephone. They must have gone out to dinner ... unless ... Mr. Fletcher won't forget to ring them up, will he?'

'No, but he has other things to do, too, remember. Oh, there goes the telephone bell again. I don't expect it's a reporter, but would you like me to take it?'

Muriel nodded. 'Yes, please.' She followed Daisy out to the hall.

This time it was the Reverend Westlea. Daisy handed over the apparatus and returned to the drawing room, punctiliously if reluctantly making sure the door latched behind her. She even put on another record to thwart her own eager desire to eavesdrop.

Ten minutes passed before Muriel crept back, her shoulders slumped, devastated. She stopped just inside the door and said in a bewildered voice, 'They blame me. How can they blame me?'

'You mean they think you did it?' Daisy

led her to a chair and made her sit down.

'Oh no, they aren't quite that... No, I ought to have looked after her better, protected her from... Daisy, what could I have done?' she cried in anguish.

'Nothing. You couldn't possibly have guessed someone would poison her, though if you ask me she brought it on herself.'

'But they don't know that,' Muriel whispered. 'I never told them about her lovers, never told them how tactless she could be – no, not tactless, spiteful! They thought she was an angel, and I could never bear to disillusion them. So it's my fault they've had such a dreadful shock.'

'Bosh! You couldn't tell tales on your sister, and if you had I dare say they'd not have believed you. There's none so blind,' said Daisy profoundly, 'as those who won't see.'

'How shall I ever face them?'

'They're coming up to town?'

'Yes, they'll catch an early train tomorrow.'

'Then you'd better get a good night's sleep tonight. Come on, old thing, time for beddy-byes. I must say, I'm good and ready to rest my weary head.'

'Oh, Daisy, I'm sorry.' Recalled to her duties as hostess, Muriel jumped up and led the way upstairs. 'I had the bed in the spare room made up for you,' she said. 'It's rather small but I didn't think you'd want to sleep in Betsy's room.'

'Gosh no!' said Daisy with a shudder.

CHAPTER 8

When Daisy went down to breakfast in the morning, she found Roger Abernathy already in the dining room, seated at the head of the table. Glancing up, he pushed away the plate in front of him, on which a pair of kippers reposed untouched. He started to rise.

'Don't get up.' She sat down beside him. 'Should you be up and about, Mr. Abernathy?'

'Miss Dalrymple, isn't it?' He gave her a shy smile. 'I'm much better this morning and I have a pupil coming at nine. I can't let him down.'

'It doesn't look as if you've recovered your appetite.'

'I'll have toast,' he said apologetically. His lips quivered. 'Bettina always had to have kippers for breakfast on a Monday, but I'm not very fond of them, I'm afraid.'

Though Daisy couldn't see why everyone had to have kippers just because Bettina wanted them, she herself liked them, so she said, 'If those are still hot, I'll eat them.' Taking the plate, she pushed towards her host the silver toast rack and the dishes of butter and marmalade.

Obedient to the gesture, he helped himself. He spread a triangle of toast, then sat looking at it as if he couldn't remember what it was for.

Embarking on the dissection of her kippers, Daisy said gently, 'Muriel will be upset if you don't eat.'

'Yes. I'm sorry, Miss Dalrymple, I'm neglecting my duties. May I pour you a cup of coffee? Or shall I ring for tea?'

'Coffee will be fine, thanks.' She handed him her cup.

Mr. Abernathy filled it and returned it. As an afterthought he passed cream and sugar. 'Sorry,' he said again.

'It's impossible to care about food, isn't it, when your world is collapsing about your ears?' All too clearly Daisy recalled the day the news had arrived of Michael's ambulance having been blown up by a land mine.

He turned to her, for the first time seeming really to see her. 'You lost someone in the War?'

'My brother was killed in the trenches.' She hesitated. Behind the distorting lenses, his eyes were kind. 'That was bad enough but then my fiancé – he was a conscientious objector and he drove an ambulance. I knew he was in danger though he was a noncombatant, but still, the shock...' The lump in her throat silenced her momentarily. Roger Abernathy patted her hand. 'For you the shock must have been ten times worse Daisy went on. 'Bettina's death was so utterly unexpected.'

'I thought I was going to die,' he said in a low voice. 'I expected – I *wanted* – to die. Bettina was my life. People never understood our marriage, how a beautiful, talented girl could put up with a duffer like me, dull, homely, so much older and not even rich. But she needed me. She was a child when I married her; she needed someone to take care of her. And I could help her. I *did* help her. I developed her voice into a glorious instrument worthy of any opera house in the world.'

Daisy said nothing. After a moment, Abernathy sighed and went on, 'My poor darling handicapped herself, sabotaged her own career. She knew her own worth and she was impatient of any hindrance. I was afraid of turning her against me, so I gave her the freedom she craved. Perhaps I should have tried to curb her?'

'Who knows? You might well have failed and lost her altogether.' Flustered, Daisy tried to correct herself. 'I mean...'

'You mean she might have left me for one of her lovers,' he said flatly, 'instead of continuing to live nominally as my wife. Did you think I didn't know? From very early in our marriage I was aware that it was only a matter of time before she was unfaithful. She was young and beautiful; she had always been pampered, always got what she wanted. I wasn't what she wanted. I loved her, but she didn't want my love. I would gladly have given her the moon, but all I had to offer that she cared for was indulgence, so that's what I gave her.'

Under other circumstances, Daisy might have told him forthrightly that he was being as wishy-washy as Mrs. Gower. It was too late. Bettina lay dead and all the firmness in the world would not bring her back to life.

At this awkward juncture, she welcomed Muriel's arrival with a hearty, 'Good morning!'

'Good morning, Daisy.' Muriel looked

much better for a good night's rest. She was wearing black, which, as Daisy had noted the previous day, suited her very well. There was even something of a spring in her step as she circled the table to take the seat on Abernathy's other side. 'Roger, how are you this morning?'

He managed a weary smile. 'Quite well enough to give a lesson or two, my dear.'

'In the drawing room. There's no need to tackle the stairs down to the music room. But I could have telephoned to cancel your lessons. You shouldn't have let me sleep in.'

'That was my fault,' said Daisy. 'I told the maid not to wake you. Your parents are coming from the wilds of Norfolk, I gather. Even if they catch the milk train, they can't be here for hours.'

'No.' Muriel blushed. 'But Mr. Levich said he'd call this morning to see if there is anything he can do to help.'

'Yakov Levich?' Abernathy looked quietly pleased, almost relieved, Daisy thought. He must be glad to have a little of the burden of being the only gentleman in the bereaved household lifted from his shoulders. 'That's good. Levich is a good fellow. Well, if you ladies will excuse me, I'll just go and pre-pare for the first lesson.'

Not until the door closed behind him did Daisy realize that he still had not eaten his toast.

Beryl brought a plate of kippers and a pot of tea for Muriel, and more toast. Her head bent over the bony fish, Muriel said to Daisy, 'I hope you don't mind Mr. Levich coming.'

'Good gracious, no. Why should I?'

'Because he's Jewish. A lot of people will speak to him, congratulate him, even shake his hand in the concert hall but would never invite him to their homes.'

'A lot of people are absolute blithering idiots,' Daisy snorted. 'Believe it or not, Lucy, who's my dearest friend, feels more or less the same about Mr. Fletcher just because he's a policeman. You're fond of Mr. Levich, aren't you?'

'Fond! I... He's just a friend. Our choir and his orchestra perform together quite often so I see him at rehearsals, and sometimes we talk. And once or twice he's given me tickets to his recitals and chamber concerts. That's all.'

'It's a good start,' said Daisy encouragingly, which made Muriel go still pinker and turn back to a close examination of her kippers.

The doorbell rang. Muriel at once lost even the pretence of interest in her breakfast.

She listened intently as Beryl went to open the door. A man's voice, words indistinguishable, was followed by the maid saying, 'Miss Westlea said to expect you, sir. Please do come in.'

'Oh dear,' said Muriel in sudden dismay, 'there isn't really anything he can help with.'

'We'll think of something,' Daisy promised.

At that moment the telephone bell shrilled. Muriel seized the excuse to go out to the hall and Daisy followed her to the door. Beryl, with Mr. Levich's rather shabby hat in her hand, answered the phone. 'It's the *Daily Sketch*, miss,' she announced excitedly.

'Newspaper?' said Mr. Levich. 'You want to speak, Miss Westlea?'

'No!'

'Then I will.' He took the apparatus from the maid. 'Allo? Sorry, plis, I no spik Inglis,' he said in a grossly exaggerated accent and hung up.

Daisy applauded. He grinned at her. When shortly thereafter the first of a flood of reporters rang the doorbell, Levich dealt with him, and he continued to answer doorbell and telephone bell with equal aplomb and incomprehension. Word got around and the flood slowed to a trickle.

In between, since Abernathy was teaching in the drawing room, they sat in the dining room. At one end of the table, Muriel and Levich conversed in low voices. At the other, Daisy made notes on the interesting conversations she had had in the choir room at the Albert Hall, so that she wouldn't forget anything she ought to tell Alec. From across the hall wafted tenor and then contralto scales and arpeggios, long drawn-out oohs and aahs on various notes, and occasional snatches of melody.

When Abernathy's two scheduled lessons were finished, Muriel and Daisy left the men together and went up to Bettina's bedroom.

'I told Elsie to pack up her clothes,' Muriel said unhappily. 'It may seem a bit precipitate, but Mother and Father will have to have her room. There's nowhere else to put them. I hope they won't mind.'

'If they do, they can always go to a hotel,' Daisy pointed out. The bedroom she'd slept in last night was certainly not big enough for two, and from the layout of the house, she thought Muriel's and Abernathy's could not be much larger.

They met Bettina's personal maid coming out of the bedroom with an armful of shoes. A spare, sour-faced woman, she looked as if she had a grudge against the world. Daisy wondered what Tom Tring had got out of her besides what he had revealed.

'I'm putting these up in the box room loose for the moment, miss,' she said. 'There's not enough room in the suitcases. And I'll be wanting to talk to you about giving my notice.'

'All right, Elsie, but not just now. Is that the last load?'

'I can't get in madam's desk, miss. That sergeant had the key from her handbag, but he checked it was locked and that there's no spare and took it away again.'

'He didn't search it?'

'Sergeant Tring wouldn't do that,' said Daisy, 'not without permission or a warrant.'

'And there's the valuables, miss,' the maid went on self-righteously. 'You didn't say...'

'I'll deal with those. Please tell Beryl she can make up the bed.'

Daisy followed Muriel into the blue and white bedroom. The wardrobe doors stood open, its bare interior too like a vast, empty coffin for comfort. Muriel hurriedly turned away and crossed to the dressing table. Among the neatly ranged brushes and combs and cosmetics were three leather jewellery cases.

'Didn't she keep her jewellery in a safe,' Daisy asked, 'or at least locked away?'

'No, she used to spend hours going through the cases and gloating over the contents. All her ... her admirers gave her jewels. It wasn't so much the value she cared about, they were more like...' Muriel hesitated.

'Trophies? They'll be yours now, won't they?'

'I think so, but how did you know?'

'Someone told me it was common knowledge Bettina left everything to you.'

'She used to threaten in public to change her will if I didn't do what she said.' Muriel sank onto the dressing-table stool and buried her face in her hands.

'How beastly!'

'That's not why I stayed. I told you, I'd promised my parents to look after her, besides having nowhere to go but back to the Vicarage. But she believed it gave her a hold over me, as well as spiting poor Roger. She said he'd taken advantage of her by marrying her when she was too young to know her own mind, and he wasn't going to profit from it. As though there was the slightest chance she'd die before him!'

'She did,' Daisy reminded her bluntly.

'Yes, she did.' Muriel raised her head, dry-eyed. 'And if it turns out I really am the one to profit, I shall give Mr. Marchenko back his blasted Russian heirlooms and sell the rest and give the money to Mr. Levich to bring his parents here from Poland!'

Too astonished either to raise practical issues or to warn her that to the police her inheritance gave her an excellent motive to do away with her sister, Daisy exclaimed, 'His parents?'

'They're stuck in Poland without the papers or the money they need to leave. Yasha – Mr. Levich, I mean – saves every penny he can to bring them here.'

'Yasha?'

'He asked me to call him Yasha.' Muriel's eyes were starry. 'It's short for Yakov.'

'I told you you had made a good start,' Daisy said with a smile, but inside she felt cold. Bettina's will had been common knowledge; Yakov Levich was badly in need of money; he had made up to Bettina's drab heir and Bettina had died.

Not for a minute did Daisy believe either Muriel or Levich had murdered Bettina, but Alec would have every reason to suspect both.

Bettina's attempts to separate the two only made matters look worse. But that had been part of Marchenko's diatribe, Daisy remembered. The disgruntled Ukrainian bass had spouted a lot of drivel not worth repeating. Besides, there were plenty of other people with reason to hate Bettina.

Muriel had gone over to the desk and tried the flap-front. 'Locked,' she said, sighing. 'Betsy kept every love letter she ever received. I suppose the police will have to see them. I can't see any hope of keeping the truth from my parents.'

'You don't have to be the one to tell them. Why don't you talk to Mr. Abernathy about it, see what he thinks you ought to do? He told me he knows about Bettina's lovers.'

'Oh yes, he's always known, poor Roger. She never tried to keep it a secret from him, only from our parents. Yes, I'll ask him,' said Muriel with relief.

'Are you going to introduce Mr. Levich to them?'

Muriel's mouth tightened. 'Yes.'

'Good. However much one loves and respects one's parents, one can't go on forever living one's life to please them.' Daisy raised a hand to her shingled head. Alec liked it; Mother would simply have to put up with it.

'But you will stay another night, won't you? At least one more? With you here, they

140

won't be able to ... to...'

'To rag you quite as freely,' said Daisy dryly. 'Yes, I'll stay, but I'll have to bring some work over. I've got an article on the V and A due next week.'

'You can use the music room. There's a desk down there, and I shan't let Roger go down for several days at least.'

Beryl came in with a duster and a pile of clean sheets and pillowcases. Daisy helped Muriel carry the jewellery cases and other odds and ends to her own bedroom, then they went downstairs.

While Muriel consulted Abernathy about what to tell her parents, Daisy talked music with Yakov Levich until the telephone rang and he went to answer it. He came back to announce that the Reverend and Mrs. Westlea had arrived at Liverpool Street Station and were about to take a taxicab to Chelsea.

Glancing at the clock, Daisy was disappointed to realize it was ten to one so she wouldn't be there when they arrived. Promptly at one, Alec's yellow Austin Seven 'Chummy' pulled up outside the house.

The small knot of reporters and photographers still lingering hopefully at the gate converged on him. Lurking behind the drawing-room curtains, Daisy saw him say something and shake his head before proceeding up the path. Two of the photographers snapped his back view with the murder victim's house as background.

'Drat!' Daisy exclaimed. 'I can't say I'm frightfully keen on appearing in the papers either as Detective Chief Inspector Fletcher's "friend" or as "helping the police with their enquiries."'

'You're both welcome to stay to lunch,' Muriel suggested tentatively as Levich went out to open the front door.

Daisy didn't think lunching with the infirm widower, two suspects, and the victim's censorious clergyman father would suit Alec at all. Nor could they very well seek privacy afterwards to discuss the case before Alec interviewed said suspects. While she hesitated over a polite refusal, Abernathy intervened.

'I expect you and the chief inspector will want to talk privately,' he said in his gentle way. 'Why don't you go out the back way through the music room into the alley, Miss Dalrymple? There are several cafés and restaurants within easy walking distance.'

'An excellent idea, Mr. Abernathy,' said Alec, following Levich into the drawing room. 'I was wondering how to avoid the hounds of the Press.' He greeted Daisy and

Muriel, then turned back to Abernathy. 'I'm glad to see you looking better, sir, well enough to answer one or two questions later on, I hope?'

'Certainly, Mr. Fletcher. Here's the key to the back door so that you can return that way. I shall be here.'

'Thank you. I'll be wanting a word with you, too, Miss Westlea, if you wouldn't mind staying at home this afternoon. And since you happen to be here, Mr. Levich...?'

'I shall remain,' said the violinist uneasily.

'Then, if you'll excuse us, Miss Dalrymple and I will be on our way.'

Passing Muriel, Daisy squeezed her hand and whispered, 'Don't worry, it'll be all right.'

As they went down the back stairs, Alec said, 'I didn't expect to find Levich letting me in. What the deuce is he doing here?'

'*Not* letting people in. He's been invaluable, pretending not to speak English so that the reporters don't pester us.'

'At least he had the goodness to speak English to me last night, though he didn't tell me anything. The other Russian, the bass, wouldn't admit to understanding either English or French.'

'Marchenko is a Ukrainian, not a Russian,

and he speaks adequate, if not brilliant, English.'

'I knew he'd been communicating with you somehow. I take it Miss de la Costa is also reasonably fluent? She managed the odd phrase in English between floods of Spanish.'

'Liberally larded with dramatic gestures?' Daisy laughed. 'She is not merely fluent but voluble in English. This way, I think.'

The wide passage was glassed on one side and wicker chairs showed it also served as a sunroom or summerhouse, pleasant even on this grey March day. It led to Roger Abernathy's music room – converted from the old mews like Lucy's studio – which contained a full-size grand piano. The walls were lined with shelves piled high with neat stacks of scores and sheet music. The desk in the corner was also neat, Daisy noted with approval, the appointment book open at the right page and ready to hand, unlike Lucy's.

'If you're not in a frightful hurry,' she said as they stepped out into the alley, 'I'll just pop into the studio and tell Lucy I'll be staying here another night or two.'

Alec consulted his wristwatch. 'As long as you don't get involved in a long conversation.'

'Come in, then you can drag me away. I'd

like to introduce you to Lucy anyway.'

'Not today. That would take longer than I can spare. I'll wait here.'

Daisy opened the back door and went into the studio, long since recovered from her last tidying. 'Lucy?'

No answer. She could ring the bell just inside the door, which sounded in the house – a convenience for clients who arrived in Lucy's absence – but Alec was in a hurry. Hastily she scribbled a note and drawing-pinned it to the open darkroom door.

'That was quick.'

'She's not there. I expect she's having lunch. I left a note.'

Alec frowned. 'No one's there? And the door left unlocked?'

'Lucy's a bit careless, I'm afraid. I suppose she's pretty lucky no one has yet pinched her cameras.'

'It's not the cameras I'm thinking about. Miss Fotheringay has a darkroom, doesn't she? Is that locked?'

'No,' said Daisy guiltily, though why *she* should feel guilty she wasn't at all sure. Except that Alec in his most policemanly aspect, fierce dark brows meeting above piercing grey eyes, was enough to make anyone feel guilty.

'Does Miss Fotheringay by any chance use cyanide of potassium as a fixing agent?' he asked, his tone caustic. 'Does she happen to know it's a deadly poison?'

'Oh Alec, you're not suggesting Bettina was poisoned with Lucy's cyanide?'

'You tell me.'

'Lucy took her portrait,' Daisy admitted, 'and it came out so well Mr. Abernathy recommended her to his friends. I should think at least half your suspects must know about her darkroom.'

CHAPTER 9

'I still think you should have tried to find Lucy instead of locking the darkroom door and taking away the key.' Over her lamb chop, Daisy glowered at Alec as he returned from the telephone.

'Miss Fotheringay needs a lesson in the proper handling of deadly poisons,' he said patiently, and reminded her, 'I did leave a note of explanation.'

'All the same, she'll be livid.' Daisy stabbed a Brussels sprout.

Alec winced. Though Daisy always skated tactfully around the subject, he was all too aware that Lucy Fotheringay strongly disapproved of the Honourable Miss Dalrymple's friendship with a mere copper. 'Tom's on his way to fingerprint the room,' he said, squeezing a slice of lemon over his fillet of plaice. 'He'll come by here to pick up the key, so she won't be kept out for long.'

Daisy cheered up. 'So he can warn her about leaving poisons lying about, instead of you.'

'I shan't have to see her at all – in the way of business – if she'll cooperate with Tom. I need a list of her clients, who was alone in the studio, whether anyone expressed interest in the darkroom or the process of developing and printing. If she won't tell Tom, I...'

'No, *I'll* get it out of her. You must admit, Alec, she's a sight more likely to tell me than you or Sergeant Tring.'

'True.' He sighed. In her inimitable way, Daisy was getting more and more enmeshed in the case. 'I gather the same applies to that lot at the Albert Hall last night. I've never met such a blank with supposedly respectable people.'

Her irresistible smile held a pardonable hint of smugness. 'Yes, they talked to me.'

She pondered. 'Or, in a way, through me. Several told me things they wanted you to know but didn't want to tell you directly.'

'Great Scott! The artistic temperament, I take it.'

'With some of them, I expect. With the Russians – Mr. Levich and Dimitri Marchenko, that is – it's partly general mistrust of the police. Fear, even.'

'Justified, I dare say, poor devils. All right, let's start with Levich and go through them in the order you spoke to them.'

'That's another thing!' Daisy had a militant glint in her blue eyes. 'Did you tell Piper always to take away whoever was with me?'

Alec grinned. 'Of course. I thought you might take it amiss, but I just wanted to make sure you circulated as much as possible.'

'Oh, I see,' she said, mollified. 'Let me see, Levich first? Yes, I went into the choir room with Muriel and he came dashing over.'

'There's something between those two, is there?'

'They're just friends,' said Daisy, unconvincingly casual. 'He was afraid you'd been bullying her – the Russian police-persecution complex. I only had time to reassure him before Piper dragged him off to the interrogation chamber. Then Muriel went to see

148

how Abernathy was doing and Olivia Blaise came over, ostensibly to cadge a cigarette.'

'Olivia Blaise – Roger Abernathy's pupil?'

'And Bettina's rival. Oh, not for Roger's affections, though she's grateful to him and fond of him – which is more than I've heard said of Bettina, come to that. But they were rivals for the mezzo part in the *Requiem*, which could have meant a big boost to someone's career.'

'Aha! And Bettina got the part.'

'By the dirtiest trick! Eric Cochran had promised it to Olivia, and Bettina threatened to tell his wife he had a mistress.' Daisy was rather pink in the face, but one way or another illicit sex had come into both the cases she'd been involved in and she didn't falter. 'Cochran used to fetch Olivia from the Abernathys' house after her lessons, I think. His car looked familiar to me, as if I'd often seen it before. I'm pretty sure he's absolutely mad about her, but *his* career depends on Mrs. Cochran's money.'

'Motives for both Cochran and Miss Blaise,' Alec mused, 'but rather thin. Murder in the middle of the concert was too late for her, and not exactly career-promoting for him, as both he and his wife were at pains to point out. Anything else from Miss Blaise?'

'She said Bettina was far from pure as the driven snow...'

'Again aha!'

'...But she refused to wash other people's dirty linen in public, so you'll just have to wait until I get to that part. Who's next?'

Alec consulted the list he'd placed beside his plate. 'Consuela de la Costa. Dare I hope she explained why she shrieked, "Assassin!" at Gower?'

'She "esplained" in considerable detail. Whether I can esplain her esplanation is another matter. She's Gower's mistress, and she admits to being wildly jealous because he was also Bettina's lover. As far as I can make out, she assumed when Bettina dropped dead that Gower had killed her so as to give himself entirely to her. To Consuela, that is.'

'So she accused him.'

'No, no, let me get this straight. She was glad Bettina was dead and she'd never have given Gower away, but he guessed she thought he'd done it and he told her Bettina hadn't been his mistress for some time. He'd continued to meet her often because she was pestering him about a promise he'd made her. So then Consuela thought he'd killed Bettina because she was making a nuisance of herself, not for Consuela's sake.

That's when she accused him of murder.'

Alec closed his eyes. 'Are you serious?' he asked in a failing voice.

'Serious, but far from certain. I think I've got it right, but this was all in a heavy accent and interspersed with bits of Spanish, remember.'

'And dramatic gestures.'

'Of course. Anyway, Gower assured Consuela he hadn't done it. She believed him, and wanted to esplain to me that she hadn't really meant it when she screeched, *"¡Asesino!"* So that I could tell you, which I've now done, and let's move on to the next, please.'

'Motive for Gower: Bettina was pestering him about some broken promise. You don't by any chance...?'

'Yes, but in its proper place or I'll get all mixed up.'

'Motive for the señorita: wild jealousy.'

'She said she wanted to scratch out Bettina's eyes. Mrs. Gower's next, isn't she?'

'First, would you like pudding? Coffee?'

Daisy had managed to clear her plate despite all the talk. Head tilted, she considered her options. 'I'd better stick to coffee,' she decided regretfully.

'Two coffees, please,' Alec said to the waitress, and added apologetically to Daisy,

'I still owe you a slap-up dinner, to make up for last night.'

'A pie and a pint'll do me, Chief,' rumbled Tom Tring, suddenly appearing on silent feet and winking at Daisy. 'You make him take you to the Ritz, miss. Got that key for me, Chief?'

'Here. If Miss Fotheringay's not there, you have Miss Dalrymple's permission to search the darkroom.'

'I never said that!' Daisy objected. 'Oh, all right, Sergeant, you have my permission. But Lucy will be there and she'll be in a tearing rage.'

'You leave her to me, miss.'

She smiled at him, transferring the smile to Alec as Tring left. 'I must say I'd like to see them meet. Never mind about dinner, Alec, we'll manage it some time. But we'd better not make plans in advance. Just give me half an hour's notice to dress up and powder my nose.'

'I'll try to give you a whole hour.' What a dear she was! Surely Belinda couldn't help liking her, nor his mother, however much she deplored his getting mixed up with the aristocracy. She was sure he'd be let down in the end. Well, maybe, but in the meantime...

'Mrs. Gower,' said Daisy, as the waitress

deposited two cups on the table and departed again. 'Poor woman, she knows about her husband's straying. She claimed to be resigned to it, since he always returns to her and their children. She said it would be unfair to make the children suffer for the sins of their father. All the same, I can't help feeling she's at least a little bit bitter. She called Consuela a Spanish hussy.'

'She saw them embracing on the stage? It's possible she hadn't realized till then that Miss de la Costa had replaced Bettina in Gower's affections.'

'Yes, but I don't think she knew about Bettina.' Daisy sounded distinctly dubious. 'She talked about foreign divas who go home to their own countries, leaving Gower to her.'

'If she poisoned Bettina, that's the impression she'd want to give,' Alec pointed out. 'Especially as Bettina, not being foreign, must have seemed a much greater threat to her marriage. A more than adequate motive for murder – if any motive can ever be considered adequate. Did she say anything else of interest?'

Daisy pulled a face. 'She and Gower and their children all had their photographs taken by Lucy.'

'Did they, indeed! Means, motive, and

opportunity, as she admits she was in the soloists' room. We'll have to take a close look at Jennifer Gower.'

'And at Gilbert Gower. He admitted to his affairs with Consuela and Bettina. Do you know, Alec, Mrs. Gower said Gower had told her how devoted Roger Abernathy was to Bettina, and the two men were supposed to be friends, yet Gower seduced Abernathy's wife!'

'Perhaps it was the other way round.'

'Bettina seduced Gower?' Daisy frowned. 'Could be, considering his preference for exotic foreigners, and ... but I'll get to that in a minute. Anyway, Gower told me it was all over between him and Bettina and he was sure Marchenko had killed her.'

'Marchenko!' said Alec, startled. 'I'd pretty much written him off, in spite of his refusal to communicate. What's *his* motive supposed to be?'

'He was in full pursuit of Bettina, gave her valuable gifts – I mean really precious stuff he'd smuggled out of Russia – and then she turned around and publicly humiliated him. Gower said she slapped his face and called him a disgusting Russian pig. It was at a rehearsal, so other people must have seen it.'

'Now I know what to ask about, I'll doubtless get confirmation. Motive for Marchenko, and opportunity. What about means?'

'I don't think Lucy photographed him. She'd have mentioned such an unusual client.'

'Well, if he bought cyanide at a chemist's, for photography or as a pesticide, we shouldn't have any trouble tracing him.'

'No, he's certainly memorable. He was the next one I talked to, wasn't he? He accused me of being a police spy. He's got spies on the brain, and Bolsheviks, and Jews, and Russians.'

'Russians?'

'I told you, he's a Ukrainian. I don't know their history much, but I dare say the Russians have been oppressing the Ukrainians for centuries. Yakov Levich being a Russian and a Jew, Marchenko's convinced he's a Bolshevik spy, too. He must have murdered Bettina because murder is what Jews, Russians, Bolsheviks, and spies like to do. Q.E.D.'

'Great Scott! He didn't accuse Levich of having an affair with Bettina?'

'No, not a hint. I wonder how he missed that one?'

'Then we can safely assume that Levich did *not* have an affair with Bettina. Unless someone else...?'

'No, no one even suggested the possibility.'

She wouldn't lie to him outright, but Alec was convinced she was withholding something Marchenko had told her. Protecting Muriel Westlea?

'Mrs. Cochran, on the other hand, doesn't believe it was murder at all,' Daisy rushed on, making Alec the more sure she had something to hide from him.

'Murder at Eric's concert would be bad for Eric's career, might even prevent his being knighted one day, therefore Bettina had a seizure.'

'So the lady informed me.'

'I asked her about the effect on the soloists' careers. She said the foreigners can always go home and Gower's career is fading anyway because he's losing his voice due to dissipation. Which ties in with what Cochran told me about...'

'Wait a minute. I can't see how it would affect the case, but does she know about Cochran and Miss Blaise?'

'If so, she won't admit it. She was frightfully condescending about what poor Jennifer Gower puts up with from her husband.'

'In any case, it wouldn't give her a motive

for doing away with Bettina.'

Daisy sat bolt upright, eyes gleaming with excitement. 'But Alec, suppose she thought it was Bettina, not Olivia, who was Cochran's mistress! I told you they used to meet at the Abernathys remember? I bet she found out he kept going there, and drew the wrong conclusion.'

'Do I gather you dislike Mrs. Cochran?' Alec asked dryly.

'Yes,' she admitted, abashed. 'She's overbearing and self-centred, and the only reason she cares about Cochran's career is that she desperately wants him to be knighted so she'll be Lady Cochran.'

'Which makes it still more unlikely that she'd wreck his concert.' He reached across to pat her hand as her face fell. 'But you could be right about her mistaking the object of her husband's affections, and jealousy might outweigh the desire for honours. It'll have to be investigated. Now what's this Cochran said about Gower's fading career?'

'He said Gower promised Bettina to land her a rôle at Covent Garden, but he couldn't possibly do so since he has no influence with the management. If they had found out about his promise, it would have put paid to his career because he's already on the way out. Cochran thought Gower had managed to string Bettina along so far, but it was only a matter of time before she went to Covent Garden to find out what was going on.'

'So Cochran's pointing at Gower. Daisy, why on earth do these people tell you these things?'

'In this case, because they want the police to know but they can't quite bring themselves to sneak on each other directly to you. I didn't ask leading questions, honestly. All I did was sit there looking interested and it all came pouring out. Eric Cochran led up to Gower's fading career by way of sympathy for Roger Abernathy, whose career he reckons is finished. He talked about conducting a benefit concert for him – it sounds charitable but I'm sure he was just thinking of the publicity.'

'Whoa!' Alec grinned. 'He'll be having you up for defamation of character. Why should Abernathy's career be over? His heart? Or because people don't want to associate with a man whose wife was murdered?'

'No, because his eyesight is so bad he can't read music any longer, apparently, and the shock of losing Bettina will make him give up the struggle. Alec, he told me himself he wanted to die when Bettina dropped dead. It was simply frightful.'

'Poor chap.'

'I suppose he's still on your list, though.'

'It's my job to suspect everyone, you know that. Hasn't anyone tried to implicate Muriel Westlea?'

Daisy hesitated, fidgeted with her empty coffee cup. 'Actually, Mrs. Cochran said if it was a murder, which of course it wasn't, then Muriel must have done it because Bettina left her everything she possessed.'

Alec studied her face. She failed to meet his eyes. Was she ashamed for having tried to keep that from him, or was she still hiding something? Surely she knew he'd find out about Bettina's will from her solicitor – as in fact he already had that morning. No, the will was a sop to Cerberus, to stop him questioning her further about Muriel.

Daisy wouldn't withhold facts from him. Hearsay or her own speculations she was more than capable of keeping to herself if she feared they might damage a friend in whose innocence she believed.

'And that just leaves Mr. Finch,' she said brightly, 'who didn't say a word to me. I don't think there's much room in his head for anything but music.'

'None,' said Alec, whose questions had somehow led to a learned disquisition on the differences between playing the organ as a solo instrument or as an accompaniment. 'That's everyone from the choir room,' he agreed, 'but surely you talked to Abernathy, Miss Westlea, and Levich last night or this morning?'

Before she could answer, the waitress brought the bill. Alec paid and helped Daisy on with her coat, and they set off back to the house. Taking out his pipe, he filled and lit it, and smoked as they walked.

The shops in the King's Road had re-opened after the lunch hour; the pavement was thronged with housewives, baskets or string bags over their arms, children in tow or running ahead. Whistling errand boys on bicycles whizzed past, dodging horse-drawn drays and motor vans. Daisy waited until they turned down a quiet side street before she responded, elliptically, to Alec's question.

'Muriel, Mr. Abernathy, and Mr. Levich aren't the sort of people to pass on gossip or make wild accusations.'

'Perhaps not, but you can't have sat in silence the whole time, and I can't believe that with the lady of the house newly murdered, you indulged in nothing but idle chatter.'

'Well, no.' Daisy sighed. 'In fact, I'd better warn you: Muriel says her parents didn't know about Bettina's lovers, so will you try not to disillusion them?'

'I'll try; no promises. Miss Westlea knew, obviously. What about Abernathy?'

'He knew. He said so, and so did Muriel. I don't think Bettina ever made any effort to keep her unfaithfulness from him. He was resigned, like Mrs. Gower, only it didn't seem to me there was any bitterness in his resignation. He pretty much expected it when he married her, being so much older. Dull and homely and not even rich, he said – it was so sad, Alec – and she was young and beautiful and talented.'

'Why on earth did she marry him?'

'To escape from home and develop her talent. Her parents wouldn't let her leave if she wasn't married. Abernathy offered marriage and voice lessons, so she accepted him. Even then, she made no secret of it. He knew what she was and loved her anyway.'

'That all ties in pretty well with what her maid told Tom,' Alec said. 'On the face of it, he has no motive for killing her now rather than any time in the past ten years. The same goes for her sister – Mrs. Cochran was right, incidentally. I saw the solicitor this morning: Bettina left Muriel everything and she hadn't changed the will in years. Odd, really, that she made one at all at her age and without vast riches to consider.'

'It's not much?'

'Not enough to live on. A nice nest egg. I expect Bettina felt Muriel was more in need of it than her husband.'

'Mrs. Cochran suggested she tried to use it to keep Muriel under her thumb,' Daisy admitted grudgingly.

'She seems to have succeeded. The maid said Bettina treated her sister as an unpaid housekeeper and general dogsbody.'

'Muriel didn't put up with it because of the will! She'd promised her parents to look after Bettina and she's the sort of person who keeps promises. And honours her father and mother, which I'm not at all sure they deserve,' she added, her tone severe.

Alec grinned. 'Be that as it may, as I was about to say, having put up with that treatment for years, why should the worm turn now? And as I was about to answer myself, in two words, Yakov Levich. Come on, Daisy, what haven't you told me about those two? I saw them together with my own eyes at the Albert Hall last night, and then there he is again this morning.'

'He's a friend, of both Muriel and Abernathy, and he came to see what he could do to help,' she insisted. Then under his sceptical gaze she conceded, 'Well, if you must know, I scent the beginning of a romance. But only the beginning, mind. There wasn't anything serious between them before last night. Certainly Levich couldn't have counted on profiting by Muriel's inheritance.'

'Perhaps not,' Alec said grimly, 'but what I ask myself is, why the sudden blossoming after Bettina's death? Is it simply that Levich now does hope to profit? Or did Muriel hope her inheritance would help friendship to ripen into something warmer? Or was Bettina so anxious to keep her unpaid housekeeper that she blighted her sister's romance? Possible motives galore; means – Lucy's unlocked darkroom next door; opportunity – your Miss Westlea poured the fatal drink.'

'No one else's fingerprints on the decanter?'

'We haven't taken anyone's yet; it's one of the things that has to be done today. But there's only one person's prints, presumably hers, a clear set on top and several blurred underneath. Which means no one wiped the decanter before she handled it for the last time.'

'The murderer probably used gloves, or a handkerchief. Everyone knows about fingerprints these days.'

'You'd be surprised how many don't know, or forget in the heat of the moment. But then, if criminals never made mistakes, we'd never catch any of them. We've considered gloves or a handkerchief, of course, though either would risk drawing attention if someone else came up.'

'With a handkerchief, you could pretend to be blotting up something you had spilled.'

'True, and ingenious. I hope you're not going to take to crime. Tom and I hadn't got any further than pretending to blow our noses.'

She wrinkled her nose at him, then turned serious again. 'Who took the glass from the soloists' room to the stage?'

'Another good point. It was an elderly usher of unblemished reputation who had never in his life exchanged a word with Bettina. Tom saw him this morning. No, I'm sorry, Daisy, the fingerprints aren't proof positive – we haven't been able to get away with that since Dr. John Thorndyke and *The Red Thumb Mark* – but Muriel Westlea has to be placed at or near the top of my list.

CHAPTER 10

As Daisy and Alec turned into the alley, she was feeling decidedly pipped. Alec had wormed out of her the romance between Muriel and Levich which she hadn't meant to reveal. Worse, he'd guessed that Bettina had tried to spoil things between the two, and Marchenko would surely confirm it now that he could no longer claim not to speak English.

Muriel hadn't killed her sister, Daisy was certain. She simply wasn't capable of it, even though she had stopped loving Bettina – at least Daisy had managed to keep that confession from Alec.

She stopped at the back door to Abernathy's music room.

'Here's the key,' said Alec. 'You go on in. I just want to see if Tom's still next door.'

Daisy took the key but followed him, stopping beside him as he paused to knock the dottle from his pipe. The door of the studio stood open. Through it floated Lucy's high, clear, irate voice.

165

'It's bad enough you should lock me out of my own premises and make a filthy mess in there with your beastly powder, which will take me *hours* to clean up. But this is really too much!'

Sergeant Tring's soothing rumble: 'It won't take but a minute, miss.'

Alec stepped in. 'Miss Fotheringay, I'm Alec Fletcher. Is there some difficulty?'

At his heels, Daisy saw Lucy look him up and down as she said coolly, 'Kindly call off your minion, Chief Inspector. I shan't... Daisy, did you really give this man permission to ransack my darkroom?'

'Yes, darling. No need to get hot under the collar. After all, he's hot on the trail of a murderer. Well, not to ransack, but to check for dabs.'

'Dabs!' Lucy exclaimed in disgust.

'What's up, Sergeant?' Alec asked.

'I've dusted for dabs, sir, and I must say there's not many, considering.'

'I use rubber gloves to handle chemicals.' Irritable yet complacent, Lucy spread her perfect, unstained hands with polished nails. 'I've no intention of messing up my fingers with your ink.'

'It comes off easy, miss. You see, sir, there's at least two different lots of prints and I need

Miss Fotheringay's for elimination purposes.'

'Most of the others are probably mine,' Daisy interrupted. 'Do say you'll take my fingerprints, Sergeant Tring.'

'It'd be an honour and a pleasure, miss,' said the sergeant solemnly, his little brown eyes twinkling at her.

While he inked her fingers one by one on his pad and took impressions on a shiny-surfaced white card, Alec drew Lucy aside. Daisy stretched her ears but Tom Tring talked as he worked and she couldn't make out the others' words. Not that she didn't know perfectly well what was being said. Lucy looked haughty, then furious, then sulky, then alarmed.

'Ta, miss, that's it,' said Tring at last. 'Soap and water should get it off in a trice.'

'I'll wash in the darkroom.'

Crossing the room, she heard Alec say, 'I don't want to give the impression that the cyanide which poisoned Mrs. Abernathy was definitely yours. It's just a possibility. A strong possibility,' he added as relief lightened Lucy's alarm.

'I'll get rid of the blasted stuff,' Lucy snapped. 'I practically always use hypo anyway.'

'Other dangerous chemicals are used in

your business, Miss Fotheringay. Silver nitrate, for one, can be deadly.'

'Oh, all right,' she said with an exaggerated sigh. 'I'll try to be more careful about locking up.'

'Thank you, you ease my mind,' Alec said dryly. 'I hope you're now ready...'

With the water running, Daisy didn't catch the rest of his sentence, but the explosive reply sounded distinctly negative.

She stuck her head back round the door. 'Don't be an ass, Lucy,' she said. 'The ink comes off, and if you don't show Alec the appointment book, I'll pinch it and make a list myself.'

Stiff with annoyance, Lucy stalked over to the desk and presented her hand to Tom Tring. She was even more annoyed when she was kept waiting while Alec took his sergeant aside for a quiet word. Then Daisy and Alec left them together.

'I haven't endeared myself to your friend,' Alec said regretfully as they returned to the house next door.

'It's not quite the first meeting I'd have chosen for you, but never mind. Lucy will come round.' She unlocked the music-room door. 'It's a bit *outré* sneaking into someone else's house the back way like this.'

168

'It was Abernathy's idea. He seemed much recovered. Would you say he's well enough to answer questions without a doctor present?'

'Keep an eye on his lips. I've noticed the first sign of trouble is that they turn blue. Like Bettina's,' Daisy added, striving to banish the horrid image. 'Is that why the third doctor wondered whether she was having a heart seizure?'

'Probably. I'd forgotten about that.' Alec frowned – a grimace always lent a peculiar significance by his dark, thick eyebrows – then shrugged his shoulders. 'The post-mortem was done this morning and the pathologist confirmed cyanide poisoning over the phone.'

'Dr. Renfrew?' Daisy remembered the impatient, irascible man who had shouted at Detective Constable Piper over the phone at Wentwater Court.

'No, he's on holiday. His junior did the autopsy. It didn't seem worth calling in Sir Bernard Spilsbury for such a straightforward case. He revels in complications.'

'Sir Bernard's the Home Office chief pathologist, isn't he? I read something about him. Here we are.' She opened the door at the top of the stairs. 'Alec, are you going to talk to Bettina's parents? Because if so, please don't forget they don't know about her misbehaviour. Muriel went to a lot of trouble not to disillusion them.'

'I shan't forget. Now, how do we announce ourselves?'

'As I'm staying here, I'll just march into the drawing room and tell them we're back.' Daisy paused with her hand on the brass door handle. From within came the sound of a harsh, denunciatory diatribe. 'Oh, poor Muriel!' she whispered. 'I'm so glad you're with me. I never did cope very well with ranting clergymen.'

'I'll protect you,' Alec whispered back with a smile, squeezing her hand. 'Courage!'

Picturing a tall, gaunt, severe parson, Daisy was decidedly taken aback when the Reverend Westlea turned out to be small and chubby, with a rubicund face above his dog collar. However, he stood before the fireplace with his right hand thrust into his coat and his chest puffed out in an unmistakably Napoleonic pose.

Muriel, drooping before him like a naughty child, jumped up and almost ran to meet Daisy. 'Thank heaven you're back,' she murmured. 'I'd almost forgotten how frightful... Mother, Father, this is the Honourable Daisy Dalrymple, and Detective Chief Inspector

170

Fletcher of Scotland Yard.'

Daisy hadn't known Muriel was even aware of her honorary title. She had certainly never mentioned it before, but it seemed to be the right thing to do now, for the Reverend Westlea came forward rubbing his hands and bobbing his head.

'How d'ye do, Miss Dalrymple. I'm delighted to find my daughter has made at least one respectable friend in London.' He gave Alec a frosty nod.

Mrs. Westlea scuttled up behind him. Daisy wasn't surprised she had overlooked the vicar's wife, who was an older version of Muriel, two or three decades more faded and downtrodden.

Once all the polite words proper to a bereavement had been uttered, Mr. Westlea addressed Alec. 'I hope you can tell me, Inspector, since my daughter has no idea, when shall we be able to hold the funeral?'

Daisy opened her mouth to correct Alec's title, but he shook his head at her.

'The inquest will be held tomorrow morning, sir,' he said. 'I imagine the ... er ... remains of the deceased will be released for burial at that time, though I can't vouch for the coroner's actions.'

'Then I shall arrange the funeral service for

171

Wednesday morning.' He turned back to Daisy. 'I shall have to apply to you, Miss Dalrymple, for the name of the incumbent of this parish. I have been shocked to find Muriel so neglectful of Elizabeth's spiritual as well as her physical welfare that she is not...'

'Chief Inspector!' Muriel broke in with an air of desperation – to Daisy's unspeakable relief as she wasn't at all sure which was their parish church, let alone the vicar's name. 'I know you want to talk to me, and to Roger. He's gone up for a rest but I'm at your service. Will the dining room do?'

'Perfectly.' If Alec was disconcerted to have his chief suspect practically throw herself into his arms, Daisy saw no sign of it in his expression. 'Did Detective Constable Piper arrive during my absence?'

'Yes, a few minutes before you. He went down to the kitchen. I'll ring for Beryl to send him up.' She pressed the bell. 'Daisy, you'll come with me, won't you?'

'If you feel in need of support, Muriel,' said her father, 'I am quite prepared to accompany you.'

Muriel looked aghast.

'I'd prefer Miss Dalrymple's presence, sir,' Alec intervened, earning glances of burning gratitude from both Daisy and Muriel. 'She

172

is acquainted with many of the other people involved in the case.'

'I hardly consider that a recommendation,' the disgruntled vicar said stiffly.

Before he could insist on his right to attend his daughter, Muriel sped out to the hall, in her haste almost catching Alec's heels in the door as he brought up the rear behind Daisy. They settled at the table in the dining room, with Piper in an inconspicuous corner taking notes.

'First, Miss Westlea,' Alec began, 'will you confirm that Mrs. Abernathy drank from the decanter during the interval?'

'Oh yes. The first thing she wanted when I joined her in the ladies' dressing room was a glass of ratafia.'

'And she drank it?'

'She didn't gulp it, as she did when ... later. She sipped it, but by the end of the interval she had finished it.'

'Thank you, that's a great help.'

No wonder Alec looked pleased, Daisy thought. Muriel had eliminated the need to hunt down everyone who arrived late for the concert. She didn't seem to realize she had limited the list of suspects to those in the soloists' room during the interval.

'Before I went back to the choir room,' she

went on, 'I refilled the glass and gave it to one of the ushers to put under her chair on the stage. Father says I should have known something was wrong with it, but how could I?' She gazed at Alec pleadingly.

'You couldn't, Miss Westlea ... unless you had added the cyanide.'

'I *told* him I couldn't possibly have guessed.' Muriel appeared far more concerned about her father's reproaches than Alec's suspicions. 'It looked and smelled just the same as usual. There was no way to tell someone had tampered with it.'

'But someone did. Why did you tell me Mrs. Abernathy had no enemies?'

'"Enemies" sounds so very malevolent. Betsy sometimes upset people, but she wasn't the sort of evil person who has enemies.'

'Would you say Eric Cochran was upset when she threatened to tell his wife about his affair with Miss Blaise?'

'She didn't exactly *threaten* him. She said it wasn't right to keep his wife in ignorance, but she didn't see how she'd ever find time to tell her if she had to rehearse for the Verdi *Requiem*.'

Alec's lips twitched. 'I see. Neither Cochran nor Miss Blaise retaliated by suggesting Mrs.

Abernathy's affair with Gilbert Gower ought to be disclosed to their respective spouses?'

'They already knew. Betsy never tried to keep her affairs secret from poor Roger, only from our parents.' Muriel threw a nervous glance backwards at the dining-room door. 'And the way Mr. Gower carried on with foreign sopranos was notorious.'

'Mrs. Gower knew about the foreign sopranos,' Alec agreed. 'Did she know about Mrs. Abernathy?'

'Yes, she actually asked Betsy to leave Gilbert alone. Betsy said she was in a state because he'd taken up with an English mistress who wouldn't go away after a few months.'

Just as Alec had surmised. He flashed Daisy a smug glance as he asked, 'Did Mrs. Abernathy comply with Mrs. Gower's request?'

'No, she refused to stop seeing him. In fact, I'm afraid she thought it was very funny because they had already ceased to be lovers. I tried to persuade her to set Mrs. Gower's mind at rest, but ... well, Betsy could be rather stubborn, and I didn't quite like to approach Mrs. Gower myself on such a subject.'

'Do you know why Mrs. Abernathy kept meeting Gower when they were no longer lovers?'

Muriel reluctantly confirmed the Covent Garden story. Alec went on to ask her about Consuela de la Costa's threats against Bettina, and then about Marchenko's grudge, both of which she admitted, growing more and more unhappy.

'And your parents still regard your sister as an angel?' he said at last, sceptically.

'They never used to come up to town and don't know anyone here. The only way they could have found out what she was really like was if I told them. Why should I shatter their illusions?' A note of yearning entered her voice. 'It wouldn't make them love me any better. They'd probably not have believed me, but if they did they'd be devastated.'

Daisy didn't believe anything was capable of devastating the Reverend Westlea's tyrannical self-righteousness, unshaken by his favourite daughter's death. As for Mrs. Westlea, she was already thoroughly devastated by life with him. Muriel had been on her way to the same pathetic state of submissiveness, but now that Bettina was dead, perhaps Yakov Levich would rescue her. He didn't seem at all the brow-beating sort, but whether he'd support Muriel against her parents was another matter.

As if he had read Daisy's mind, Alec

asked, 'Were your parents disturbed by Mr. Levich's presence here this morning?'

'Yes.' Muriel looked mutinous. 'Father stared down his nose as if Mr. Levich were a ... a cockroach and asked in a perfectly horrid voice if he was a Hebrew. Then Roger, the dear, said very firmly that Mr. Levich was his friend, but I said he was mine, too. And then Yasha, Mr. Levich, said he ought to be going. I asked him to stay but he insisted. When I showed him out, he told me he didn't want to add to my parents' distress at such a time. So I said what about my distress and I made him promise to come back for dinner!' she finished in triumph.

'Bravo!' said Daisy.

As Muriel turned to her, Alec's eyebrows warned her against interrupting. 'Miss Westlea,' he said, recapturing Muriel's attention, 'what did your sister think of your "friendship" with Levich?'

'Betsy made things as difficult as she could,' said Muriel candidly, sadly. 'She was even ruder than Father to Yasha. But he ignored her, and anyway, she was hardly ever there when we met at rehearsals. Most of her engagements were in the provinces, you know. I'm afraid she blamed poor Roger for that, too, though it was her own fault.'

Seizing the opening, Alec asked her about Roger Abernathy's relations with Bettina. Nothing new emerged, as far as Daisy could tell. Despite all provocation, Abernathy had remained patient and kind, not so much forgiving as accepting his beautiful wife's vagaries.

'He was still in love with her,' said Muriel with absolute certainty, 'don't ask me why.'

After that, Alec took her through what little she recalled about people's movements in the soloists' room, from which one useful fact emerged: After her arrival, Consuela de la Costa had only left the ladies' dressing room briefly to see Eric Cochran. She had brought bottled spring water with her, the way Continentals did, not trusting tap water. Her maid had a glass of it ready.

'Her maid?' said Alec, dismayed. 'I've heard nothing about a maid!'

'She stayed in the dressing room. The usher at the door wouldn't have seen her. And I expect Miss de la Costa sent her home at the end of the interval.'

'Yes, probably. At least, she left before the room was locked. That's all for the present, then, Miss Westlea, except that my sergeant should be here by now to take your fingerprints, and Mr. Abernathy's. It's routine procedure, for elimination purposes.'

Without hesitation, Muriel rang for the maid. Beryl appeared with Tom Tring in tow, and was sent to see if Roger Abernathy had risen from his rest.

Abernathy came in just as Muriel's fingerprinting was finished. He still looked pale and strained, but by no means in imminent danger of dropping dead. Like Muriel, he presented his fingertips to Sergeant Tring without hesitation.

'I needn't detain you any longer,' Alec said to Muriel, with a glance at Daisy which said plainly, 'and that goes for you, too.'

'Have you got your pills, Roger?' Muriel asked anxiously. He felt in his pocket with his free hand and produced the little bottle. 'Oh dear, you only have a couple left, and this is the spare bottle from the cloakroom. I must get your prescription renewed at once.'

Daisy hissed a reminder at Alec: 'Watch his lips!' Alec nodded, and she and Muriel went out.

Muriel telephoned Abernathy's doctor. As she hung up the receiver after talking to him, Tom Tring came out of the dining room.

'I've Mr. Abernathy's permission to have a look through Mrs. Abernathy's desk, miss,' he said.

'Oh dear, I've put Mother and Father in there, and I was just going to send Elsie out for Roger's prescription.'

'I'll clear it out and take the contents downstairs to examine, if that's more convenient, miss.'

'Yes,' Muriel said gratefully, 'you can go to the music room. I'll take you up now. Daisy, would you mind frightfully...?' She gave the drawing-room door an edgy glance.

'Right-ho,' said Daisy nobly, and went to beard the vicar.

She didn't suffer alone for long. Muriel returned, and shortly thereafter the front doorbell rang to announce the first of a stream of visitors.

The Reverend Westlea proved most adept at dealing with the mixed condolences and curiosity of acquaintances, leaving to Muriel her brother-in-law's many genuinely sympathetic friends. Choir members, pupils past and present, others who had worked with Roger Abernathy, all surprised Daisy with their evident fondness for the quiet, unassuming man. He put in a brief appearance, but he was not at all well. Just before he retired upstairs again, he told Muriel and Daisy – to Daisy's annoyance – that the police had left.

Olivia Blaise came specifically to find out how Roger was. 'I can't bring myself to offer sympathy,' she murmured to Daisy, 'because he's much better off without her, but I do hope he'll take care of his health.'

'Muriel will look after him. It's a frightful thing to say, but if you ask me he ought to have married her, not Bettina. Then they both could have been happy for the last ten years instead of miserable.'

Olivia smiled but shook her head. 'Bettina would have battened on them and ruined everything anyway.' She looked round as Beryl announced Mr. and Mrs. Cochran. 'I'm off. Don't forget to tell Roger I asked after him.' Turning, she found Cochran close behind her: 'Oh, Eric! What do you want?'

'To offer you the Verdi part.' A muscle twitched in his cheek and his eyes pleaded with her. 'Browne has arranged for a repeat performance next Monday. Please, Olivia.'

Her gaze searched his handsome face. 'Do you really want me?'

'You know I do!'

Olivia's expression softened and she laid her hand on his arm. 'We'll give it a try,' she said gently.

Daisy slipped away unnoticed. She joined the group around the Reverend and Mrs. Westlea in time to hear Mrs. Cochran offer the use of her house for a reception after the funeral.

'Mrs. Abernathy was well known in musical circles and you will certainly need more space than you have here,' she said. 'In my youth we always lent our grounds for church picnics and fêtes. My father, Sir Denzil Vernon, considered it his duty.'

The Reverend Westlea eagerly accepted. 'Mrs. Cochran, have you met the Honourable Miss Dalrymple?' he went on.

'The Honourable!' Mrs. Cochran's nostrils flared as she stared at Daisy with pursed lips, to the detriment of her *maquillage*. 'Yes, Vicar, Miss Dalrymple and I have met. I was not aware...'

'I find titles quite superfluous in artistic circles, don't you, Mrs. Cochran?' Daisy struggled to keep a straight face.

'Why, yes, perhaps. Modern young women are casual about such things, I know. I fear I was not aware that you are Lord Dalrymple's daughter.'

'Cousin.'

Before Mrs. Cochran could rally, her husband joined them to express his condolences to the bereaved parents and second the offer of hospitality after the funeral. Daisy saw Olivia say a word to Muriel and depart.

No doubt Cochran would tell his wife he had arranged for Olivia to sing the mezzo part in the *Requiem*. Not for a moment did Daisy suppose they had reached agreement only on musical business. Surely Mrs. Cochran must have realized by now how matters stood between the two.

CHAPTER 11

Alec and his henchmen managed to steal away from Abernathy's house without seeing Daisy. She had been very helpful but he had no intention of discussing the case with her any further, since she chose to champion his prime suspect.

'Muriel Westlea seems an unlikely murderer,' he admitted to Tom as the Austin Seven pulled away from the kerb, leaving a couple of disconsolate reporters behind. 'Can she be clever enough to make me believe she's candid and ingenuous at the same time she's stupid enough to have left those prints on the decanter?'

'There's only the one set of dabs all right, Chief,' was Tom's unhelpful response. 'Clear as a bell, the last lot on the stopper. They'd more'n likely be smeared if summun other'n you had used gloves or a hankie over 'em.'

Young Ernie Piper was still less helpful. 'She seemed like a nice lady, Chief.'

'And her brother-in-law's a nice gentleman,' said Alec acidly. 'Abernathy's motive is stronger. He's not faking that dicky heart. Is he faking the sorrow? He put up with her shenanigans for years, but so did Crippen with *his* wife until Ethel le Nève came along. Any hints from the servants why he might have cracked now, Tom?'

'More t'other way about, Chief. Mrs. Abernathy was between lovers, 'ccording to her maid, and she was that taken up with practising for the big concert she didn't bedevil the poor bloke as much as usual. It was more her sister she was badgering, over the Yid.'

'The Jewish gentleman,' Alec reproved him. 'Another nice gentleman, and highly talented, I understand.'

'We going to see him next, Chief?' asked Piper.

'No, we'll tackle Marchenko first. I want to leave time to find an interpreter today if he persists in his claim to speak no English in spite of having chatted to Miss Dalrymple. Anything else of interest, Tom? What did you find in the desk?'

'Bundles of love letters, Chief, all tied up with pretty pink ribbon. I swiped the ones from Marchenko and Gower, like you said. They was the only ones mixed up in this. None from Mr. Cochran. Beryl, the house parlour maid, confirmed he used to come here to meet Miss Blaise. She had her eye on his chauffeur, good-looking chap like his master, she said, but he never came in. They'd drive up in front, then Mr. Cochran'd dismiss him and he'd go off on foot.'

'Did he, now! I wonder if he went home and reported to Mrs. Cochran that he'd taken her husband to Mrs. Abernathy's house? Have a word with him, Tom, when we call on them.'

'Right, Chief. The only other thing – can't see what it's got to do with what but it struck me as a bit odd – Elsie said Mrs. Abernathy's doctor came round while the family was at lunch. He wanted whatever was left of some medicine he'd made up for her

'What, why, and did he get it?' Alec asked,

interested. 'And what's his name?'

'Some cough syrup, Chief, he said he'd made it special for her and it wouldn't do Mr. Abernathy any good if he was to take it. Elsie'd already thrown all that stuff out, clearing out the bathroom cabinet for the vicar and his missus, and the dustbin men came around noon. But the oddest thing of all, it was that Dr. Woodward, who was at the concert.'

'Very odd.' Alec frowned as he drove into a narrow, dingy street lined with tall, narrow terrace houses. 'Here we are. What's the number Major Browne gave us, Ernie?'

Piper, with his phenomenal memory for numbers, had Marchenko's address on the tip of his tongue.

As they climbed out of the little motorcar, which rocked as Tring extracted his bulk, Alec continued, 'Woodward never said a word about being Mrs. Abernathy's doctor, though he was the only one of the three who thought it might be a seizure, not poisoning. I'll have to see him.'

Ernie Piper rattled off the doctor's address and telephone number.

'Showing off, young 'un?' said Tom indulgently, adding in a low voice, 'Curtains twitching inside, Chief, and both sides and opposite, too.'

'They're all wondering how we stuffed you into the car in the first place, Sarge.'

'Cheeky bugger. You want me to talk to the neighbours, Chief?'

'Not at this stage, Tom. There's no question of alibis. Come in and take his prints, then you can buzz off and find a telephone booth. Make me an appointment with Dr. Woodward for tomorrow morning, before the inquest. I'm not going to have time to see him today.'

'I'll write down his number for you, Sarge,' said Piper, grinning.

'All right, Ernie, see what you make of this,' said Alec. He pointed at the row of bell pushes beside the front door. Like most in this area, the once respectable middle-class house had been divided into flats and bed-sitters. Each bell was labelled with the name of the tenant – every one written in Cyrillic script.

'Easy, Chief.' The young constable thought better of his certitude and hedged, 'Least-ways, I'd try the ground floor. See, the first two letters looks like an M and an A, and the last two's K and O. Near enough, isn't it? I mean, it's not like it's Chinese.'

Alec pressed the bottom bell.

Dimitri Marchenko's flat was sparsely and cheaply furnished. On the rack of an elderly upright piano a vocal score stood open. Having admitted the three detectives, the bass stood by the deal table in the middle of his untidy room, glaring at them. By the light of a single naked electric light bulb – the curtains were tightly closed – he looked more than ever like a bear. An angry bear, but Alec thought he saw wariness in the big man's eyes.

'I'm hoping you have remembered your English, sir,' he said in a matter-of-fact tone, speaking clearly. 'Otherwise, we'll come back with an interpreter from the Soviet legation.'

'Soviet, *nyet!*' What little of Marchenko's face was visible among the hair turned dark red, a pulse beating at his temple.

'English I spik some. *Vchera* – yesterday – was shock, make to forget.'

'I quite understand, sir. First, if you wouldn't mind, my sergeant will take impressions of your fingerprints.'

Marchenko whipped his hands behind his back, an interesting response, as well as one which made it clear he followed English more easily than he admitted to speaking it. At once he thought better of his reaction and sheepishly held out both hands as Tom Tring stepped forward. The two large men stared hard at each other, then, as if by mutual agreement, both dropped their eyes to the fingerprint kit which Tom set on the scarred, ringed table.

That messy business completed, the sergeant departed on his errand. Alec and Marchenko sat down at the table and Piper took up his usual unobtrusive position slightly to the rear of the suspect, notebook at the ready.

Alec scarcely had to prompt Marchenko before the accusations against Yakov Levich poured out. He was a Jew, a Russian, a Bolshevik spy, what more did one need to know?

'Much more,' said Alec. 'Why should a Bolshevik spy – supposing Mr. Levich to be one – choose such an unlikely victim?'

'I hear, I see! Always she stop him talk to sister: "Come sew button, Muriel"; "Go fetch coat, Muriel"; "I tell father you like Jew, Muriel." This I hear. And to him, *oscorbleniya...*'

'In English, if you please, sir,' Alec requested as Piper chewed his pencil in despair.

'Insults, much insults.'

'I understand Mrs. Abernathy insulted you, too, sir, after accepting a number of gifts.'

Paltry trinkets, Marchenko claimed, or at least that's what his muddled explanation, scattered with Russian phrases, amounted to. As for the insults, what else could you expect from a 'veetch?' (Bitch? Witch? Wasn't one Russian letter written B but pronounced V?) A sensible man took no account of such things.

Marchenko spoke calmly but his eyes glittered. Better take a look at those gifts, maybe have them appraised, Alec decided.

'And what did you *see*, sir, which roused your suspicions of Mr. Levich?'

'I see him at table in soloist room. What he wants there? Has own room for orchestra, *nyet?* Own refreshment, also.'

'Did you take a drink from the table, sir?'

'*Da.* To sing make thirst. Take samovar for tea. English tea *otvratitelny.*'

Alec didn't bother to ask for a translation of that. He went on to ask about everyone's movements in the soloists' room.

'After *Lacrimosa* we come from stage, I get glass tea, bring to men's room. Gover already in room, drinks Scotch veesky from flask. Never he goes out, always drinking and pimping.'

A muffled gasp turned into a cough came from Piper.

'Perhaps *primping is* the word you want, sir?' Alec suggested.

Massive shoulders shrugged. 'Pimping, prrrimping – you English swallow letter errrr.' He gave it the full rolling Russian sound, like a bear's growl. 'Gover sits at mirror, plays with hair.'

'You are quite sure Mr. Gower never left the men's dressing room during the interval?'

'Quite very sure. Only drrrinks and prrrimps,' Marchenko said with scorn. 'When Cochran comes, quickly he hides flask.'

It looked as if the tenor was out of it. 'What did Mr. Cochran want?'

'Has new idea to phrase *"quam olim Abrahae."* Is not bad idea, but too late to rehearse. We talk, sing few notes. When he leaves dressing room, I go with to get more glass tea. There is *gospozha* Cochrana looking after him.'

'Mrs. Cochran looking for him?' Alec proposed, more for Piper's enlightenment than his own.

'*Tak.*' Marchenko nodded. 'They talk. I go to samovar. Then Cochran knocks on ladies' door. Out comes Miss de la Costa, Miss Vessstlea,' – he hissed the name – 'and sister. Miss Vestlea has glass in hand. Like Gover, always taking nipples.'

Momentarily stumped by the possibly apposite but presumably misapplied word, Alec glanced at Ernie Piper. 'Taking nips, sir,' the young detective said, wooden-faced.

'I stay to listen to music talk.' Once started, the bass seemed suspiciously eager to co-operate. 'I see Miss de la Costa stay at end of room.'

'She did not go anywhere near the table?'

'*Tak*. Next comes in young woman – Bless is name, *da?* Olivia Bless? – short dark hair, much *chic*. Miss Muriel goes in ladies' room, brings out papers to her. I am talking about *"quam olim,"* not see if Miss Bless goes near table, but notice later she still there, talking to Muriel. Then comes Abernathy, also talks music. Soon he goes to table, brings cup tea for wife, *English* tea. "Peeg sveel," she says. "I not drinking that peeg sveel."' Marchenko's relish made clear his hearty concurrence.

'Cochran and wife go away,' he continued. 'Miss de la Costa go into dressing room. This is when Levich arrives. At door he talks to Cochran, one moment, then he looks round room, goes to table, and puts poison in Bettina's drink.'

'You actually saw him put some substance in the decanter, sir?'

His eyes shifting, Marchenko backed off a little. 'I know this is what he does. He is filthy, murdering Jew.'

'Yes, well, sir, we've been through all that. Was anyone else in a position to see what he was doing?'

'Miss Bless goes to him at table on way out. But plenty time before to put in poison.'

'Was Miss Blaise with him long?'

'Just moment. Two ticks of lamb's tail, as you say. After, he goes quickly to Muriel. At once Bettina finds loose button. "Muriel, sew on button!" like I tell you.'

'So you did, sir.'

'Like I tell you, never she lets Levich talk to Muriel, so Levich kills her.'

'That remains to be seen, sir. What happened next?'

'I go back in dressing room,' said Marchenko, disgruntled by Alec's scepticism. 'See nothing no more. That is all.'

Except where Levich was concerned, Alec saw no reason to doubt his word. In fact, he had turned out to be an excellent witness. Abernathy had already mentioned the cup of tea for his wife, and most of what Marchenko had said could be checked with other people.

As for his own innocence or guilt, the most

telling points would be the value of his gifts to Bettina and whether the team presently trudging from chemist's to chemist's found evidence of his having purchased cyanide. The name he signed in the Poison Book, required of everyone buying dangerous substances, might be false, but no one who had seen and spoken to him could possibly forget him.

Alec thanked Marchenko for his help and warned him not to leave London without informing the police. Then he and Piper went out to the car, where Tom awaited them.

'Got you an appointment with Dr. Woodward, Chief. But whatever he has to say, I reckon it was that Russian done it. A nasty piece of work, he is, and you 'member the mad monk, Rasputin? It was cyanide they tried to put him away with, afore they up and drowned him.'

'You didn't meet the Spanish singer, Sarge,' Piper said as Alec started the car. 'She's a regular Loo-creature Borger. If you was to ask me, she done it.'

'She never went near the table,' Alec pointed out. 'Anyway, Lucretia Borgia was Italian, and Marchenko is Ukrainian, Tom, not Russian. And we're on our way to see

194

Gower, who's Welsh. Any takers?'

'Nah, the Taffies'll scrag you in a scrum,' said Piper, a keen sportsman, 'but they're not the poisoning sort.'

'There's always Mrs. Gower, Chief,' Tom put in. 'Poison's a woman's weapon.'

'There, what did I say, Sarge? Loo-creature Borger it was! She used one of them slow-acting poisons.'

Alec laughed. 'It was cyanide, Ernie. Besides, I think Miss de la Costa is more the dagger sort, and still more likely to scratch out her rival's eyes, as she threatened. Tom, assuming the Gowers are at home, have a chat with the servants after you've taken their prints. See if Mrs. Gower was unusually on edge in the weeks before the concert. She may well deny that she knew about Mrs. Abernathy being her husband's mistress. We've only Miss Westlea's word, and Miss Westlea has every reason to try to throw suspicion elsewhere.'

'Right, Chief.'

The Gowers' house, in South Kensington, was a solidly respectable Victorian semi-detached, shielded from the street by laurels. A neat, elderly parlourmaid opened the door to the three detectives. After informing them that the master was out but expected back any moment, she went to see whether her mistress was 'at home.'

She returned to usher them into a sitting room where Mrs. Gower stood waiting, her plain, pudgy face pale, her hands twisting, amid comfortably shabby furniture. The inevitable piano had *Für Elise* open on the rack and a dozen framed photographs on top. On tables and walls were displayed more photographs. Most were snapshots of two boys and a girl in various combinations, from babyhood to late adolescence; a few showed Gilbert Gower in one or another of his operatic roles. In pride of place over the mantelpiece hung a studio portrait of the three youngsters. The girl was about twenty, the boys perhaps eighteen and sixteen.

Would a woman so obsessed by her off-spring risk being convicted of murder and taken from them for ever?

'Fine children,' said Alec, walking over to study the portrait after greeting Mrs. Gower and receiving a shaky response.

'Aren't they?' she responded eagerly. 'My daughter is engaged to be married, to such a nice boy. My sons are still at school, of course, but growing up so fast!' She sighed. 'I have plenty of time to spare for my volunteer work now. They don't need their mother as they used to.'

And there was his answer. He remembered himself at that age, the long, serious talks with his father about his future. For a year or two his kind, fussy mother had seemed irrelevant, often irritating. He hoped he had hidden it better than the Gower boys seemed to have. If Mrs. Gower felt herself less necessary than their father to her children, for their sakes she might have struck out at the woman she feared was tearing him away.

'But I expect you want to ask me some questions, Chief Inspector.' She was quite calm now. 'Won't you sit down? Would you like tea?'

'No, thank you, ma'am.' As he waited for her to be seated, with a tiny jerk of the head he sent Tom out of the room. Fingerprints could wait till Gower came home. 'Tell me again, please, just what you did and whom you saw in the soloists' room at the Albert Hall yesterday. We realize everyone was in a state of shock and we're not holding it against them if they remember things today that they forgot last night.'

'I told you everything. No one was in the sitting room. I didn't want to disturb Gilbert if he was resting, so I waited a minute or two and then left.'

'Perhaps you helped yourself to a cup of tea while you waited? A very natural thing to do, and no one would have minded.'

'No, I didn't go near the table. Gilbert always said the refreshments at the Albert Hall were the worst anywhere.' Her hands twisted in her lap. 'Was that where ... where the poison was put in Mrs. Abernathy's drink?'

'So it seems. You knew about her decanter of ratafia, of course. Everyone did.'

'I didn't go anywhere near it, truly. Ratafia, is that what it was? Gilbert mentioned some liqueur. He said she was a fool to let everyone know she drank, as it didn't do her career any good. She was ruining her own chances with her temperamental outbursts anyway,' Mrs. Gower added with a touch of grim complacency.

'You appear to know a good deal about Mrs. Abernathy.'

'Not really.' She looked flustered. 'That is, I suppose so. Gilbert has worked with her before and he talks about the people he works with.'

'People like Miss de la Costa? I expect you hoped for a word with her, too, when you went to the soloists' room.'

'No, why should I? I didn't know yet... I mean, I had no reason to talk to her. I gave up years ago trying to change Gilbert or to persuade his mistresses not to take him away from his family.'

'Until it came to Mrs. Abernathy,' Alec rapped out. 'You begged her to give up your husband.'

'Begged!' she cried, jumping up. 'I wouldn't have begged that woman for a crust if I and my children were starving in a ditch!' She took an agitated turn about the room.

Standing with his hand on the back of his chair, Alec continued, 'We know you spoke to her about her involvement with your husband.'

'I suppose she gossiped.' Mrs. Gower slumped into her seat again. 'That's the sort of thing she'd do. Yes, I talked to her. I reminded her about Gilbert's responsibilities to his family, and her own to poor Mr. Abernathy. That's all.'

'You admit you knew about the affair.'

'I knew,' she said drearily.

'And that it was different from Mr. Gower's previous liaisons, which you could overlook rather than deprive your children of their father. As an Englishwoman, Mrs. Abernathy posed a real threat to your marriage.'

'I didn't kill her! Gilbert always comes home!'

'Of course he does, Jennie darling.' Gower came in, wearing an unconvincing air of hearty cheerfulness. 'What-ho, Chief Inspector.'

'Good afternoon, Sir.' Internally, Alec cursed. Another few minutes and Jennifer Gower might have confessed, saving everyone a great deal of trouble. 'I'm here to clear up one or two points. Mrs. Gower has been most helpful. Perhaps I might ask you a few questions now.'

'Of course, old chap. Er' – he gave his wife an uneasy glance – 'Jennifer, my dear, I'll take these gentlemen to my study and leave you in peace.' He led the way.

The tenor's study was dominated by a second piano rather than the usual desk, but the deep, comfortable armchairs were standard for a gentleman's retreat, as was the tantalus on a side table. Gower crossed to it at once.

'You'll have a drink, Chief Inspector? No? Constable?'

'No, thank you, sir.' Piper was at his most stolid.

'Not on duty, I suppose, ha ha. You don't object, if I "tak a wee dram"?' He poured a hefty slug of Scotch from a cut-glass de-canter. Something about the action tugged at Alec's mind, but he lost the thought as Gower continued, 'No smoking, if you don't mind. Bad for the voice.' He patted his throat, swathed in a red and blue silk Paisley cravat.

As they sat down, Alec said, his tone dry, 'I hope, you're sufficiently recovered from the shock, sir, to tell us a bit more than you were able to last night.'

Gower was not at all abashed. 'I expect Miss Dalrymple told you I said Marchenko did it,' he said breezily. 'I didn't actually see him, I'm afraid. Didn't set foot out of the dressing room, as a matter of fact, and nor did Finch, if you've got him in your sights.'

Alec had forgotten the organist. 'You'll vouch for Mr. Finch?'

'Certainly, though I don't expect him to return the favour. Lives in another world, does our Finch. Never stirred from his imaginary organ.'

'But Marchenko did leave the dressing room. What makes you think he might have murdered Mrs. Abernathy?'

'Oh, he was mad as a hornet at Bettina. With good cause, to be fair,' he added. 'She was a bloody nuisance to me, but she virtually swindled him out of a fortune in jewels and then was damn nasty on top of it – in public, too. Don't know how I ever got myself mixed up with her.' He gulped the remains of his whisky.

'An unhappy situation,' Alec agreed smoothly, 'especially for her husband and your wife.'

'Jennifer didn't know about Bettina,' Gower said, but he had the grace to look a trifle shamefaced. 'Besides, she's used to my ... er ... peccadilloes. She knows I'd never desert her and the children. You're not suggesting she poisoned Bettina? Good God, man, Jennie wouldn't hurt a fly! Look at the way she spends half her time at that East End clinic, taking care of indigent brats.'

'And Roger Abernathy?'

'Abernathy? Well, it wasn't as if I was Bettina's first lover, was it? Poor fellow, he was used to wearing the horns. He'd do anything for her, even put up with that.'

'Did she take another lover after you?'

Gower frowned. 'I wondered about Eric Cochran. I'd heard he was involved with a mezzo-soprano, and he gave Bettina the Verdi part. But if it wasn't for that, I'd have said there was no love lost between them.

He wouldn't have bumped her off, though, not in the middle of a concert. Nor would his wife. She's even keener on his career than he is.'

'So I'm given to understand. What about Muriel Westlea?'

'Who? Oh, the fair Bettina's ugly sister. In the choir, isn't she?'

'Yes.'

'That's all I know about her,' Gower said without interest.

'Yakov Levich?'

'The violinist? Well, one is more or less obliged to shake hands with the leader after a good performance, but otherwise... Not quite one of us, is he?'

'Olivia Blaise?'

'Is she the smart little filly who was hanging about? Pupil of Abernathy's? Not my style,' he dismissed her.

The tenor had little else to impart. Sergeant Tring was summoned from the kitchen and the Gowers' fingerprints were taken without incident.

Mrs. Gower showed them out. On the doorstep, she detained Alec with a hand on his sleeve and said urgently, 'You must believe me, I really am resigned to Gilbert's straying. I've learned to make allowances for the artistic temperament, not like Ursula Cochran, who just pretends it hasn't happened, though she knew perfectly well her husband was carrying on with that woman.'

'It seems certain, ma'am, that Eric Cochran and Mrs. Abernathy were not lovers.'

'Oh.' Her face fell. Misery loves company, Alec thought. 'Well, I'll have to make sure dear Ursula knows her suspicions were unfounded. Good-bye, Chief Inspector.' Shoulders drooping, she turned and went back into the house.

As the door clicked shut, Tom Tring announced, 'The servants all agree Madam's been like a cat on hot bricks for weeks.'

'She knew about Bettina all right,' Alec said grimly, 'and she was afraid if it came to a tug of war over her husband, she'd lose. She'd visited Miss Fotheringay's studio, and she was alone in the soloists' room. In the normal way of things, I'm sure she's a kind and charitable woman, but for her childrens' sake...'

They passed the laurels and emerged into the street. In the front seat of Alec's little Austin sat a stranger.

CHAPTER 12

'Detective Chief Inspector Fletcher?' The stranger stepped out of the car onto the pavement. Middling height, nondescript clothes, a trilby pulled low over a nondescript face with a small, neat, greying moustache – altogether unremarkable, yet somehow vaguely familiar. He held out a card towards Alec, shielded by his hand from Tom and Ernie.

Superintendent, Special Branch!

Founded as the Special Irish Branch in the 1880s, to combat the Fenian bombing outrages, the organization had got off to an unhappy start when its offices were blown up by the Irish terrorists. However it had then put an end to their attacks in London and gone on to the investigation and suppression of anarchist plots. Now it dealt with all crimes of a political nature.

And when Special Branch and Criminal Investigation Department crossed paths, the Special Branch had the right of way.

'I'd like a word with you, Mr. Fletcher. Five or ten minutes at most.'

'Tring, Piper, I'll meet you outside Miss Blaise's place in a quarter of an hour.'

As the two trudged off, the Special Branch man returned to the passenger seat of the Chummy, so Alec walked around and got in behind the wheel. 'What's going on, sir?'

'You're to stay away from Dimitri Marchenko,' said the clipped, public school and Sandhurst voice.

'Marchenko! But he's one of my main suspects.'

'Nonetheless, leave him alone.'

'I'm investigating a murder, sir,' Alec said angrily, 'not an unlicensed vehicle.'

The superintendent sighed. 'I was warned you wouldn't lie down and roll over at a word. I'll explain, but if a hint of this leaks out I'll have your badge and your head, not necessarily in that order.'

'I can keep my mouth shut, sir.'

'If I thought you couldn't, I'd have you taken off the case altogether. Marchenko is a member of a group of anti-Bolshevik refugees. In a sense, he's their cover: he provides a respectable front, funding, and a house. The cellar of that house is full of explosives, dynamite, glyceryl trinitrate, TNT, enough to take out every building for streets around. They're planning to blow up the Soviet

Russian legation.'

'But if they get the wind up...' said Alec slowly, chilled by the memory of the Siege of Sidney Street. In 1911, when he was fresh from university and doing his years on the beat, two anarchists who had killed three policemen had been cornered in a terrace house. Rather than be taken, they had set it on fire, regardless of the risk to the houses next door.

'If they get the wind up, who knows – they may decide to go out in a blaze of glory, taking several hundred neighbours with them.'

The two men sat in silence for a moment. Then Alec said, 'We'll stay away from Marchenko, sir. What are you going to do?'

'You know better than to ask that,' the Special Branch man said mildly. He opened the car door and strolled away down the street, the very image of unconcern.

Alec's mind raced. He had better stop the uniformed branch enquiring after Marchenko at chemists' shops, but he'd go on asking the other suspects about him. They would think it odd if he didn't. Nor did he see any reason not to have the jewellery valued. If the Ukrainian's motive was as strong as Gower seemed to think, and if no convincing evidence against any of the others turned up, he would do his best to get his man. Once the plot was foiled, once Marchenko and his fellow conspirators were safely in custody, the Special Branch might even be glad of a murder charge to hold him on.

He drove to a telephone booth, where he rang up the inspector in charge of the chemists' enquiry team. Fortunately, he felt justified in taking Finch and Miss de la Costa off their list as well as Marchenko, so Inspector Wardle saw nothing noteworthy in his request.

Tom Tring was going to be another matter. He'd want to know just why they were dropping his favourite suspect from the investigation, and he wouldn't be slow to connect it with the mysterious stranger. On the other hand, very likely he had seen the superintendent around at the Yard, knew perfectly well who he was, and would not only button his lip but keep Piper's buttoned, too.

When Alec reached Miss Blaise's address, a light rain was falling and there was no sign of his men. They had had plenty of time to walk here. He looked around in irritation to see where they might have taken shelter.

'Hoy, Chief!'

He glanced up. Ernie was hanging out of a third-storey window, waving and beckoning. Still more irritated, Alec went up. He was sure he had told them to wait outside.

Olivia Blaise opened the door to him. 'Don't blame them, Chief Inspector she said, regarding his sour expression with sardonic amusement. 'I came home to find them waiting and as it had just started to rain I persuaded them to come in. You'll have a cup of tea, won't you? Otherwise I'll think you're about to arrest me. The kettle's on the boil.'

'Thank you, Miss Blaise, I won't say no.'

His arrival crowded the tiny room. As sparsely and cheaply furnished as Marchenko's, it was brightened by opera posters drawing-pinned on the walls, vivid-hued cushions scattered about, and colourful curtains. The curtain in one corner probably hid Miss Blaise's clothes, that in another a washbasin. The kettle steamed on a gas ring beside the metered gas fire. Tring sat on a kitchen chair painted scarlet, Piper on a couch-bed covered with a patchwork quilt.

A working girl making the best of things – Alec felt an immediate sympathy for her. He joined Ernie on the couch.

Tom had already taken fingerprints, so

once the tea was poured, Alec started asking questions. Olivia Blaise frankly admitted to her affair with Eric Cochran. She was 'pretty sure' Mrs. Cochran had not known about it.

'We were fearfully discreet,' she said with a grimace. 'He took me to the most ghastly cafés and we always came back here, never to a hotel, let alone dancing. But dear Ursula may guess now, if she hasn't already. Eric's asked me to sing in the repeat performance.'

'Congratulations.'

'Which means I gained by Bettina's death precisely what she denied me in life. It's all right, Chief Inspector, I didn't poison your tea. I didn't poison Bettina, either. It was by no means a sure thing that there would be a repeat performance, nor that Eric would offer me the part. We had quarrelled, as I'm sure you're aware. In spite of that, I suppose I might have considered doing in the bitch before the concert, in the hope of a reconciliation. I didn't, though. The idea never crossed my mind, and if it had I'd have chased it out.' Her sharp-featured face and cool eyes softened. 'I couldn't have done that to Roger.'

All she'd say about the others was that Muriel, likewise, would never deliberately do anything to distress Roger Abernathy, and that Eric would not have sabotaged his own concert. 'Nor would *she*,' Miss Blaise added sourly.

She hadn't noticed what anyone else did while she was in the soloists' room. She'd been talking to Muriel. When Muriel went into the dressing room to fetch her music, she had listened to Eric arguing for a last-minute change in the *'quam ohm Abrahae.'* (Piper's flying pencil hesitated at the phrase and she kindly spelled it out for him.) She hadn't gone anywhere near the table.

'Except just to tell Mr. Levich that Muriel wanted a word with him.'

'I assume you didn't observe Mr. Levich putting something in the decanter?'

She laughed. 'No, certainly not. And if it's gossip you want, well, I've enough on my own plate without poking into other people's business. That's not a dig at your profession, Chief Inspector,' she assured him with a smile, but she adamantly refused to say more, until, as they left, she said in a reflective voice, 'Roger should have married Muriel. Her voice would have been as good if it had been trained, and she's good and kind. But men always fall for golden curls.' She flipped her own dark, glossy cap derisively. 'Good-bye, gentlemen. Do call again some time.'

Following Alec down the narrow staircase, Tring's ruminative rumble observed, 'If there's anything I hate, it's seeing a bright young woman madly in love with a married man.'

'Olivia Blaise in love with Eric Cochran?' said Alec, surprised. 'She's very off-hand about him.'

'Ah, she's not the sort to wear her heart on her sleeve. You was watching her with an eye to Mrs. Abernathy's murder, Chief.'

'And you with an eye to a pretty girl?'

'That's as may be.' Tom preened his luxuriant moustache as they emerged into the street. 'Take it from me, Chief, she's pining for him. Now if we was to find Mrs. Cochran dead...'

'Then I'll arrest Miss Blaise.' Alec took his place behind the Austin's wheel and pressed the self-starter. 'I'm inclined to doubt she murdered Mrs. Abernathy. If you're right, Tom, she might even have hoped for Mrs. Cochran to be told about the affair in hopes of cutting her lover loose.'

'Cochrans next, Chief?' asked Piper.

'Yes. We can rule out Miss de la Costa, at least provisionally. Levich is going to dinner at Abernathy's and I'd quite like to run him to earth there. Tom, unless I miss my guess, the Cochrans will make a fuss over the fingerprinting so we'll leave it till last. You talk to the servants first, especially Mrs. Cochran's lady's maid and the chauffeur.'

'Right, Chief.'

The Cochrans' imposing residence overlooked the Thames. A smart, pretty parlour maid let them in out of the rain. In the hall, several stags' heads stared down in glassy-eyed disapproval at an antlered hattree, an elephant's-foot umbrella stand, and a stuffed fox on a pedestal. From the ceiling dangled a cock-pheasant in full flight. Facing the door hung a portrait of a patriarchal gentleman of the hirsute period of the previous century – full beard, moustache, and whiskers – in a shooting jacket. He was flanked by two suits of armour.

'Crikey!' breathed Ernie Piper, and blushed as the pretty parlour maid smiled at him.

'I'll see if the mistress is home,' she said primly, remembering her place. Alec, who had no intention of being denied, followed hot on her heels. She opened a door, glanced back at him, and announced, a bit flustered, 'It's the police, madam.'

Entering the spacious drawing room, Alec

winced. Elegant Sheraton and Hepplewhite, hideously disfigured by Victorian bobbles and fringes and antimacassars, mingled with the latest tubular steel and aluminium. Someone with no natural taste knew what was 'good,' what was fashionable, and what her father had liked. Wryly aware of his own snobbery, Alec guessed Sir Denzil Vernon attained his baronetcy and his country manor by making a fortune in beer, or perhaps pig feed, and donating large sums to the Tory party.

Averting his eyes from a stuffed fish in a glass case on the mantelpiece, Alec met the almost equally cold gaze of Mrs. Cochran.

'The striking portrait in the hall, is that Sir Denzil?' he asked.

'Yes, that's my father.' The atmosphere thawed perceptibly. 'No doubt you wish to speak to my husband. He's rather busy but...'

'Later' Alec said quickly, and repeated his line about last night's shock and today's recovered memory.

Mrs. Cochran confirmed most of Marchenko's report of people's movements in the soloists' room while she was there. She had been alone for a few moments before her husband came out of the dressing room, but she hadn't gone to the table.

'The refreshments were for performers, not visitors,' she pointed out astringently. A fact liable to be overlooked by anyone so crass as to follow a maid into the drawing room before he was invited, her tone implied. 'Miss Blaise didn't appear to realize she had no right to help herself - unless she had some other purpose at the table.'

'You saw her there?'

Under the piercing gaze which made his subordinates jump to attention and crooks shake in their shoes, she backtracked. 'I thought so. I couldn't swear to it.'

Alec took this as evidence that she had now guessed the true identity of her husband's mistress. He was the more certain when she hurried on:

'Roger Abernathy was only at the table very briefly, just long enough to pour the cup of tea he brought for his wife. Not that you can possibly suspect the unfortunate man. So kindly and gently he offered it to her, and the vulgar creature pouted and called it pig swill!'

Had all his suspects not been at daggers drawn, one way or another, Alec might have wondered if there was a conspiracy among them to exonerate Roger Abernathy. Conscious of the influence of the weight of opinion, he reminded himself that the man was by no means exempt from the rule that a murdered wife was most likely to have been killed by her husband. Kind, gentle, long-suffering, he'd not be the first worm to have turned. Yet the rejection of a cup of tea hardly qualified as a trigger for murder.

Mrs. Cochran started to bemoan the *Times* music critic's article on the concert, which had been more an obituary for a promising young singer than a review. Eric had scarcely been mentioned. Worse, several of the prominent musical personages who had received complimentary tickets had telephoned not to praise his conducting but to commiserate over the débâcle.

'And not all of them are able to come again on Monday,' she lamented. 'It's a serious setback to his career. I trust you'll do all in your power, Chief Inspector, to catch the culprit.'

Whose major misdeed in her opinion was clearly not murder but disrupting the concert. She appeared to be perfectly sincere, and oblivious of anything to cavil at in her viewpoint.

Alec remembered Daisy telling him of Mrs. Cochran's obsession with her husband's career. If she had wanted to dispose of Bettina, she'd never have done it in the middle of an

216

important concert. He decided not to broach the subject of Cochran's infidelity, at least until he had a firmer indication of whether she had believed Bettina to be his mistress.

In the meantime, he'd take advantage of her words. 'You can be sure we shall do our utmost to "catch the culprit," ma'am,' he assured her blandly. 'You and Mr. Cochran can be of assistance by allowing my sergeant to take your fingerprints, for elimination purposes.'

She blustered a bit but gave in. Tring and Cochran were sent for, fingerprints obtained. Then Cochran, a wary eye on his wife, invited the detectives to join him in his music room, a large room with French windows in one wall.

The expected piano was a concert grand, its black curves reflected in the polished parquet floor, but the most impressive object in the room was an American Victrola gramophone with a huge horn. The walls were lined with shelves bearing a vast collection of records and orchestral scores, interspersed with busts of the great composers. In one corner, a group of straight chairs and music stands suggested chamber music gatherings. Otherwise the furnishings were typical of a well-to-do gentleman's den – leather armchairs, superb antique rolltop desk, drinks cabinet.

'My chains,' said Eric Cochran bitterly, with an all-encompassing gesture. 'Sit down, Chief Inspector. Drink? No? Do have one of my cigars – I don't smoke them.'

Tring, an occasional cigar smoker who would deeply regret missing a genuine Havana, had slipped off back to the servants' quarters. Alec preferred his pipe, which he filled and lit; Piper, in his unobtrusive corner, took out a packet of Woodbines, but put it away when Cochran offered his silver cigarette case. An expensive cylinder of the finest Turkish tobacco between his lips, Piper produced his pencils and opened his notebook.

Cochran was ready to talk. Excited by his new idea for the '*Quam olim Abrahae*,' he hadn't paid much heed to what people did in the soloists' room. Except for irritation at his wife's following him, he had only noticed Olivia's arrival.

'I'm sure you know about me and Olivia,' he said wryly. 'I was always conscious of her whereabouts in the room and she didn't go to the table, though I don't expect you'll believe me. I love her, dammit! When Bettina Abernathy threatened to expose us to

Ursula, I was afraid for my career and – let's face it – for my life of luxury. Now I'm wondering whether it's worth it if it means I can't have Olivia. Surely you can understand that, Chief Inspector?' he pleaded.

'We can't condone adultery, sir.'

'No.' Cochran sank his head in his hands. 'And Ursula's always been kind in her own way, not to mention more than generous. But she'd never give me a divorce, and Olivia won't take me back without. What shall I do?'

Though he could not like him, Alec admitted to himself a sneaking sympathy for the unhappy man as well as for his betrayed wife.

'Do you think Mrs. Cochran is now aware of your involvement with Miss Blaise?'

'There's nothing to know *now*. She may have guessed that there *was* something, and she knows I've given Olivia the part.'

Cochran said nothing else of interest. They soon left him to his miserable life of luxury, collected Tom Tring, and went out into the damp dusk. As they stood for a moment watching a brightly lit boat chug down the river, Tom reported.

'A sly sort of chappie, the chauffeur, Chief. He used to drive Mr. Cochran to the Abernathys' house, right enough. Cochran'd dismiss him, give him the afternoon or evening off, the which he'd take, then go home and peach to the missus. Seems she always had to know just where hubby went, and seeing she paid the bills, this chappie blabbed.'

'Did he know about Miss Blaise?'

'Not him. Thought it was Mrs. Abernathy.'

'Then the chances are Mrs. Cochran did, too. I still don't see her – or him, come to that – wrecking the concert, but we'll keep them in mind. All right, Tom, you'd better get back to *your* missus, or she'll have my head – which reminds me, I'd best call home and say I shan't be in for dinner. I'll drop you at the nearest Tube station. Leave the fingerprint kit. Ernie's been watching you, and I dare say he and I between us can manage Levich's dabs. I'll want you at the Yard early enough to read over Ernie's notes before you come with me to see Dr. Woodward.'

'Hey, Chief,' protested Piper, 'you want it all typed up tonight?'

'That's right, laddie. But first we get a bite to eat and head back to Abernathy's house to see Levich.'

Piper groaned and Tom grinned.

'The inquest's tomorrow,' Alec reminded them. 'The coroner is going to want to know what we've been doing.'

CHAPTER 13

Daisy would have liked nothing better than to sneak off home to her typewriter. Contemplation of the long evening ahead filled her with dismay. The Reverend Westlea's silent disapproval of Yakov Levich and equally silent censure of his remaining daughter were so eloquent as to be painful.

They'd dined early as Monday was the Pro-Musica Choir's rehearsal night. Against Muriel's protests, Roger insisted he was well enough to direct it, though she assured him no one would expect it of him. Quietly stubborn, he was determined to carry out what he saw as an obligation, though he quite understood that she could not face it. She made him take a taxicab instead of his usual bus.

Adding to Daisy's restlessness was an urgent need to talk to Alec, so when the front doorbell rang and Beryl announced that the p'leece were back, she was delighted.

'The chief inspector wants to see Miss Muriel first, then Mr. Levich,' the maid continued.

'You will go with her, Miss Dalrymple?' Levich asked anxiously.

'Please, Daisy,' Muriel pleaded. The vicar pursed his lips and looked the other way.

Daisy was only too ready to comply. They went out into the hall, where Alec and Piper were waiting, and Muriel led the way into the dining room. Alec looked resigned when he saw Daisy. Containing her impatience, she decided he would not be pleased if she produced her revelation in Muriel's presence. She found it easier to hold her tongue when she heard what he wanted to talk about.

'Miss Westlea, I've been hearing a good deal about the jewellery Dimitri Marchenko gave your sister. I should like to see it, if you have it to hand.'

'Yes,' Muriel faltered, 'it's in my bedroom. I didn't think it would matter if I moved it out of my parents' way, and since she left it to me ... didn't she?'

'I believe so, and it doesn't matter in the least that you moved it. I may want to have it appraised.'

Daisy perked up. Marchenko was under suspicion, then, his motive presumably in proportion to the value of his gifts to Bettina.

'I'm sure it's very valuable,' said Muriel. 'I'm going to give it back to him. It seems only fair.'

Alec raised his eyebrows. 'More than fair. That's up to you, as long as you don't dispose of it before the will is probated.'

'Yes, that's what Roger said when I told him.'

'How is Mr. Abernathy?'

'Quite well.' Muriel frowned. 'Physically, at least. He … he seems to have lost interest in everything. He's just going through the motions because one can't let people down, wouldn't you say, Daisy?'

'Yes, he's awfully listless and he hardly eats a thing.'

'I'm sorry to hear it. Was your sister in good health, Miss Westlea?'

'Oh, yes, Bettina was never ill. That's why she wasn't quite sympathetic about Roger's heart.'

'She took no medicines?'

'A cough elixir, I think. Singing a lot, one's throat gets dry and scratchy. Otherwise, an occasional headache powder. I don't know of anything else.'

'Thank you. That's all for now, though I expect I shall need to talk to you again at more length sometime. If you wouldn't mind fetching the jewellery while I see Mr. Levich?'

'I've got something to tell you,' Daisy said to Alec in a low voice as Muriel turned to leave.

'Later, please, Daisy. I don't want to keep Levich waiting.'

'Gosh no!' she agreed, thinking of the poor man alone in the drawing room with the Westlea parents. 'But don't go away till I've told you.'

He smiled, wearily. 'As long as it's short. Ernie and I still have a long night ahead of us.'

'It won't take long. Yes, I'm coming, Muriel.'

While Muriel went upstairs, Daisy returned to the drawing room to summon Yakov Levich. He was obviously not at all happy about talking to the police again, still influenced more by early experience than by his previous encounter with Alec's innocuous methods of interrogation.

'Shall I go with you?' Daisy offered impulsively.

His long, bony face lit up. 'Please, you will?'

'If you like, as long as you tell Mr. Fletcher you want me there.'

At the sight of her, Alec's expression went from incredulous to long-suffering. He voiced no protest but his eyes demanded, 'How the deuce do you do it?' He glared at Piper, on whose face Daisy caught the remains of a grin, quickly wiped off. When she next glanced at Levich, she saw he had followed at least some of this byplay, for he looked faintly amused and much more relaxed.

Alec asked him about whom and what he had seen in the soloists' room. 'I hope you will remember better now that the first shock of Mrs. Abernathy's death is past,' he added, as if reluctance had played no part in yesterday's reticence. A clever touch to set his victims at ease, Daisy thought.

Levich thought a moment. 'First, I saw Eric Cochran and Mrs. Cochran,' he said. 'We met at door. Already Cochran speaked – spoke to me about new idea for next part of *Requiem*, but I have one question more, so I ask. You understand, I have looked for Cochran in conductor's room and not found. This is why I went to soloists' room.'

'I see, sir. So you left after speaking to Mr. Cochran?'

'No.' Levich flushed. 'When I saw Miss Westlea was there, I have hopes to exchange some words with her. But she talked with Miss Blaise. I not liked to interrupt. So...'

'Just a minute, sir. Was anyone else in the sitting room?'

'Mr. and Mrs. Abernathy only. They too talk together. This is why I not liked to appear as if I wait for Miss Westlea, so I got drink of water.'

'We'll need to take your fingerprints, sir,' Alec said at this point, 'just so as to be sure which glass you used and what other people touched.'

'I had mine taken,' said Daisy cheerfully as Levich quailed.

He looked a bit less alarmed and Alec gave her a nod of near approval. Just let him try to claim she wasn't helpful!

'Miss Blaise spoke to you as she left?' Alec asked next.

His thin cheeks pink-tinged, Levich said, 'She spoke to me that Miss Westlea is happy to see me. So I went to Miss Westlea.'

'You're fond of Miss Westlea, sir?'

'*Da*, fond. Am affectionate friend of her, is right word?'

'A very good word, sir. As you might say, you're in love.'

'Love, *nyet*. Love is not allow to me. By me is nothing to offer Miss Westlea, not money for home, for children. Miss Westlea has *krasivaya dusha* – beautiful soul. I admire, I like to talk, but to marry I cannot. This Miss Westlea knows.'

Alec didn't appear impressed by Muriel's beautiful soul. 'But she'll have some money now, her sister's money,' he said.

'Not enough for family to live. She will give back jewels to Marchenko. Is right, perhaps, but...' Levich spread his hands and shrugged. 'Also, I begin think like English. In my country, to marry wife with money is good. Here I see how people talk of Mr. Cochran. Is not good. I must become Englishman.'

'You mean,' Daisy burst out indignantly, 'you'll let poor Muriel wither away into an old maid living in some frightful cheap boarding house at some ghastly resort...'

'Daisy, please!' said Alec.

She ignored him. 'You might at least give her a choice!' she snapped. Levich looked bewildered, then thoughtful.

Alec ran his fingers through his hair. 'Miss Dalrymple, I shall have to ask you to leave.'

'I'm sorry, Chief. I'll keep quiet. But really, the way men ruin people's lives with their idiotic scruples! It makes my blood boil.'

'As long as it boils silently, I've no objection. Mr. Levich, tell me please what happened next.'

'Mrs. Abernathy ask Miss Westlea to mend

button, so I go.'

'Did Mr. Abernathy go with you?'

'No. He had cup of tea in hand. Perhaps he stay to drink?'

'Perhaps.' Alec was singularly blank-faced. Daisy wondered what was the significance of the cup of tea.

She was tempted to ask, but just then Muriel arrived with one of Bettina's jewellery cases. 'I hope I haven't kept you waiting, Chief Inspector,' she said breathlessly.

'Far from it, Miss Westlea.' He sounded rather annoyed, and Daisy guessed he had intended Muriel to wait until he summoned her when he had finished with Levich.

'I was transferring all the pieces Mr. Marchenko gave Betsy into the same case,' Muriel explained. 'I'm pretty sure this is the lot.'

She set the case on the table in front of Alec. Opening it, he whistled.

Daisy stood up and leaned forward to peer around the raised lid. 'Gosh!'

Alec closed the lid, cutting off her glimpse of gleaming red and green stones in hideously ornate old-fashioned settings. 'I'll have to have these valued, Miss Westlea. Would you mind making up a list which I can sign as a receipt? I dare say Miss Dalrymple will help you while I finish up with Mr. Levich.'

He returned Daisy's fulminating look with one of limpid innocence. Since she was really rather keen to see the jewels properly, she changed her mind, smiled sweetly, and said, 'Of course I'll help you, Muriel.'

They went back up to Muriel's bedroom since she didn't want her parents to see the loot. The gems were as stunning, the elaborate gold and silver settings as frightful as Daisy's quick glimpse had suggested. 'Did Bettina actually wear these?' she asked.

'No, I told you, she liked to gloat over them. If I kept them I'd sell them, but I can't think it would be right,' Muriel said wistfully.

'It's very noble of you to give them back.' Daisy was far from sure she would have been quite so noble.

They listed each piece with a brief description, then returned to the dining room to find Alec and Levich chatting about life in Russia.

Alec signed the list and took charge of the jewellery case. 'You haven't mentioned your intentions to Mr. Marchenko, have you?' he asked Muriel. 'Please don't, nor, of course, that I'm getting an appraisal.' Politely dismissed, Muriel and Levich reluctantly returned to the drawing room and the Reverend Westlea.

'Shouldn't you have checked the stuff against the list?' Daisy asked.

'If you hadn't helped prepare it, I would have.'

'Oh, I see,' she said, enlightened. 'So you weren't just getting rid of me.'

'Not just.' He grinned. 'Though as a matter of fact Levich didn't tell me anything new – except that you have persuaded him.'

'I've what?'

'After consulting me about the proper, gentlemanly thing to do, he's going to propose to Miss Westlea. But not until this business is cleared up,' he warned her as she started to crow, 'so not a word to your friend. Apart from anything else, remember I may yet have to arrest her.'

'Oh no, Alec! It must have been someone who couldn't get close to Bettina in private. Why should Muriel murder her sister at the Albert Hall when she could have done it much more easily at home?'

'Ernie?'

'Because this way gives us lots more suspects, Chief?'

'Exactly.'

'If she was clever enough to think of that,' Daisy protested, 'she'd be clever enough not to leave all those fingerprints on the decanter. And by the way, what was all that fuss about a cup of tea? The poison was in the ratafia, not tea, wasn't it?'

'Abernathy took a cup to Bettina but she didn't want it,' Alec explained.

'Oh, that's happened to me at formal tea parties. One stands there with the wretched cup and saucer in one's hands, wondering what to do with it, before one finally decides to abandon it. Alec, listen. The Reverend Westlea poured the sherry before dinner, and guess what he did? He took the top off the decanter like this.' She held out her right hand palm up, a gap between forefinger and the other three. 'You see? With the neck of the stopper between his fingers he wouldn't have left any prints.'

'That's what Gower did! Something caught my attention but I wasn't sure what.'

'Which means Muriel didn't do it.'

'It means nothing of the sort,' Alec said dampingly, 'but I admit it does open other possibilities. Definitely worth keeping Ernie and me up late for.'

'It's not very late.'

'Not now, but while you're dropping off to

sleep, Ernie will be typing and I'll be studying chemical lab reports and autopsy reports.'

'Ugh.' She screwed up her nose.

'You may hear them yourself. You'll be at the inquest, I take it?'

'No,' said Daisy regretfully. 'I have some work I simply must finish tomorrow morning. Too, too tiresome!'

The reams of obscure medical terminology of the autopsy report boiled down to no more than that the symptoms observed were consistent with death by cyanide poisoning. Alec had an uneasy feeling about it. He re-read the statements taken from the three doctors who had offered their services at the Albert Hall. Dr. Woodward had suggested Bettina might have had a seizure, and now she turned out to be his patient, and there was this odd business of his wanting her prescription returned.

Woodward would probably clear it all up in the morning. All the same, Alec wished Dr. Renfrew had not gone off to the Italian Riviera.

Rubbing his tired eyes, he turned to the report from the forensic laboratory. The carpet and the slivers of broken glass had provided too little material to be tested. The dregs in the decanter were scarcely better. A trace of cyanide was detected, but not enough to tell if the concentration was strong enough to kill.

Hydrocyanic acid, also known as prussic acid, was a natural constituent of almonds, and of the peach, apricot, or cherry stones often used to make almond-flavored liqueurs. Another of these, noyau, had caused at least one accidental death when the oil of bitter almonds, risen to the top of a bottle left sitting for years, had been poured out in the first glassful. Though the present case was different, as the ratafia had been decanted, it all went to show that the trace of cyanide found meant precisely nothing.

Alec groaned. The almond smell from the decanter could have been just the liqueur. Therefore the poison might have been put in Bettina's glass. If so, did it make any difference to anything? Did the almond smell from the broken glass and spilled liquid mean equally little? No, with his own eyes he had seen Bettina drink from that glass and drop dead.

'Mr. Fletcher?' The inspector from Fingerprints put his head round the door. 'I'm glad to see you're keeping yourself up late, sir, as well as me.'

'You've compared the dabs?' Alec asked eagerly.

'Here's the darkroom prints, and here's the Albert Hall lot. All checked against the ones you brought in, sir, and I've labelled 'em, like so.'

Everyone's fingerprints were precisely where Alec expected them to be – and nowhere else. He sighed. 'Thanks. Can you tell whether someone took out the stopper of the decanter this way?' He demonstrated Daisy's discovery.

'I might be able to tell if it's been done, but there's no way to identify who did it.'

'Right. Try it for me, please, but it can wait till morning. I'm off home to bed.'

Too tired to drink the cocoa his mother had left him in a Thermos flask, Alec was up in the morning in time to have breakfast with his mother and Belinda before she went to school. At nine, his daughter was putting on a spurt of growth, and he worried about how skinny she looked in her navy blue uniform tunic and black stockings. Her reddish-blond hair – Joan's hair – was thick and glossy, though, exuberantly trying to escape its pigtails, and she ate voraciously. Like Daisy, but less restrained.

'Daddy,' she said, swallowing a last morsel of heavily buttered toast with a quarter inch of strawberry jam on top, 'I know I'm not to ask about your case and I won't, I promise, but are you working with Miss Dalrymple again?'

'You could put it that way,' Alec said cautiously.

'I do so want to meet her. Will you ask her to tea?'

He glanced at his mother, caught her look of dismay. 'That's up to your gran,' he said.

'*Please*, Granny. On Saturday, when I'm not in a rush, and I'll bake rock cakes. Golly, I must fly or I'll miss the bus. Please may I be excused, Gran, and where's my satchel?'

'I must be off too. I'll drive you to school, Bel.'

'Oh, topping!'

'We'll talk later about inviting Miss Dalrymple, Mother.' He bent to kiss her soft, lined cheek. 'I'm afraid I may not get home for dinner again. I'll telephone later and let you know.'

He delivered Belinda to the Victorian Gothic red brick pile of her school and watched her disappear among a swarm of navy coats and hats. Then he drove on to meet Tom Tring at Dr. Woodward's.

The door was opened by a plump child a year or two younger than Belinda, blond-pigtailed and red-nosed.

'I've got a cold so I can't go to school,' she announced. 'And I can't play with the baby 'case he gets it, too. And Tommy's a *boy*.' This in a tone of ineffable scorn. 'Do you want to see my daddy? Dr. Woodward, I mean. It's too early for the surgery.'

'He's expecting us.'

The doctor looked tired, edgy, far from well. 'Come into my office, gentlemen,' he invited. 'I can spare you a little time before my surgery hours. What can I do for you?' Sitting down behind his desk, he took off his gold-rimmed spectacles and polished them on his handkerchief. Without them he seemed younger, with an uncertain, vulnerable air.

'Just a few questions, sir.' Alec glanced around the room. The usual medical references, neatly shelved; a glass-fronted cabinet full of case-books; his gaze fixed on a door in the corner with a sign which read *Dispensary*. 'You won't mind if I ask, Doctor – it's a subject on my mind at present – you do keep that door locked, I hope?'

'Always, Chief Inspector. I have small children.'

'You make up all your own prescriptions, do you?'

Woodward's pale cheeks paled further and he fumbled with his spectacles as he put them on. 'Just a few of the simpler remedies,' he said. 'I got into the habit in my first practice. It was in the country, rather remote, and I dispensed medicines as a useful service to my patients.'

'Quite, sir. Now Mrs. Abernathy's cough remedy, that would be one you put up yourself?'

'Yes.'

'Why didn't you tell me you were her doctor? Why did you ask her maid for the remains of the medicine? What was in it?'

'I should have known you'd find out.' He buried his haggard face in his hands. 'The prescription contains prussic acid. In an extremely dilute solution, it's an excellent specific for a dry, scratchy cough, the kind Mrs. Abernathy occasionally suffered from. I've been having nightmares.'

'You're afraid you didn't dilute it enough.'

'I can't believe it!' He looked up, earnest now. 'I'm always careful, of course, but I was especially careful in this case.'

'Why?'

'I knew Mrs. Abernathy often took the

mixture with that damned liqueur she was so fond of, and the effect of both prussic acid and alcohol is depressant. I advised her not to. She wasn't the sort to take advice, and the stuff worked, so she refused to take something else instead. I can't believe it, I tell you! I feel as if I'm *living* in a nightmare. This could ruin me, and my family.'

'So that's why you argued that Mrs. Abernathy might have had a seizure.'

'Partly wishful thinking,' Woodward admitted. 'And partly, I suppose, because I can't smell cyanide. I've been thinking of nothing else ever since, as you can imagine, and naturally my mind's been running on poisons. Do you know, an overdose of trinitrin would produce much the same symptoms?'

'Trinitrin, Doctor?' Suddenly alert, Alec heard Tring's abrupt intake of breath. Ye gods, had they been barking up the wrong tree? Had the bitter almond smell come solely from the ratafia?

Had Dr. Renfrew's assistant found evidence of cyanide only because that was what he was asked to look for?

'It's a heart medicine,' the doctor explained. 'Combined with alcohol it can cause a disastrous fall in blood pressure, as well as

238

asphyxia, cyanosis, convulsions, and all the rest.' His shoulders slumped again. 'But Mrs. Abernathy's heart was perfectly healthy. *I* certainly never prescribed trinitrin.'

Bettina's heart was healthy. Her husband's was not. What were those pills he kept always to hand? Alec had to talk to his doctor, to the pathologist, to Daisy ... but first, before the inquest, he had to talk to the coroner.

'Thank you for your frankness, sir, though I wish you might have spoken up sooner.'

'Yes. I'm sorry.' Dr. Woodward's face was a mask of despair.

'I'm not saying you're in the clear, Doctor, but I can tell you that no cough medicine bottle was found at the Albert Hall, and Mrs. Abernathy had already consumed a good deal of ratafia before the glass which killed her. So unless a cumulative dose...'

'No,' said Woodward eagerly, 'cyanide doesn't work that way. If she'd taken a dangerous dose, it would affect her at once.'

'I'll have to take independent advice on that, sir. I'll let you know as soon as possible.'

'Thank you, Chief Inspector. Anything I can do to help, anything at all, call on me day or night.' Much cheered, Woodward showed them out.

'Damn! Damn! Damn!' Alec thumped the

steering wheel in time with the expletives. 'I'll have to ask Sir Bernard Spilsbury to redo the postmortem exam, and he's going to want to know why the devil I didn't call him in in the first place!'

CHAPTER 14

'And I don't like to speak ill of the dead, miss,' said Mrs. Potter, obviously about to do just that, 'but me friend Mrs. Wick, which obliges next door, she says Mrs. Abernathy weren't no better than she should be, and a nasty piece of work as they're well shot of. Not but what I wouldn't wish such an 'orrid end on me worst... Ah, there's the doorbell. Your young man, I 'spect?'

'My young man?' Daisy tried to assume an innocent expression.

'That copper what's after Mrs. Abernathy's murderer. Mrs. Wick says he's a real good-looker and a proper gentleman, too.'

'Oh, Mr. Fletcher.' Gulping down the last of her tea, Daisy pushed back her chair and started for the kitchen door. 'No, I shouldn't think it's him. He'll still be at the inquest.'

All the same, on the way to the front door she paused to glance in the hall looking glass and dab powder on her freckles. Her shingled head still gave her a shock every time she saw her own reflection. She opened the door.

'What-ho, Daisy.' On the doorstep, hat in hand, stood Phillip Petrie, tall and loose-limbed, fair hair sleeked back above a face which was handsome in an indeterminate sort of way. 'My sainted aunt, what have you done to your hair?'

'Hallo, Phillip. Don't be an ass, I had it cut, of course. Come in. I haven't seen you in ages. What brings you to this neck of the woods?'

'I was down in Dorset for the weekend. Just got back. What's all this about a singer being murdered next door?'

'Not next door, Phil. At the Albert Hall.'

'Oh, then you're not mixed up in it,' he said, relieved.

'As a matter of fact, I was at the concert.'

'You would be!'

'Along with several thousand other people. Including Alec Fletcher, who's investigating the case.'

The doorbell rang again. It was Muriel, looking flustered. 'Oh, Daisy, you have a visitor? I'm so sorry, I...'

'It's all right, Muriel, come in. This is Phillip Petrie, an old friend of the family. Phillip, Miss Westlea, my next-door neighbour.'

'Westlea? Next door!' But Phillip was equal to any social occasion. He said all the proper things to Muriel, then turned to Daisy and went on with a touch of grimness, 'I'll take you out to dinner tonight.'

'Not tonight, old dear. I just popped home to do a bit of work, but I'm staying next door with Muriel until this ghastly business is over.' From the corner of her eye, Daisy saw Muriel's mouth open. She silenced her with a glare. 'Not that I wouldn't love to go out to dinner with you one day, Phil. I'll telephone when I'm free again, so start saving up your pennies. I expect you're due back at the office, aren't you?'

It was his turn to wilt before her speaking gaze. 'Yes, I'd better get back,' he said lamely, then he rallied, 'but I'll be in touch.'

'You can always telephone Daisy at our house, Mr. Petrie,' Muriel said hesitantly, and told him the number.

'Thank you, Miss Westlea.' He looked upon her with approval. 'Cheerio then, Daisy.'

'Cheerio, old bean. See you soon, and

don't *worry*.' Closing the door behind him, Daisy brushed aside Muriel's mumbled apologies for intruding. 'You've saved me from a ragging,' she said cheerfully. 'Phillip doesn't approve of Alec Fletcher, and since Phillip was my brother's best friend, he feels not merely entitled but obliged to try to make me see the error of my ways. I didn't expect you home yet. Is the inquest over already?'

'Yes, it was very short. I thought there would be lots of evidence given, everything Mr. Fletcher has found out so far, but he just asked for an adjournment to allow the police to pursue enquiries. All I had to say was that it really was Betsy – they let me do it instead of poor Roger – and a doctor confirmed that ... that she really was dead. Father's absolutely furious because the coroner wouldn't release her ... her body for burial.'

'How odd,' Daisy mused. 'Does it mean the funeral can't be held tomorrow?'

'Father decided to have a memorial service at the parish church here tomorrow, as Mrs. Cochran has so kindly made all the arrangements for afterwards. He and Mother will go home then as planned, thank heaven, and he'll have poor Betsy shipped home to be buried in his churchyard. Imagine being stuck for all eternity in the place she was so glad to leave!'

'At least her ghost is more likely to haunt the Albert Hall. Oh Muriel, I *am* sorry!'

But her tactless remark had surprised her friend into a smile. 'Oh dear, I hope she doesn't start interrupting concerts with snatches of Verdi's *Requiem*. I must be going. Will you be long?'

'I've another hour or so's work I really must get done. I'll be over by lunchtime.'

'You can't possibly realize what a comfort it is to have you there. If Mr. Fletcher arrives before you come, I'll send him here, shall I? He stopped me after the inquest and asked me to tell you he must see you. And Roger wants to see him. He's in a state over something; he wouldn't say what.' Muriel sighed. 'See you at lunch.'

Daisy retreated to the tiny back parlour where her massive, aged second-hand Underwood typewriter reposed in state on an elegant Georgian writing table from Fairacres. She had all but finished transforming her notes on the V and A into an article when once again the doorbell shrilled.

Her mind on her article, this time she forgot to glance in the hall mirror. Of course this time it was Alec on the doorstep, but if her freckles had emerged through the powder he didn't seem to care.

'Miss Westlea says you're working. Can you spare me a moment?'

'Yes, but just let me finish off the last paragraph before I forget how I was going to put it. Come on back to my den.'

Alec stood at the window, gazing out at the narrow strip of garden and the forsythia blooming on the studio wall, while Daisy finished the last few lines. 'There,' she said, straightening the pile of paper, all done. What's up?'

Turning, he grinned. 'I expect your friend Miss Fotheringay will be happy to hear that it may not have been cyanide after all.'

'No?' said Daisy, astonished. 'But the doctors said the symptoms ... and the almond odour?'

'I'm an absolute idiot, as Sir Bernard Spilsbury hasn't hesitated to tell me.'

'The Home Office pathologist? How dare he!'

'He has every right. I've had to ask him to redo a botched autopsy and he says it's far too late to find the proof he'll be looking for. Something called methemoglobin, which disappears from a cadaver within a few hours. You see, I assumed the murderer had relied on the almond smell of the ratafia to cover the cyanide smell, but it may have been irrelevant. The smell was there whether there was cyanide or not.'

'But the doctors said it was cyanide!'

'They jumped to the same conclusion as I did. At least, two of them did. Dr. Woodward has drawn to my attention that the symptoms of an overdose of a certain heart medicine are very similar to those of cyanide poisoning. Daisy, do you know what's in those pills of Abernathy's? I can't get hold of his doctor.'

'They're trinitrin. It's another name for nitroglycerin, the same stuff as the explosive, believe it or not.'

'The explosive? Great Scott! I don't suppose you know if yet another name for it is glyceryl trinitrate?'

'I haven't the foggiest. Why?'

'Oh, I just wondered,' said Alec evasively.

'Is trinitrin what Dr. Woodward told you about?'

'It is. Who, besides Abernathy, has access to his pills? Miss Westlea, of course.'

'Anyone who has visited the house. He tends to forget to carry them, so Muriel keeps a spare bottle in the downstairs lav. I was there once when she asked Olivia to fetch them for him. Cochran was there too. There's a bottle in the music room, too, I think.'

Running his fingers through his hair, Alec pulled a wry face. 'Almost as accessible as Miss Fotheringay's darkroom. But while she might not miss the small amount of cyanide needed for a fatal dose,' he added thoughtfully, 'Abernathy or Miss Westlea would surely have noticed if a whole lot of his pills had disappeared.'

'He's absent-minded, remember. But don't go trying to make out that Muriel must have done it,' Daisy begged. 'She wouldn't necessarily notice, not unless Roger needed one from the lav and was too ill to get it for himself.'

'How often does he take them?'

'Just when he needs to, not on a regular schedule. They're an emergency remedy for an attack of angina. Which reminds me, Mrs. Gower told me they hand out trinitrin pills at the East End clinic where she volunteers, though it's the children she works with.'

'Do they, now! I must find out if any have gone missing.'

'Mrs. Gower is still on your list of suspects? Who else?'

'Daisy, you know I can't...'

'Blast, there's the doorbell again, and Mrs. Potter's downstairs cleaning the kitchen. I'll have to see who it is. Half a mo.'

An agitated Roger Abernathy was just raising his hand to ring again. 'I hope I'm not disturbing you, Daisy. Is the chief inspector here?' he asked.

'Yes.' Daisy studied his lips for a trace of blue. 'Do you need to take a pill?'

'How kind of you to ask. Yes, I took one before I came. May I see him?'

'Come in.' She led the way down the narrow hall and preceded him into the back parlour. 'Alec, Mr. Abernathy would like a word. Do sit down, Roger.'

'Perhaps I'd better,' he said apologetically.

Daisy did her best to fade into the wood-work, but Alec said, holding the open door, 'Thank you for lending us your den, Miss Dalrymple.'

Roger stopped her. 'No, please don't go, Daisy. You ought to know what's being said, too. Mr. Fletcher, someone at the inquest showed me some newspapers – the *Daily Sketch*, the *Graphic*, I can't remember, not the sort of papers one reads. Their reporters claim that Yakov Levich killed my wife. You must stop them!'

'I doubt they're printing that, sir. That would be libel, and they're pretty careful on the whole not to lay themselves open to a suit for damages.'

'They don't say it openly. They talk about foreigners and Jews in the most bigoted way, making it perfectly obvious to whom they refer.'

'I'm afraid there's nothing I can do, Mr. Abernathy. It's the penalty we pay for a free Press.'

'It's abominable!' Abernathy cried. 'Levich's reputation will be ruined, his future destroyed.'

'I shouldn't worry, Roger,' Daisy said soothingly, coming forward to lay her hand on the anguished man's shoulder. 'After all, the people who read that sort of paper go to music halls, not serious concerts. True music-lovers won't care about beastly insinuations in the penny papers.'

'Do you think not?' he asked, eager to believe her. 'Levich is such a good fellow, as well as a brilliant violinist. I couldn't bear it if he were to be injured by my ... by my loss.'

'Miss Dalrymple is very likely right, sir. Assuming Mr. Levich is not our man, he'll weather the storm. Now, since you're here, I'd like to go over people's movements in the soloists' room once more, just to make sure I've got it all clear. And since you're here, Miss Dalrymple,' Alec added with a sardonic glance, 'will you take notes for me?'

'I'll be glad to,' Daisy said promptly. She hadn't yet heard the full story of who went where when.

To her disappointment, Abernathy had been one of the last to arrive in the room. As far as she could tell from Alec's questions and the glimpses of his demeanour she caught between shorthand scribbles, he learned nothing new.

'That's that, then,' he said at last, leaning back with a sigh. 'Mrs. Abernathy and Miss Westlea returned to the ladies' dressing room and you and Mr. Levich left together.'

'Not quite together. I still had the cup of tea I'd fetched for Bettina in my hands. I suppose I stood there for a few moments wondering whether I ought to drink it.' Abernathy smiled faintly. 'I was brought up in a waste not, want not household, Chief Inspector. But it was tepid by then, and not at all appetizing. I decided since the rest of the contents of the urn would undoubtedly go down the drain, to leave the one cup would not be too great a sin.'

'No sin at all. By the way, why did you pour it for her in the first place? She didn't ask for it?'

'No. I continued to hope she'd come to find tea a sufficient stimulant in place of the liqueur she favoured.'

Just as he must have gone on hoping to the end that Bettina would stop taking lovers and turn to him, Daisy thought sadly. Poor little man, he had given her the best years of his life and now he wasn't well enough to enjoy the freedom her death had brought him. He sat huddled in his chair, drained, somehow shrunken since she first met him.

'Are you ill, Mr. Abernathy?' Alec asked sharply.

He shook his head. 'No. Only tired. I seem to be tired all the time now, I'm afraid.'

'You have your pills with you? You must worry about running out.'

'It's very easy to renew the prescription. My doctor knows what I need, and it's a common medicine; the chemist always has the pills to hand. If my supply gets low, I just tell Muriel and she sees to it for me. My sister-in-law has been extraordinarily kind to me over the years, as well as quite devoted to her sister.'

'I'm sure she has, sir. Well, I shan't keep

251

you any longer just now. I expect your lunch is waiting. Thank you for your patience, and I shouldn't worry about Mr. Levich. Those Grub Street rags will move on to some new scandal, real or invented, in no time.'

Daisy neither saw nor heard from Alec again until the memorial service at Chelsea Old Church on Wednesday morning.

To go with the grey silk dress she hated, because it reminded her of the deaths of Michael, Gervaise, and her father, she had borrowed a frightfully smart little black hat from Lucy for the occasion. She was wondering whether in spite of its colour it was a bit too dashing for a funeral when she spotted Alec. She knew he hadn't been invited. No doubt he had waved his C.I.D. identification at the ushers – they had strict instructions not to admit anyone who might conceivably be a reporter.

He nodded to her gravely but made no attempt to speak, so she proceeded with the family to the front pew.

The service was extremely well attended. Roger Abernathy being in no state to deal with the matter, the Reverend Westlea had gratefully left it to Mrs. Cochran to issue invitations. She was acquainted with all the important musical personages who ought to be included, he pointed out when Muriel objected.

Muriel ceased to object when she discovered Mrs. Cochran had invited Yakov Levich. At that point the vicar had second thoughts, but by then it was too late.

Glancing back as she sat down, Daisy saw everyone who had been in the choir room that night, except Marchenko and Consuela de la Costa, which was not surprising. Both had loathed Bettina; both were foreigners with little to gain by a show of doing the proper thing; neither was well enough acquainted with Roger or Muriel to want to show sympathy.

The last explained the arrival of Olivia Blaise, looking simply stunning in black. Mrs. Cochran wouldn't have invited her, presumably, but she had asked Muriel for a list of friends who might otherwise be left out. She couldn't very well strike any names off that list.

After the service, when they emerged from the church's dimness into the sunny but wind-chilled day, Olivia was waiting to speak to Muriel and Roger. 'I shan't go to the Cochrans' she said, 'but I did want you to know I was here, and feeling for you.'

'Do come. Please.' Roger looked distraught rather than ill. 'If I must go through this, I need another friend to help fend off all these well-meaning people. I can't ... I can't...'

'Of course I'll come,' Olivia said quickly, 'if it will help.' She joined them in the hired motor.

Daisy saw Alec's little yellow Austin Seven taking its place in the procession. If he chose to attend the reception, she was sure he'd weasel his way in, whether Mrs. Cochran wanted him or not.

Once Daisy had recovered from the defunct wildlife in the front hall, she had to admit that Mrs. Cochran had done a good job. Double doors between drawing room, dining room, and music room stood open. The dining-room table had been moved against the wall and covered with funeral baked meats in the form of appetizing hors d'oeuvres. Two maids and a hired waiter passed among the guests with trays of sherry. A hired waiter? Daisy stared. She had almost not recognized Ernie Piper in formal black and white, a napkin over his arm, instead of his usual cheap brown serge. He had such an ordinary face. Was it really him?

Handing her a glass of medium-dry sherry, he winked fractionally before turning to

Muriel, who scarcely glanced at him. Olivia looked vaguely puzzled for a moment, then joined Muriel in persuading Roger that a glass of sherry would do him good.

Daisy stood on tiptoe and peered over heads. 'I'll be back in a moment,' she murmured to Muriel. Slithering between elbows, she came up behind Alec and in an undertone demanded, 'How did you get Mrs. Cochran to let Piper play waiter?'

'I sincerely hope she knows nothing about it. He's not easily recognized, is he? People don't really look at waiters, and they say things in the presence of a waiter which they'd never say to a policeman.'

'But *how?*'

'I found out which agency she generally used for her parties and prevailed upon them to hire Ernie. They wouldn't take Tom,' he added regretfully.

Daisy laughed. 'And how did you get in?'

'Trade secret. Now go away, Daisy, before you draw attention to me.'

'They'll all recognize you, by the eyebrows if nothing else.'

'I just want to keep an eye on things from a distance. You'd be surprised how often a funeral makes a murderer let down his guard – or hers, as the case may be. So buzz off;

there's a good girl.'

Daisy buzzed. She made a detour via the laden table, where she heaped two plates with a variety of tidbits; she was hungry and she was sure a bite to eat would help Roger survive the ordeal. He hadn't been eating enough recently to keep a sparrow alive.

When she reached the protective group around him, the Reverend Westlea was addressing Olivia. 'I understand you are a singer, Miss Blaise? A mezzo-soprano like Elizabeth? Would you be so very kind as to sing a little something for us *in memoriam?*'

'Oh, I don't think...'

'Please do, Olivia.' Roger looked on his father-in-law with a more kindly eye than was his wont. 'I'd like that.'

'Then of course I'll be happy to. If you will play for me, Roger. If Eric ... Mr. Cochran doesn't mind us using his piano.'

Unsurprisingly, Mr. Cochran didn't mind at all. As Olivia and Roger made their way into the music room, followed by those who had heard what was afoot, Daisy found herself beside the conductor.

'It's a great opportunity for Olivia,' he said to her in a low voice. 'There are people here who can do much more for her than I can.'

Accompanied by Roger, Olivia sang 'Ye

now have sorrow,' from Brahms's *German Requiem*, simple words of comfort very different from Verdi's visions of hellfire. Her voice had the cool, pure clarity of a mountain stream. Her last note was followed by a long hush, during which Daisy, blinking hard, saw more than one handkerchief surreptitiously touched to the corner of an eye.

Olivia stood with bowed head. Roger rose from the piano bench and went to take both her hands and kiss her cheek. Daisy heard murmurs behind her of musical personages informing each other that here was a talent to be watched. They began to move forward to congratulate Olivia.

Olivia reached for the tumbler of water standing on a doily on the piano in anticipation of her need. As she raised it to her lips, Roger dashed it from her hand, crying, 'Don't drink that! Can't you smell it? Cyanide!'

CHAPTER 15

For a frozen moment the music room was utterly still. Then Ernie Piper appeared from nowhere, dropped to his knees, righted the unbroken glass, and started to mop up the spilled puddle with his napkin.

'Don't get it on your hands, Piper!' Alec's command rang above the sudden clamour from the guests. 'And try not to breathe in any fumes. Major Browne, Mr. Levich, front and back doors, please. No one is to leave. Ladies and gentlemen, I am a police officer. I'll ask you to return to the other rooms at once, if you please.'

Piper was holding his napkin by one dry corner, lowering the sodden cloth into the glass. Roger Abernathy dropped down onto the piano bench and Muriel hurried to his side. Olivia stood alone by the piano, white-faced, shaking. Hurrying towards her, Daisy thought she looked fearfully fragile, almost brittle, alone and defenseless.

Before Daisy reached Olivia, Eric Cochran was there. 'Darling!'

Olivia held him off. 'Don't be a fool, Eric she said in low, tremulous voice. 'You'll ruin yourself.'

'I don't care. My poor sweet!'

She collapsed into his arms, sobbing help-lessly.

'Piper, is it cyanide? Alec arrived, having chivvied everyone else out of the music room and closed the double doors.

'Smells like it, sir. I got quite a bit sopped up here.'

'Good man. Get it into something with a lid from the kitchen, take the Austin and rush it to the lab, top priority, then the glass to Fingerprints. Miss Dalrymple, keep an eye on the French windows for me, please. Cochran, are there any other exits? Good. Where's your telephone?'

'Front hall, under the stairs.' Eric Cochran spoke without turning his head, his cheek resting on Olivia's sleek, dark hair. 'Miss Dalrymple, may I prevail on you to pour a brandy for Olivia? In fact, we'd better have brandy all round. We've all had a shock.'

At that, Olivia looked up. 'Is Roger all right?'

'Not too bad,' Muriel assured her.

Before fetching brandy, Daisy intercepted Alec on his way to the hall door. 'Mrs.

259

Cochran?' she whispered.

'Could be,' he said grimly. 'She's being a good hostess in very difficult circumstances at present.' He nodded towards the double doors. 'That may be enough to account for the desperation in her eyes, but I doubt it. I'll be right back.'

The brandy had just time enough to bring a little colour back to Roger's and Olivia's cheeks before Alec returned.

'My sergeant's on his way with several men,' he announced. 'I had him in reserve at the local station, though I need hardly say I didn't expect anything like this. Until he arrives, the best I can do is ask those of you in here a few questions. Miss Blaise, it wasn't arranged beforehand that you should sing, was it? Whose idea was it?'

'Mr. Westlea. The Reverend Westlea.'

'Yes, it was Father,' Muriel confirmed.

'He didn't happen to say, "So-and-so suggested I should ask you"?'

'No.' Olivia thought. 'He said, if I remember rightly, "I understand you are a singer, a mezzo-soprano like Bettina" – no, – "like Elizabeth".'

Daisy and Muriel nodded.

'You had the impression someone had mentioned your profession to the vicar?'

260

'Yes, I suppose so.'

Eric Cochran, looking rather sick, said quickly, 'I'd pointed Olivia out to a number of people as the mezzo soloist for the repeat performance of the Verdi.'

Alec nodded. 'Mr. Westlea will be able to tell me who told him ... and whether that person also suggested Miss Blaise should be asked to sing.'

Now Olivia was comforting Cochran as he clung to her hand. By this time they had all caught the drift of Alec's questions.

'Wait a minute,' said Olivia suddenly. 'I met Mr. Westlea at Roger's house. I don't specifically remember, but I may well have been introduced to him as a singer then.' She looked round at Roger, Muriel, Daisy. None of them remembered.

'It's likely she was introduced as one of your pupils, Abernathy, isn't it?' Cochran pleaded.

'More than likely,' Roger agreed kindly.

'Miss Blaise, did you request a glass of water?' Alec changed tack.

'No.'

'Did any of you see who put the glass on the piano?'

Murmurs of 'No,' shakings of heads.

'Did anyone notice it earlier, before the

question of Miss Blaise's performance came up?'

No, but no one could swear it wasn't there.

'Miss Blaise, Mr. Abernathy, would you mind coming over by the piano, just as you were when she finished singing? One of you bring your brandy glass. Is that doily in the same position as it was with the tumbler on it?'

'I think so,' Olivia said. 'I didn't move it.'

'Put your glass on it, please. Then stand as you were, pick it up, and raise it to your mouth.'

Olivia obeyed, reaching back between herself and Roger. Her hand bearing the empty glass passed close to Roger at chest level, perhaps nine inches below his nose.

'So that's why Mr. Abernathy smelt it,' Alec said with satisfaction. 'I presume you are unable to detect the odour of cyanide, Miss Blaise?'

'I suppose so. I've never before had any occasion to wonder. But surely, Mr. Fletcher, this may all be a horrible mistake? Perhaps Roger was mistaken, having the beastly stuff on his mind?'

'Detective Constable Piper smelt it too, I'm afraid. It's just conceivable the smell came from something other than cyanide.

We shall soon find out, I hope. It's not a difficult test, when there's enough of the stuff there. Mr. Cochran, is there somewhere we can go for a private word? I'd like the rest of you to stay here, together, for the moment.'

Cochran stared at him, aghast. 'You don't think she'll ... the person will try again, do you? Try to kill Olivia?'

'I doubt it, sir, but I'd rather she wasn't alone.'

'She'll come with us,' the conductor said firmly. 'Anything we have to say to each other, she can hear.'

Alec conceded, and the three of them went out, leaving Daisy, Muriel, and Roger.

'Mr. Fletcher thinks it was Mrs. Cochran, doesn't he?' Muriel said to Daisy as Roger sat down at the piano and began to play softly, aimlessly.

'So does Cochran. At least, he's afraid it might be.'

'I'm so sorry for him ... for her ... for all three of them, though I can't quite bring myself to like him. Daisy, does this mean Mrs. Cochran killed Betsy?'

'Possibly,' Daisy said with caution, 'but not necessarily.'

Muriel shuddered. 'How frightful to think

263

there may be two murderers about!'

'It is rather, isn't it?' Involuntarily, Daisy gave a quick glance around. They were alone, of course, except for Roger. No sinister figure crept towards the French windows – and just what did Alec expect her to do about it if the murderer tried to escape that way? she thought indignantly. Hit him or her over the head with a music stand? Call on Roger to help her tackle him?

Roger was playing something quiet and sad, deep lines of sadness carved in his face. He had aged immeasurably over the past few days, not troubled more than usual by angina but sinking into apathy. The news-papers' nasty hints about Yakov Levich had roused him, as had Olivia's singing and the attempt on her life. Now he was slipping back, the notes coming softer and slower until he sat with his hands resting on the keyboard, head bowed.

'Muriel, I'd like to go home,' he said sud-denly in a low voice, raising his head with an obvious effort. 'Do you think the chief inspector would let us go, Daisy?'

'I expect so, but I don't like to interrupt to ask. I'm sure Sergeant Tring will be here any moment, if you can hold on.'

'Come and sit in one of these comfortable

chairs, Roger,' Muriel said anxiously. 'You're not feeling ill, are you?'

'No, just tired. So very, very tired.' He moved to one of the leather armchairs and at her coaxing drank a little more of the brandy left in his glass.

A few minutes later, Alec returned with Cochran, Olivia, and a uniformed constable whom he posted at the French windows.

'Yes, you can go,' he told Muriel, 'though I'll need to talk to you both again. Miss Dalrymple, I want you to go home with Miss Blaise if you would. Otherwise I'll send for a woman police officer.'

'No, I'll go.' She was more pleased to have the opportunity of talking to Olivia than annoyed at his high-handedness.

'Thank you. Lock the door and don't open it until you hear from me...'

'I'll take Miss Blaise home,' interrupted Eric Cochran, who looked utterly wretched.

'Sorry, sir, I need you here. Is there a telephone in your house, Miss Blaise?'

Olivia shook her head. She was still pale, but calm and self-possessed. Though she stood a little apart from Cochran, not touching him, the link between them was almost tangible.

'I'll send an officer to let you know what's

going on,' Alec decided. 'I phoned for a taxi. Here's for the fare, on the Yard.' He handed Daisy a ten bob note.

'We'll drop Muriel and Roger on the way, shall we? They'll want to leave the hired motor for the Westleas.'

Alec gave Muriel and Roger one of his searching looks, then nodded. 'Yes, that'll do. I must talk to the vicar and Mrs. Westlea before they leave here.' He held Daisy back as another policeman came in to announce the arrival of the taxicab and usher them out. 'Daisy, may I take you out to dinner tomorrow?' he said softly.

'Yes, spiffing!'

'Don't get too excited.' He grimaced. 'Unless this is all cleared up by then, it'll be a mixture of business and pleasure, I'm afraid, but on Saturday, if you're free, Belinda and my mother hope you'll come to tea. I promise to be there, if I have to disconnect the phone!'

'Tea on Saturday?' Don't be ridiculous, she admonished the butterflies which suddenly took flight in her middle. 'Please tell them I'll be delighted and I look forward to meeting them.'

'Good. Belinda will be thrilled. Off you go, now. Don't worry, I don't really think Miss

Blaise is in any further danger, but she ought to have someone with her.'

As she hurried after the others, Daisy wasn't worrying about Olivia. She was thinking that he hadn't said Mrs. Fletcher would be pleased – let alone thrilled – by her coming to tea.

The policeman showed them out by the back door, through the kitchen where Tom Tring was already ensconced at the table with a cup of tea and several excited servants. He lumbered to his feet as the ladies passed, giving Daisy a wink as infinitesimal as Ernie Piper's. Clad in funereal black instead of his usual wild checks, he looked slightly less bulky and much less vulgar, more like an undertaker than a second-hand car sales-man.

In the taxi, Olivia insisted on Roger settling on the forward-facing seat while she perched on a pull-down seat. Daisy told the driver to take them to Mulberry Place, and they set off.

'My dear,' Roger said to Olivia, 'I'm so very sorry.'

'I don't mind sitting here in the least, honestly. I was going to walk or take the bus.'

'No, no, about the dreadful fright you've had. I feel responsible.'

'Good heavens, Roger, why? I owe you my life.'

He looked a bit nonplussed. 'Well, I... Suppose it was a false alarm, as you suggested?'

'I only said that for Eric's sake.' Olivia continued seriously, 'I simply can't think of anyone other than his wife who might want me dead, you know. It's too frightful for the poor darling.'

'Yes, but ... if it was indeed Mrs. Cochran, the idea must have been put into her head by ... what happened to Bettina.'

The three women exchanged glances. It would be too cruel to remind him that Mrs. Cochran had probably imagined she had the same motive for murdering Bettina as she had for Olivia.

'If so,' said Daisy, 'you can hardly be blamed for that, Roger. Olivia's right, she owes you her life, and if by some outside chance you were mistaken, I'm sure she's jolly glad you didn't wait until she dropped dead to cry wolf.'

'That goes without saying,' Olivia agreed dryly.

Roger seemed not entirely reassured, but the taxicab pulled up outside the house so it was left to Muriel to set his mind at rest.

They got out and Olivia gave the driver her address.

She moved across to sit beside Daisy. 'Thank you for coming. I couldn't have borne some grim police matron. I must say, your pet policeman's a pretty decent chap.'

'Isn't he? He said he doubts you're actually still in danger, by the way.'

'Better safe than sorry. We'll have a cup of tea. I could do with one!'

'To tell the truth, I'm starving. You started singing before I had time to start eating.'

'Sausages and toast?'

'Spiffing. I don't want you to think I'm a complete Philistine, though. Your singing was absolutely heavenly, and everyone around me was frightfully impressed. I'm looking forward no end to the repeat Verdi concert.'

'It's a great chance for me.' Olivia sighed. 'I just wish it had come to me some other way. Poor Roger! Poor Eric!'

'What did Alec want to ask Mr. Cochran, if you don't mind telling me?'

'He wanted to know if there was any cyanide in the house. Eric's a bit vague about domestic matters, but he remembered talk of poisoning a wasps' nest in the attic last summer.'

'Oh gosh!'

269

'Then Mr. Fletcher asked again whether Ursula knew about Eric and me before last Sunday, whether she could have suspected Bettina, all that stuff. And Eric tried to persuade him she'd never have wrecked his concert like that, whatever she suspected. Neither of us could think of anyone else who might have it in for me, though.'

'No, it does look awfully as if it must be Mrs. Cochran.'

'Eric blames himself terribly, and though Mr. Fletcher was perfectly polite, I could tell he holds Eric to blame for the whole mess. You don't like him either, do you?'

'Oh dear, does it show?' Daisy demanded, dismayed.

'Not to anyone who doesn't care as much as I do,' Olivia assured her. 'I know he's weak, and he's let me down before, and all the rest of it. I know he's not perfect, but nor am I, and I can't help it, I love him desperately.'

Despite the dim light in the taxicab, Daisy could see Olivia's lips firmly compressed in an effort to stop the tears overflowing her swimming eyes. She took the unhappy girl's hand and pressed it.

'Like Roger,' she said, commiserating. 'However badly Bettina behaved, he went on loving her to the end.'

Olivia drew a long, shuddering breath as the taxi pulled up outside her digs. Daisy paid the driver, giving him a very decent tip 'on the Yard.' They went upstairs and Olivia locked the door of her room behind them before she spoke again.

'Perhaps it would have been better for Eric,' she said then, 'if Roger hadn't stopped me drinking from that glass.'

'Bosh! Alec would have caught Mrs. Cochran anyway, and she'd have been hanged, and Eric wouldn't have had you there to comfort and console him. Though I must say it does complicate matters, your having survived.'

'Doesn't it?' Olivia picked up the kettle from the gas ring by the fire and went behind a curtain in the corner to fill it. Daisy stuck one of Scotland Yard's shillings in the meter. As it dropped with a satisfying clunk, Olivia turned back with a smile. 'Sergeant Tring fed the meter when they all came here. He didn't think I saw but I heard, of course. Thanks.'

'It's on the Yard,' said Daisy grandly. 'But I expect the sergeant's was his own – he'd have a hard time claiming it as expenses. He's a nice chap, Tom Tring, a friend of mine.'

Lighting the gas ring, Olivia looked at her curiously. 'You're rather democratic for an Honourable, aren't you? I've met one or two before, and Lady Thises and Thats, and they were all fearfully stuck-up.'

'I can't help it. I'm interested in people, and lots seem to want to talk to me, and once one talks to someone and likes them one can't just discard them because they're not out of the top drawer. At least I can't. My friend Lucy – oh, she took your portrait, didn't she? – she's always ragging me about it. Not that she's even an Honourable, but her grandfather is an earl. As if it made the slightest difference to what people are like!'

'Speaking of which,' said Olivia, continuing the preparations for lunch, 'what do you think Eric will do if Ursula's convicted of attempted murder? If he stands by her, everyone will say he doesn't want to lose her money. If he applies for a divorce, everyone will say he's deserting her.'

'It's a bit late to worry about what everyone says,' Daisy pointed out. 'Don't forget to prick those sausages or they'll explode. Shall I slice the bread?'

'Yes, will you? I'll light the fire. It takes a while to heat up enough to make toast. I suppose you mean I should have thought about what people would say before succumbing to Eric's charms.' Her sardonic tone showed she had recovered her poise in spite of returning to the difficult subject. 'You're quite right, and it's no use crying over spilt milk. I should have considered Ursula's point of view, too. I was so sure she didn't love him, only cared for the chance of a title he represented.'

'One can be possessive, and jealous, without love, don't you think? I can't imagine Bettina being complaisant if Roger had strayed, though she doesn't seem to have cared a hoot for him.'

'She didn't care a hoot for anyone but herself. All the same, it will be too beastly if it turns out Ursula killed her by mistake because of Eric and me.'

Daisy could only soberly agree, while privately feeling that for everyone but Olivia and Cochran it would be even worse to have two murderers on the loose. She wished she knew what Alec was discovering back at the Cochrans' house.

'It was cyanide they used on that wasps' nest all right, Chief,' Tom Tring reported, padding across the music room to the desk where Alec sat. 'They stored what was left in a tin in the potting shed, up on a high shelf out of the way, clearly marked 'POISON" with a skull and crossbones. I oughter've caught that last time, when I came about the chauffeur.'

'We weren't seriously considering either of the Cochrans as Mrs. Abernathy's murderer then.' Alec frowned. 'I'm not at all sure I am now. Does Mrs. Cochran garden?'

'She potters, picking flowers, pruning roses, and such. No one wouldn't think twice to see her pottering into the potting shed, as you might say.' He paused to allow Alec to appreciate this *bon mot*. 'But what's more to the point, Chief, there's a loverly set of dabs on the tin, on the sides *and* on the lid. It's a bit dusty, a bit rusty, easy to see the prints are recent. I sent one of the local laddies to take it over to Fingerprints.'

'Good.'

'Only thing is, the gardener doesn't come Wednesdays. Could be he used it for rats or summat.'

'You can track him down later. Anything else that can't wait?'

'Just that both the maids swears neether of 'em put that glass on the pianner.'

Alec nodded. 'About all I've learned is that it was Mrs. Cochran who suggested to the vicar that he ask Miss Blaise to sing.'

'Ah,' said Tom, 'was it now.'

'All right, I want you to help me with these interviews or we'll be here till midnight and the natives are already restless. This room's big enough, you can take them at the other end. I want to know were they previously acquainted with Miss Blaise, when the glass appeared on the piano, who put it there, did anyone go near it, all the obvious things.' He could count on Tom to follow up anything significant and draw it to his attention.

'Right, Chief.'

'Warn them we might be in touch again, and let 'em go. It's a good job I had you wear black. You look quite respectable for once.'

'Want me to talk la-di-da?'

'Just don't drop your haitches.'

'As if I ever did,' said Tom, his tone injured, but a grin lifted his luxuriant moustache.

Alec told the uniformed constable at the dining-room doors to send in two guests, and the Gowers came in together. The officer directed Gilbert Gower to Tring, his wife to Alec.

Plump, untidy, sallow in black, Mrs. Gower was agitated, but remembering their previous interview he couldn't hold that against her.

This was no time to ask her about nitro-glycerin, either, whatever his hunch about the attempt on Miss Blaise being an imitation, not a second effort by the same murderer. Besides, he hadn't yet heard from either Sir Bernard or the lab on that question.

He opened his mouth to ask about the glass, but she forestalled him. 'Gilbert had never even met Miss Blaise, Chief Inspector,' she said with nervous determination.

The tenor's voice, penetrating though slurred, came from the other end of the room assuring the sergeant of the same thing.

'We have no reason to suppose your husband was in any way involved with Miss Blaise,' Alec assured Mrs. Gower.

She was quicker-witted than she looked. 'Oh dear, then it *was* she and... I told Ursula you believed Eric Cochran wasn't Mrs. Abernathy's lover, but I swear I never said it was someone else, let alone mentioning Miss Blaise. I didn't know! Did she...?'

'We don't know yet just what happened,' Alec said firmly, and moved on to his questions about the glass. Nothing useful emerged.

Gilbert Gower came over, a trifle unsteady. 'All done, Chief 'Spector? C'mon, darling, le's go home.' He took her arm and they left.

'Sozzled,' said Tom succinctly. 'He swears he's broken off with Miss de la Costa and he'll never touch another bit on the side.'

The next two came and went, and the next. It began to look as if they'd get to Mrs. Cochran, deliberately left till last, before Alec heard from Piper. Then the constable on duty in the hall stuck his head round the door. 'Telephone call for you, Chief Inspector, sir.'

He made his excuses to a stout gentleman in gold pince-nez, the umpteenth to swear no glass stood on the piano when he first arrived in the house – unless he simply hadn't noticed it. And he wouldn't have noticed anyone putting it there, either, Alec reflected as he went out to the hall. Practically everyone in the three reception rooms had been holding a glass.

Ernie Piper was on the line. 'They done the test, Chief. They was that glad to get plenty to work with this time.'

'Thanks to your quick action, Ernie. It was cyanide?'

'Enough to kill an elephant, they reckon, if the glass was full.'

Alec averted his eyes from the elephant's-foot umbrella-stand, met the fox's glazed gaze, and turned his back. 'And the glass?'

'Miss Blaise's prints, Chief, plain as the nose on your face 'cos it'd been wiped before she touched it. But... Hold on a jiffy, Chief.' Down the wire came a distant murmur, then Ernie's excited voice returned. 'That tin of poison Sergeant Tring sent in, Chief? With the dabs on it? And what I was just going to say: When the glass was wiped there was one print missed, at the bottom.' He paused dramatically. 'It's the same as on the tin, and they're Mrs. Cochran's.'

CHAPTER 16

'It is my duty, ma'am, to warn you that anything you say will be taken down and may be introduced in evidence in a court of law.' From the corner of his eye, Alec saw Tom's pencil dash across the paper as he recorded the utterance of the required caution. 'Do you wish to send for your solicitor?'

'That won't be necessary, I'm sure. None of my guests has complained of being given the third degree.' Mrs. Cochran gave a brittle, artificial laugh. 'As the Americans put it, I believe.'

Alec glanced at the constable by the hall door, who shook his head slightly. No departing witnesses had been permitted to take their leave of their hostess, let alone to tell her anything about their interviews with the police.

'I'm sorry people were kept waiting so long,' Alec apologized in a conversational tone.

She relaxed visibly. 'No harm done, Chief Inspector, except to Eric's cellar. Gilbert Gower – well, the less said the better! I quite understand, you had to be certain no one else had a hand in that foolish young woman's attempt to dramatize herself.'

'Dramatize herself?'

'By pretending she meant to commit suicide. I must say it was a disgraceful trick to play on poor Roger Abernathy.'

'Why should Miss Blaise pretend to commit suicide?'

'To catch Eric's attention.' Mrs. Cochran leant forward. 'I must explain,' she confided, 'that Miss Blaise is rather taken with Eric. Or perhaps she simply hopes to further her career, I can't claim to be sure which. In any case, recently she has been positively throwing herself at him, and the poor dear can't bring himself to be so cruel as to reject her outright. He isn't always able to avoid her – you saw for yourself how blatantly she threw herself into his arms when his duty as host forced him to approach her after that silly show.'

Was she trying to convince herself, or him? 'I'm afraid that was not a silly show, ma'am. Not pretence. The glass contained a large dose of cyanide.'

No sign of surprise, of shock, behind the mask of make-up. Mrs. Cochran's story was as slipshod as her crime, the fingerprints missed, the reactions unplanned.

'No doubt Miss Blaise would have found some excuse not to drink, had Mr. Abernathy not prevented her. Unless she really meant to kill herself? In my house!' The indignation at least had been practised, but was belied by Lady Macbethian hands, writhing in her black silk lap. 'Thank heaven she failed.'

'Why should she kill herself?'

'Eric must at last have told her plainly to leave him alone.'

'On the contrary, he offered her the mezzo-soprano part in the Verdi *Requiem*.'

'I imagine that was by way of a parting gesture.'

'A parting gesture? A farewell gift? Implying the end of a relationship. What was the relationship between your husband and Miss Blaise?'

'I didn't mean a parting gift!' She was beginning to get flustered.

Alec gave her a hard look. 'I think you did, Mrs. Cochran.'

'Oh, very well, I did,' she said sulkily. 'Eric is too kind for his own good; he found it impossible to repulse her. He treated her as a friend and she tried to take advantage of him.'

'And you were angry about their "friendship"?'

'Eric is a brilliant conductor. Any scandal could put paid to his future. Of course I was angry. But it was over, so even if I had wanted to kill her, why should I try now?'

'Because it isn't over. Because the Verdi part signalled reconciliation, not goodbye. Because Eric Cochran is deeply infatuated with Olivia Blaise and on the verge of abandoning his career and his wife for her sake.'

'Rubbish! His career is the most important thing in the world to him, and he needs my support. He knows I'd do anything to help him rise to the top of his profession.'

'Anything?' Alec spoke softly, yet she blenched. 'Your fingerprint is on the glass.'

'It can't be!' She stared at him aghast, then

made a quick recovery. 'I mean, of course it can. This is my house, after all, and my party.'

'Your maids handed around the glasses.'

'The sherry glasses, yes. But when I heard Miss Blaise was to sing, I told one of the girls to bring a glass of water specially, in case she needed it. Then I made a point of taking it from her tray myself and placing it on a doily, to make sure the surface of the piano was not marred. Maids are so careless these days. One simply cannot get decent servants since the War.' Mrs. Cochran looked pleased with her clever improvisation.

For the moment Alec let lie the question of how she had managed to leave only a single print when she picked up the tumbler, not to mention the lack of the maid's prints. 'You gave the maid the order to fetch a glass of water when you heard Miss Blaise was to sing? That was quick work. I understand she went straight to the piano when she was asked.'

'Oh. Well, perhaps it was when Mr. Westlea expressed his intent to invite her to sing. Yes, that's it. I wanted to be prepared in case she accepted.'

'I believe you were prepared before that. Even before you proposed the notion to the reverend gentleman.'

'I? It was entirely his own idea.'

'Mr. Westlea says you pointed out Miss Blaise to him and suggested that a song from her would be a suitable memorial for his daughter.'

'What if I did? That's no crime!'

'Odd, though, you must admit, since you disliked and despised Miss Blaise. However, that is only a part of the preparations I referred to. A full set of your fingerprints has been found on the tin of cyanide in the potting shed.'

'Oh Lord, I forgot,' she groaned, her shoulders sagging. But she wasn't done yet. She straightened again, stiff as a backboard. 'That is, I forgot I had moved the tin up to a high shelf. I noticed the gardener had carelessly left it within easy reach. As I said, good servants are impossible to find nowadays.'

She was a game fighter. Alec admitted to himself a sneaking admiration. He glanced at Tom.

'Prints on the lid, sir,' the Sergeant murmured.

Mrs. Cochran heard. 'Naturally I checked the lid to make sure it was on tightly.'

'Well, we shall of course check with your

gardener as to where he left the tin.' He noted her alarm with satisfaction. Still, the gardener might well not remember. The evidence all pointed towards her, yet he'd prefer some sort of admission before he charged her. 'Both maids have already denied bringing the water glass to the piano.'

'They would, wouldn't they,' she said contemptuously. 'Really, Chief Inspector, what's all the to-do about? Miss Blaise didn't die. She came to no harm whatsoever.'

'Bettina Abernathy died.'

'That has nothing to do with me. I had no reason to kill *her*.'

'No, but you thought you did. You didn't know about Miss Blaise. Mr. Cochran met her at the Abernathys' house, and you had every reason to believe his affair was with Mrs. Abernathy.'

'What if I did? However much I wished to be rid of her, I'd never have poisoned her in the middle of Eric's concert, and such an important concert!'

Much against his will, Alec believed her. How neat it would have been to wrap up both cases at once with a single arrest, he thought regretfully, though he'd never counted on it. Bettina's murderer was still unidentified.

His tone deliberately casual, he said, 'So Mrs. Abernathy's murder just gave you the idea of poisoning Miss Blaise.'

'Yes, it... No! I want my solicitor!' Mrs. Cochran demanded belatedly.

'By all means, ma'am. He can join us at the police station, where you will be charged with attempted murder. I suggest you ask your maid or your husband to pack up a small suitcase for you.'

'Not Eric.' The heavy cosmetics no longer disguised her years. 'I don't want to see him. This is his fault, all his fault!'

Pitying her, Alec could not altogether disagree.

When Eric Cochran arrived at Olivia's digs, the sausages were long gone, a second pot of tea brewed and consumed. To stop Olivia's nervous pacing, Daisy had persuaded her to practise for the *Requiem* and she was singing the *Agnus Dei* when her lover rang the bell.

Daisy had a sudden qualm about letting him in. 'Alec said he'd send an officer,' she remembered. 'What if it's a ruse to get at you?'

'If Eric wants to kill me, I'd just as soon be dead.' Olivia unlocked the door.

Cochran looked almost shell-shocked.

285

'They've arrested Ursula,' he said dully. 'I can't believe it. I simply can't believe it.'

Though Daisy was dying to ask whether Mrs. Cochran had been arrested for Bettina's murder as well, she opted for discretion. The moment his face was buried in Olivia's lap, she hopped it, waving good-bye as Olivia raised her head to mouth a silent, 'Thanks!'

She went home first, to tell Lucy the latest news.

'Darling, you do get mixed up with the most peculiar people,' Lucy drawled. 'I trust your tame copper doesn't think the woman pinched the cyanide from my darkroom?'

'I shouldn't think so,' said Daisy, a bit disgruntled because Lucy wasn't all agog. 'After all, the Cochrans patronized a posh West End photographer.'

'Some people imagine they must get something better if they pay more. Phillip dropped by this morning. The poor prune rang up next door and panicked when he didn't get answer.'

'The maids were told not to answer the phone because of reporters. What did Phil want?'

Lucy waved a languid hand. 'Just to know whether you were still in the land of the living. If they've arrested this Cochran person, you'll be coming home, won't you?'

'I expect so. Not because of the arrest; because the ghastly vicar's supposed to flee the wicked city today so Muriel won't need protection from him. I'd better go and see what's going on. Toodle-oo, darling.'

Daisy found Muriel alone with her afternoon tea. Roger was lying down in his room and the Reverend and Mrs. Westlea had already departed.

'Father was furious that I wouldn't go with them,' Muriel said. 'Have a biscuit while I ring for another cup.'

'I couldn't touch another drop. Olivia and I drank tea till my insides started sloshing about.' She took a chocolate biscuit though. 'Why on earth did your father expect you to go back to the wilds of Norfolk?'

'He couldn't decide whether I was more likely to be compromised by Yasha or by Roger. I suppose it will look a bit odd, my going on living in Roger's house now Betsy's gone.'

'Bosh! You're practically brother and sister, and he'd never survive without you. Today was a bit much for him, was it?'

'He's just so tired. And he still seems to feel the attempt on Olivia's life was somehow his fault. Do you know what's happening?'

'Golly, I nearly forgot to tell you. Alec's arrested Mrs. Cochran.'

'Oh dear, that's what Roger's afraid of. He doesn't believe she killed Betsy, so she must have copied whoever did.'

'Which doesn't make it his fault.'

'No, but you know how one imagines all sorts of frightful things when one's ill and overwrought. He must wish he'd been able to stop Betsy behaving in such a way that someone decided to poison her. Anyway, whatever is bothering him, he's in a dreadfully morbid state. He even... Daisy, promise you won't tell Yasha?'

'Tell him what? All right, I promise.'

'Roger's made an appointment with his solicitor for tomorrow morning. He's going to change his will and leave the house to me, which would be wonderful if it didn't mean he's feeling absolutely rotten.'

'He told me he didn't expect to survive losing Bettina,' Daisy said slowly. Muriel looked so appalled, she quickly added, 'But I dare say he'll live for years yet. Why don't you want Mr. Levich to know about the house?'

'It's this impossible business about not wanting him to marry me because I have a bit of money, and not wanting him *not* to

288

marry me for fear I'll believe ... you know.'
Muriel sighed. 'Not that I really expect him
to propose, but he's so... He has a rehearsal
this afternoon, but he came straight here
from the Cochrans', as soon as Mr. Fletcher
had finished with him, to make sure Roger
and I were all right. Oh Daisy, he was so
sweet, so pleased that Mr. Fletcher had
trusted him to guard the back door.'

Daisy refrained from pointing out that Alec
had no earthly reason to suspect Levich of
wanting to bump off Olivia. 'I hope it means
Alec's cleared him altogether,' she said, 'but
don't count on it. Once you're on his list of
suspects, it's frightfully difficult to get off. I
wish I knew whether he's charged Mrs.
Cochran with Bettina's death too!'

'So you don't think she did in Mrs.
Abernathy, Chief?' Ernie Piper asked from
the back seat of the Austin, which he had
driven over to pick up Alec and Tom at the
Divisional Police Station. The formalities
over, they were at last on their way back to
New Scotland Yard.

'No, and even if she did we've not a
shadow of proof to justify a charge against
anyone. Great Scott, we don't even know for
sure whether Mrs. Abernathy died of cyan-

ide or nitroglycerin poisoning! I hope Sir Bernard's report is waiting for me.'

'It is, Chief, and the lab's, and the jeweller's. I knew you'd want to know, so I went and had a quick glance at your desk.'

'No dinner, and supper in the canteen again,' said Tom with a lugubrious sigh. 'A man could starve to death.'

'Not on what you pack away, Sarge,' said Ernie cheekily. 'I'd like to see what you eat at home, I would.'

'Then you'd better come round to tea one of these days, young'un. See what a good home-cooked meal is like and put a bit of meat on them bones of yours. The missus likes to have summun extra to cook for.'

'Really?'

'After a meal prepared by Mrs. Tring you won't need to eat for a week,' Alec assured him, 'and that's if you turn up without notice. Her steak-and-kidney pud has to be tasted to be believed. You can both count on tomorrow evening free, barring emergencies.' Because tomorrow, come hell or high water, he was taking Daisy out to dinner.

He turned towards the river and New Scotland Yard rose before them, its red and white stripes glowing in the sunset. Since he was a small boy Alec had been determined to belong there, ever since his father had pointed from the river steamer and told him that was where the best detectives in the world worked. Now he belonged, and despite the inconveniences of his job he wouldn't give it up for anything.

Joan had accepted the inconveniences, the uncertainty as to whether he'd be home for dinner or dashing off to some out of the way corner of the country. His mother put up with it stoically – but she was of a generation of women raised to put up with the vagaries of their men. Daisy appeared to understand and forgive, but as yet she was only a friend, minimally affected. She couldn't fully grasp the demands on a copper's wife.

Not that she was going to have to find out unless he plucked up his courage to propose. He wasn't ready for that yet.

Taking her home for tea with his mother and daughter was a step in that direction. Was he mad to have agreed to invite her? Could she possibly be as pleased as she had seemed when she accepted?

His wandering mind returned to the case as they reached his office. He and Tom sat down at their desks and Piper pulled up a chair. Alec tossed the lab report to Tom, the jeweller's to Ernie. Turning to the last page of Sir Bernard Spilsbury's, he was relieved to find a summary in comparatively plain English.

'Crikey!' said Ernie, who had also turned straight to the last page. 'Twelve thousand nicker! The Russian bloke had a motive, all right.'

'Twelve thousand pounds?' Alec said, dismayed. He had hoped the jewellery would turn out to be paste. As if it wasn't bad enough not to be able to investigate Marchenko further, how was he to explain his neglect to his men?

At least they didn't know about the nitroglycerin in the cellar – assuming Spilsbury and the lab agreed on nitroglycerin as the cause of Bettina Abernathy's death. What was more, the way Lord Curzon was carrying on in Lausanne, the Soviet trade mission might not be around much longer to be blown up.

'Twelve thou, give or take,' Ernie confirmed. 'Mr. Feinstein says he's kept the stuff in his safe as you asked, Chief.'

'See if you can get Miss Westlea on the telephone, Ernie.' Alec and Tom returned to their more complicated reading.

The chief pathologist's conclusion was that the signs found at the second autopsy were slightly more in favour of nitroglycerin than cyanide. Very slightly, he emphasized. He wouldn't swear to either in court. The most positive indication was the word of Dr. Renfrew's assistant, who thought he remembered the victim's blood being brownish at the first autopsy. Since he hadn't noted it in writing, let alone investigated whether the cause was the presence of methemoglobin, his word was hardly useful as evidence. However, Sir Bernard trusted it would help the chief inspector in his investigation.

'Miss Westlea, Chief.'

Alec took the phone. 'Miss Westlea, this is Alec Fletcher.' Damn, now he was thinking of her as a friend of Daisy's, not a suspect. 'Chief Inspector Fletcher,' he amended. 'The jewellery you let me take for appraisal is worth approximately twelve thousand pounds.'

'Oh no! Are you quite sure?'

'Isaac Feinstein, the jeweller who valued it, is both reliable and discreet. In fact, I've left the stuff in his care and I'd appreciate it if you'd let him look after it for the present, just in case it should be needed as evidence. However, you have every right to insist on its return.'

'Oh no. I'd absolutely hate to have it in the house. As I can't give it back to Mr. Mar-

chenko yet, I'll be glad it's somewhere safe
She hesitated. 'Mr. Fletcher, this may sound
funny, but would you mind not telling Mr.
Levich it's so valuable?'

'Of course not.' He could think of no conceivable circumstances which might require
telling Yakov Levich. Poor woman! Whether
she returned the goods to Marchenko or
not, they were liable to cause complications
in her life.

But she was still a suspect. Means, motive,
opportunity, she had them all in abundance.

'Do you want a word with Daisy?' she
asked.

'She's with you?'

'No, she's moved back next door, but I
could fetch her.'

'That's all right, thanks. If you happen to
speak to her, please tell her I'll see her tomorrow evening. Good-bye.'

Hanging up, he glared at the grins on Tom
and Ernie's faces.

'Miss Dalrymple safe home, Chief?' Tom
asked innocently.

'Yes. What does the lab say?'

'Too little for proper testing, but some indication of a substance which could be nitroglycerin. Reading between the lines, they're
convinced but won't swear to it on oath.'

'Sir Bernard says much the same. For the present, we'll work on that basis. Let's get something to eat while we go over the list.'

Over steak-and-kidney pie – more kidney than steak, as Tom remarked – with chips and greyish tinned peas, they discussed the suspects. Gower, Finch, and Miss de la Costa were out of it. No sign of a motive for Browne had emerged.

'Of the rest,' Alec said, 'Abernathy has trinitrin pills and Miss Westlea has easy access to them. Miss Blaise and Cochran knew a spare bottle was kept in the down-stairs cloakroom. Cochran's access to the house was limited after Mrs. Abernathy forced him to give her the part, but Miss Blaise continued to frequent it for her lessons. Levich never visited until after Mrs. Abernathy's death.' He interrupted himself to take a forkful of gravy-sogged pastry and rubbery kidney such as Mrs. Tring would never have allowed on her table.

'What about Mr. Abernathy, Chief?' Piper asked.

'I don't think there's any doubt that he loved her, which doesn't mean he didn't poison her. He's still top of the list, if only because statistics prove husbands are the most frequent killers of wives.'

'Don't say much for marriage, does it.'

'Ah,' said Tom, 'now if everyone's trouble and strife was like mine!'

Alec smiled at him. 'Some of us are luckier than others. Abernathy was not one of the lucky ones. He had means, motive, opportunity. The trouble is, like Miss Westlea he had all three in abundance for a long time. Why there and then? I've yet to hear anything which even hints at an explanation. Any ideas?'

The others shook their heads.

'Think about it. Unless we come up with something, I wouldn't put any money on him.'

'That leaves Mrs. Cochran, Mrs. Gower, and Marchenko,' Tom said. 'Didn't you say Miss Dalrymple told you Mrs. Gower could get at the pills?'

'Yes. She does volunteer work at an East End clinic and actually mentioned to Miss Dalrymple that trinitrin is one of the drugs dispensed there, though she herself works mostly with children. Ernie, I'll leave this one to you.'

'Really, Chief?'

'If Mrs. Gower is at the clinic, she's unlikely to recognize you and take fright – don't mention her name if you can help it.

We need to know whether they keep their drugs locked up and if so, who has keys.' He paused as Ernie whipped out his notebook. 'Also whether they keep proper records and, if so, has an unusual amount of trinitrin been used recently.'

'Trinitrin's the same as nitroglycerin, Chief?'

'Yes, and easier to spell. If the clinic's not open tomorrow morning, try to find out who's in charge and get them to show you around. Refer them to me if necessary. I want to know soon.'

'Right, Chief.'

'You really think she could be the one, Chief?' Tom enquired, pushing away a practically spotless plate and replacing it with a dish of spotted dog liberally doused with lumpy custard.

With a shudder, Alec gave up on his bullet-like peas and took out his pipe. 'You can have my pudding, Tom. Yes, Mrs. Gower's near the top. She was afraid Mrs. Abernathy was going to break up her family, harm her children, who are her whole life. She was alone in the soloists' room. Ernie, when you're done with the clinic, find the usher who was on the door and pin him down as to how long she was in there.'

'Right, Chief.'

'Not that it'll make much difference. A few seconds would suffice. I'll have to see her again, and I'll deal with Marchenko. Tom, I want you to trace the Cochrans' and Levich's doctors and find out if trinitrin was ever prescribed for any of them. I'm inclined to write off all three, but we need to know.'

'I doubt it was Miss Blaise eether, Chief. Like she said, bumping off Mrs. Abernathy during the performance was too late to do her much good.'

Alec's pipe caught at last and he puffed at it for a few moments before he said contemplatively, 'There's another reason, less tangible perhaps, why I'd be inclined to write off Miss Blaise, and Miss Westlea, too. Whether they're genuinely in love with Cochran and Levich respectively I don't pretend to guess, but I do believe their affection and concern for Abernathy is sincere. They're both very much aware that any severe shock could kill him. To my mind, that would be enough to stop either killing his wife.'

'D'you think so, Chief?' Tom said, his large face dubious.

'"I'd be inclined," I said,' Alec laughed. 'You know better, Tom, than to think anyone drops off my little list without more

298

reason than a hunch.' Or intervention by the Special Branch. 'There's something else in Miss Westlea's favour, though, those finger marks on the sides of the stopper. Why should she grasp it that way when her prints are all over the knob?'

'If she didn't, someone else did,' Piper observed profoundly.

'Exactly, and no one but the murderer had a reason. Ernie, you can go home now. Tom, you've today's notes to write up, and I have three or four other cases to catch up on. We'll all meet in my office tomorrow at five – no, try to make it half past four.'

Tom winked. 'Give you time to spruce up before you take Miss Dalrymple out, eh, Chief?'

CHAPTER 17

The yellow Austin Chummy pulled in to the kerb promptly at seven thirty. Daisy hurriedly dropped the curtain to close the tiny gap she'd been peering through.

'Lucy, do I look all right?' she asked hopefully, twitching the belt which clamped the rose charmeuse to her unfashionable, undeniable hips.

'Topping, darling,' Lucy drawled. 'Much too smart for the Strand Corner House.'

'He won't take me there, and if he does I don't mind. All sorts of people eat there.'

'Precisely.'

Daisy pulled a face at her maddening friend, then grabbed her handbag and powdered her nose as the doorbell rang. Dashing out into the hall, she opened the door. There was Alec, looking frightfully suave, in fact altogether scrumptious, in a perfectly decent dinner jacket. Hardly daring to acknowledge to herself that she'd been afraid he'd turn up in a suit – not that she cared, but what Lucy would say! – she took him into the front parlour.

'Good evening, Mr. Fletcher.' Lucy was coolly antagonistic. 'I hope you're prepared to spring for champagne. Daisy has some news to tell.'

'I was going to save it for later,' Daisy said crossly.

'You can't keep me in suspense now.' Alec smiled at her. 'I can do with some good news.'

'I took my museum article, the one about the Victoria and Albert, to the editor this morning.' Elation frothed up inside her again. 'There was a magazine editor from America in his office, visiting, and he looked at it and liked it and bought American rights on the spot.'

'Congratulations!'

'Wait, that's not all. He wants a whole series of articles on the museums of London, and he's paying simply pots of money!'

'Daisy, that's wonderful!' His pleasure set the seal on her accomplishment.

'So the champagne's on me,' she said grandly, picking up her coat from the back of a chair.

'Not on your life.' He held the coat for her. 'Tonight's my treat. My honour: Miss Daisy Dalrymple, the well-known international journalist, was seen dining with an un-known...'

Daisy laughed. 'With the celebrated Chief Inspector Fletcher of Scotland Yard, reports of whose feats of detection have often graced these pages. I'll see you later, Lucy.'

'Cheerio, darling, have fun.' Lucy's smile was genuine and included Alec.

Alec waited until the front door closed behind them to comment. 'Do I detect a slight thaw?'

'You're the detective. Yes, I think the liberated woman may yet overcome the blue blood. You were suitably impressed by my brilliant achievement, unlike Phillip.'

'Philip Petrie?' he said guardedly, opening the Austin's door for her.

'Yes.' Sitting down with a grace worthy – she hoped – of a Daimler, she looked up at him. 'You see, I met Phil for lunch afterwards and his response to my news was that it would only encourage me in this tommy-rot about earning my own living.'

'Silly juggins.'

By the light of the streetlamp on the corner, she saw his broad grin. Could he possibly be jealous of Philip?

'I was livid, and so was Lucy when I told her,' she said as he got in beside her. 'But it's pointless, really. The dear old duffer just doesn't understand. Enough of that, though. What's going on with the case? I gather from the papers that Mrs. Cochran hasn't been charged with Bettina's murder?'

'Let's leave that till later. Listen, I've booked a table at a rather different little place in Soho, but your news calls for the Ritz, if you'd prefer.'

'Oh no, let's go somewhere different and interesting. Maybe I could write a series on unusual places to eat in London, for the

American magazine. I bet Mr. Thorwald would swallow it. Where are we going?'

'Wait and see.'

He took her to the Cathay. Daisy had noticed it before, when dining at the popular Monico, next door, but none of her set had ventured to delve into its Oriental mysteries. In fact, she had never tried Chinese food. The proprietor himself welcomed Alec by name and showed them to one of the best tables. To Daisy's disappointment, the Chinaman was dressed in ordinary black tails, not an embroidered robe, and the only accent she detected was the merest hint of Cockney. At least he bowed in proper Oriental fashion.

The meal was exotic enough to satisfy her – dishes containing bamboo shoots and bean sprouts among commoner ingredients. With strange and delicious flavours tickling her palate and champagne bubbling her nose, it was hard to concentrate on all the questions she wanted to ask.

'It was really Mrs. Cochran who tried to kill Olivia?' she said at last, the immediate pangs of hunger assuaged.

'Indubitably. Faced with incriminating fingerprints, she confessed.'

'How on earth did she hope to get away

with it?'

'Like most criminals, she hadn't really thought it through. She says she expected whoever murdered Mrs. Abernathy to be blamed, and since she didn't do that...' He shrugged. 'She's quick-witted at times, but she's not a levelheaded woman or she wouldn't have married a man fifteen years younger and tried to mould him into a knight-able conductor.'

'It's most unfair.' Daisy went off at a tangent. 'It's perfectly acceptable for a man to marry a girl fifteen years his junior and try to make her an able singer, like Dame Nellie Melba.'

'If you mean Abernathy, I'd have said the ambition was hers, not his. He just wanted *her*, for what she was worth.'

'Yes, but the principle is the same. It's awful, Alec, he's absolutely pining away. He doesn't seem to want to live without her. It's hard to fathom, but he truly loved her.'

'Re-reading my notes, the word people most often used was "doted," with its suggestion of foolishness and blindness.'

'Foolish, yes; blind, no. She broke his heart – yet losing her has broken it all over again. It may sound fearfully soppy and old-fashioned, but it's true. On top of everything else, he has this weird idea it was his fault Olivia was nearly poisoned. The only thing keeping him going is preparing her and his chorus for the repeat performance on Monday. You will be able to go, won't you?'

'I expect so. No promises.'

'Well, at least you've kept your promise tonight not to desert me before dessert,' Daisy said with a smile as the waiter removed empty plates and offered the menu. 'What do you recommend?'

'Both the lychees and the ginger in syrup are good.'

'Hmm. I can't decide.'

'I'll order both and we'll swap halfway if you like.'

She nodded. With champagne singing in her head, the intimacy of sharing sounded simply heavenly.

'And coffee, sir?'

'Jasmine tea, please. If you don't care for it, Daisy, we can always ask for coffee.'

After a few mouthfuls of fiery ginger, she was glad of the cool succulence of the lychees. Sipping the fragrant tea, she returned to business.

'If it wasn't Mrs. Cochran who killed Bettina, do you know yet who it was?'

'There's a good chance it was Jennifer

Gower, I'm afraid.' Refilling her tiny, handleless cup, he failed to meet her eyes. Was he being evasive? 'The drug cupboard at her clinic is only locked at night and their records are in a hopeless mess. You know how Piper is with figures? He glanced over their books and came back with a list of discrepancies as long as my arm. Mrs. Gower could have walked out with anything from trinitrin to morphine without its being missed.'

'You don't have any proof she took anything though?'

'None. Frankly, at this stage I can't see how we'll ever find proof. The best I can hope for is a confession, and if it's her I've an idea how to wring one from her.'

'It sounds beastly.'

'Murder is beastly. Remember that, Daisy, because I want your help.'

Her qualms vanished. 'You do? Oh, spiffing! What do you want me to do?'

'Are you free tomorrow, late afternoon? There's to be a rehearsal of the Verdi *Requiem* at the Albert Hall, so most of the suspects will be there anyway.'

'Everyone *except* Mrs. Gower.'

'Yes, but I've told her I want to gather everyone together to give them news about the case. She'll come, and I don't imagine anyone will be surprised to see you there.'

'They'll all think you're going to tell them Mrs. Cochran did it, but I can't see how that would induce anyone to confess.'

'No, what I shall announce is that the only way Mrs. Abernathy could have been poisoned by cyanide...'

'But I thought you'd decided it was trini-trin!' Daisy interrupted.

'Hold on a minute. Let me finish. The only way she could have been poisoned *by cyanide is* if her doctor made a mistake in putting up a prescription for her, a prescription for cyanide in a very weak solution to soothe a cough.'

'Dr. Woodward?'

'Yes, though I shan't mention him by name.'

'I should hope not! He could be ruined.'

'Exactly. That's why I have to hedge, and why I'm hoping it will flush out a confession, and why you can help. And, incidentally, why I've already asked his permission to try this.'

'He's letting you do it? She was outraged. 'Doesn't he have a family? What about his wife and children being ruined too?'

'Perfect!'

Daisy glared at him. 'What do you mean, perfect?'

'If you'll just stop going off half-cocked and let me explain, you'll find out! You see, the nitroglycerin theory is still theory, not fact, so Woodward has a stake in getting the case cleared up. And his children are the whole point.'

'Mrs. Gower is mad about children,' Daisy said slowly.

'Right. Woodward has three young 'uns.'

'So when you say he ... you want me to... And you think she'll confess for their sake? Yes, she might.'

'Only don't, for pity's sake, announce his name in case she doesn't. I can't squeeze another drop from this teapot. More? All right, then, we'll work out on the way home exactly what you have to say.' Alec summoned the waiter with a glance and asked for the bill.

Instead of the waiter returning, the proprietor came over. 'Please, Mr. Fletcher, I 'ope ... *h*ope you will accept your dinner on the *h*ouse, sir,' he said, beaming and bowing.

Alec firmly, though politely, insisted on paying. On the way to the car, Daisy asked what he had done to be so favoured, but he shook his head.

'Come on, Alec, be a sport!'

He laughed. 'No, that was one case of

mine you didn't manage to horn in on. We'll keep it that way. Be satisfied with a vital part in this one.'

So there they all were in the choir room again. Daisy had attended the rehearsal. Her head still buzzing from the thrill of the *Libera me* with its dramatically hushed ending, she sat with Muriel, Roger, and Yakov Levich.

Nearby, Mr. Finch played on his imaginary keyboard. Olivia and Cochran were together, the conductor looking harrowed, uncertain, as if he had lost his place in the score of life and now had to improvise on an unknown tune. His performance on the podium hadn't been affected, though, as far as Daisy could tell. The rehearsal had gone well.

Dimitri Marchenko again sat alone, brooding. Consuela de la Costa paced, a tawny, impatient cat, studiously ignoring and being ignored by the Gowers. Gilbert and Jennifer Gower sat very close to each other, heads together. Daisy had seen them holding hands as they came in. She couldn't help hoping that Alec was wrong and Mrs. Gower innocent.

Of all those present, Daisy would have preferred to see Marchenko unmasked as the murderer, but he'd never confess to save

Dr. Woodward. If he was the one, how on earth was Alec to prove it?

Major Browne came in, red-faced and tubby as ever, and bustled from group to group, assuring all and sundry that the chief inspector would be here any minute. When he reached Daisy and her friends, he winked at her and said in a roguish aside, 'I've got a new tin of biscuits if you'd like to join me afterwards, Miss Dalrymple? Haw, haw!'

Daisy smiled at him but was saved from having to answer by Alec's arrival.

As he moved to the centre of the room, very self-assured and official in his dark suit, he caught Daisy's eye. She gave him a tiny nod. She hoped Jennifer Gower wasn't a murderer, but if she was...

Tom Tring and Ernie Piper followed Alec in and took up positions on either side of the door. Piper took out his notebook.

The sergeant was wearing black again. This time it made him look formidable. The bulk which clad in his usual violent checks appeared to be adiposity was revealed as solid muscle. A match for Marchenko, perhaps. Daisy remembered her impression that Alec had been evasive last night. Did he have something up his sleeve?

'Would you like to sit down, Miss de la

Costa?' he said politely as Consuela stalked up to him, spitting in Spanish.

'Why I am here?' she demanded. 'I not kill *esta maldita*, and not care who is murrrtherer. Tonight I rehearse opera. Must have rest!'

'This won't take long, ma'am. Please sit down.' He waited until she sulkily complied, then went on, 'Good evening, ladies and gentlemen, and thank you for coming. I'm sure all – most – of you are anxious to hear the results of our enquiry into the death of Mrs. Roger Abernathy, or Bettina Westlea as she was known in musical circles.'

One or two heads nodded. Finch, prompted perhaps by the word death, began to play what looked like a funeral march on his silent organ. Beside Daisy, Roger stared down at his hands, clenched but trembling on his knees. He shouldn't be subjected to this, Daisy thought as Muriel laid a hand on his arm.

Alec continued remorselessly. 'Mrs. Abernathy used to take a cough mixture consisting of an extremely dilute solution of prussic acid, that is, hydrocyanic acid. She was in the habit of taking this medicine in her favourite liqueur. The only way she could have been poisoned by cyanide is if her doctor made an error in dispensing his prescription.'

'How dreadful!' Daisy cried. 'One frightful mistake and the poor man will be ruined for ever. What will become of his wife and those poor little children?'

Mrs. Gower looked horrified. But she made no move to speak.

The silence lengthened – to be broken by Roger Abernathy's voice, low and weary. 'It wasn't cyanide.' With an immense effort he got to his feet and took a step forward. His hands hung at his side, limp, as if he didn't know what to do with them. 'It was trinitrin. I killed her.'

Stunned, Daisy stared. Beside her Muriel gave a horrified gasp, the only sound in the stillness.

Alec's steady gaze was unsurprised. 'Why?' he said levelly. 'Why now, after all these years? You realize anything you say may be used as evidence.'

Roger did not seem to hear the warning. He spoke in a monotone. 'She was ruining her sister's life. I made the mistake, it was right that I should suffer. I loved her and married her instead of Muriel. To my shame, I gave in to her demand that I not teach Muriel.'

'Oh, Roger!' Muriel sobbed.

Again he seemed not to hear. 'And then

Muriel met Yakov Levich and Bettina did her best to ruin that, too. I still loved her, but I couldn't allow it. You must understand, she was always unhappy, discontented, until her great opportunity came with this concert. At last she was satisfied. She thought it was the beginning of a wonderful new life and I hoped for her. But happy as she was, she went on bullying her sister. That day, when she stopped Muriel exchanging a few words with Levich, I knew she'd never change. She'd never have a chance to earn the recognition she craved. She died happy, before the disillusionment...'

The door burst open, flattening Piper behind it. Half a dozen men rushed in. 'Special Branch!' the leader bawled. 'Dimitri Marchenko, I have a warrant for your arrest on a charge of conspiracy to...'

'*Chort vozmi!*' Marchenko bellowed, surging to his feet. He charged towards the door. '*Svobodnaya Ukraina!*'

Alec, swinging round to protest the invasion, took a fist between the shoulder blades and went flying. The invaders closed in on Marchenko, who bulled onward dragging them with him, all shouting. Tom Tring slammed the door shut. Consuela screamed, piercingly, again and again. Daisy saw Olivia cross to her and slap her face. The screams abruptly cut off.

'Roger!'

At Muriel's cry, Daisy turned her head. Not more than a yard from her, Roger Abernathy stood with one hand clapped to his mouth, the other flailing the air. A shudder convulsed his body. He bent double, retching helplessly.

Muriel sprang to his side, tried to support the contorting figure. 'Yasha, help! Daisy, his pills. In his inside pocket. Quickly!'

But the little brown bottle lay on the floor. Daisy picked it up. 'Empty.'

'It can't be. I checked. It was full!'

No pills on the floor, and Roger clutched at his throat, writhing in Levich's grasp. Blood suffused his face. His glasses fell off and his eyes bulged as he fought for breath.

Daisy pulled Muriel away. The dying man's struggles weakened and Levich gently lowered him, twisting still but more and more feebly. Muriel broke from Daisy's arms and knelt beside him. She took his twitching hands in hers.

'Roger.' Her voice choked on sobs.

Roger Abernathy lay still at last. Again Daisy pulled Muriel away, and this time Olivia was there to help. Levich closed his staring eyes.

'He never expected, nor wanted, to survive Bettina,' Daisy murmured.

'The ruddy bastards!' Alec stood looking down at the body, his mouth tight with anger. 'Miss Dalrymple, Mr. Levich, take Miss Westlea home, please, at once. There's nothing more any of you can do here.'

Taking the empty pill bottle from the pocket where she had slipped it, Daisy silently handed it to him. He nodded his thanks. 'Piper, find them a cab.'

Ernie Piper sported an incipient black eye. Tom Tring's wide face was undamaged but for a ruffled moustache. He seemed to be trying to disguise a certain smugness. Marchenko was gone, and with him the Special Branch men. Stepping out into the passage, Daisy saw a ragged phalanx marching away round the curve, the Ukrainian's shaggy, dishevelled head in the middle, protruding above the rest.

Major Browne watched them go, wringing his hands. 'What are we going to do without a bass?' he moaned.

'So there the major stood,' said Daisy, pulling on her gloves, 'with bodies strewn all over the place like in grand opera - well, practically – in despair because his blasted bass was being dragged off in chains. Alec, what did Marchenko *do?*'

'Conspired.' He grinned, rather sourly, as she glared at him. 'I can't tell you any more. Official Secrets Act.'

'Bosh! Those men who ruined your denouement were about to announce it when he started roaring about.'

'"Disrupt the security of the realm" they were going to say. Did you see Tom down him when he broke away from them?'

Daisy allowed herself to be distracted. 'I thought Sergeant Tring looked pleased with himself. No, I missed it.' Sobered, she waited until the Austin pulled away from the kerb before she went on, 'Roger was collapsing by then.'

'I could have prevented that,' Alec said savagely, 'if those congenital idiots hadn't made a mess of it! I've had an apology from their super, by the way. They were supposed to wait until Marchenko left the choir room.'

'I don't see why you're so upset, though. You had his confession and that way was better than hanging.'

'They don't hang dying men. At worst he'd have gone out peacefully in a prison hospital. Don't forget, though, Daisy, his motive may have been unselfish but he murdered his wife. Whatever she was, she didn't deserve that.'

Daisy sighed. 'No. It's just so hard to believe that of him. He seemed such a gentle, kind little man.'

'Oh, he was. I don't doubt it. It was his dismay, his horror, when the daily rags went for Levich which gave me the idea of suggesting the danger to Woodward and his family.'

'Then you were aiming at Roger all along? You led me to believe it was Mrs. Gower!' she said indignantly.

'I didn't know for sure. It was between her, and Abernathy, and Marchenko, and there wasn't a damn ... dashed thing I could do about *him*. I'd been warned off by the Special Branch.'

'How madly frustrating. Muriel's decided she can't possibly give him back the jewellery if he's a criminal. He might use the proceeds to blow up Parliament, or Buck House, or 10 Downing Street or something.'

Alec laughed. 'He might, at that. Very wise of her.'

'I said she should give it to Mrs. Gower's clinic, so she's going to split it between them and the Musicians' Friendly Society, or whatever it's called. She'll just keep enough to send for Yasha's parents. They're engaged, you know.'

'Miss Westlea and Levich? That was quick work.'

'*She* proposed to *him* last night. She's got a lot more spunk than I ever gave her credit for. Roger wanted it, she said, and she couldn't bear that his awful sacrifice and poor Betsy's death might go for nothing. I'm jolly glad for them, but I must say this whole affair has been frightfully wearing!'

Alec reached across the gear lever and squeezed her hand. 'Never mind, you can relax now and enjoy the tea party.'

'Relax!' Daisy sat bolt upright. The daffodils of Hyde Park were already behind them and St. John's Wood was no more than three minutes away. 'Relax! I'm absolutely terrified! I shan't be able to eat a thing!'

'You must. Belinda's baked rock buns and I understand she's trying her hand at scones. She'll be devastated if you don't like them.'

'Oh, then I shall eat lots and lots,' said Daisy stoutly, consigning terror and her waistline to oblivion. 'And afterwards I shall ask her to teach me how to make them.'

The publishers hope that this book has given you enjoyable reading. Large Print Books are especially designed to be as easy to see and hold as possible. If you wish a complete list of our books please ask at your local library or write directly to:

Magna Large Print Books
Magna House, Long Preston,
Skipton, North Yorkshire.
BD23 4ND

This Large Print Book, for people
who cannot read normal print,
is published under the auspices of

THE ULVERSCROFT FOUNDATION